I0733244

1966 FOREVER

VICTORIA MAXWELL

Magic Pizza Press

Copyright © 2021 by Victoria Maxwell

All rights reserved.

No part of this book may be reproduced in any form or by any electronic or mechanical means, including information storage and retrieval systems, without written permission from the author, except for the use of brief quotations in a book review.

ISBN: 978-1-9163114-1-1 (Paperback)

Any references to historical events, real people, or real places are used fictitiously. Names, characters and places are products of the authors imagination.

Front cover image and book design by Victoria Maxwell

First printing edition 2021

www.victoriamaxwellauthor.com

Also by Victoria Maxwell

Class of 1983 | Santolsa Saga Book 1

Summer of 1984 | Santolsa Saga Book 2

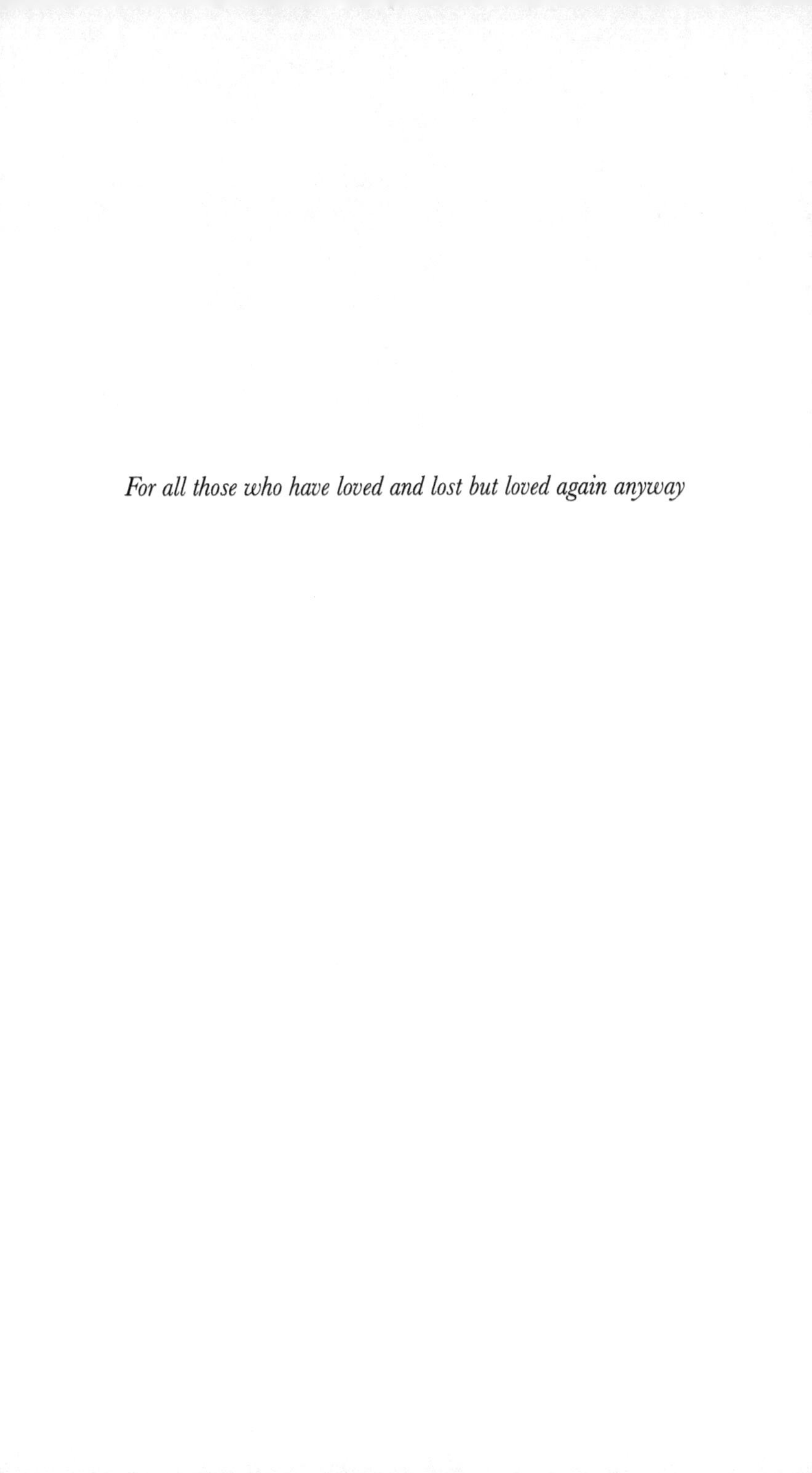

For all those who have loved and lost but loved again anyway

PART ONE

Prologue

Santolsa
   1985

It was a balmy Saturday evening and Janet was already dressed in her electric blue satin pajamas and looking forward to having the house to herself for the night. They had run out of frozen pizza, but she was too tired to go to the store, so she had ordered one from Super Pan. While she was waiting for it to arrive, she had made a huge bowl of popcorn sprinkled with one of Jack's special popcorn spice mixes. She poured herself a large wine glass of Mello Yello and sat down in front of the TV. She had been looking forward to watching the video of *Private Benjamin* she'd rented all day.

Peggy had enrolled in night classes to study special education teaching and Janet couldn't have been prouder. Teaching was such a rewarding profession, even if it was thankless at times, and she knew Peggy was going to be a wonderful teacher. Peggy and Sammy had finally worked things out and for the first time in a long time, it felt like life was going smoothly for everyone. Peggy was still working at the bowling alley and if she wasn't busy with school or work, she was usually off somewhere with Sammy. Janet was glad they were so happy, but her own break-up with Ray last year had been tough.

Not because she had been heartbroken, but because she hadn't.

She enjoyed spending time with Ray, she liked his company, but it wasn't *love*. And it wasn't fair to keep it going when she knew it was never going to be more. Ray still had time to meet someone who wanted to get married and have a family. Deep down Janet knew that path wasn't hers. She loved her work, and she already had a family - Peggy, Sammy, Jack and Lacey had become like her children in so many ways.

Peggy and Sammy were so in love, and it brought back so many bittersweet memories for Janet. She had felt like that once, many years ago, but since then her relationships had involved a lot of settling and not very much magic.

Jack and Lacey were just as happy. After spending some time in L.A., they had moved back to Santolsa and into their own apartment. It had caused a real stir in the small desert town of Santolsa. Lacey's mom had been livid about her "living in sin" (even though she was one to talk), but they were in the throes of young love and that mattered more than what the townsfolk, or even Lacey's mom said. Jack was back working at Dee's diner, although he was assistant manager now. It was only temporary of course, just while Lacey was taking photography classes at Salt Valley community college and getting a portfolio together. They were planning to return to L.A. when Lacey was done with school. She had big dreams to work as a free-lance photographer in the L.A. clubs and music venues and Jack had fallen in love with creating vegetarian versions of Santolsa's favorite diner dishes and was dreaming about taking them to L.A. where he hoped they might be appreciated a little more.

Everyone was landing and finding their way in the world, and Janet was watching from sidelines. She'd lost count of how many times she'd said, "I'm so happy for you". And she *was* happy for them all, of course, but she couldn't remember the last time someone had said that to her.

Things were changing. Peggy didn't need her like she used to, and Janet knew that Peggy wasn't going to want to live with her forever. Sammy was a bit of a traditionalist so she knew they wouldn't move in together anytime too soon, but she also knew Peggy wasn't going to live with her fake Aunt Janet forever.

And then there was the other thing.

The thing that Janet hadn't been able to forget since the first day she'd met Peggy.

The name that Peggy had called her.

Mrs. Willis.

Maybe that was the thing that had stopped her from really trying with Ray, or with anyone who's last name wasn't Willis.

Maybe it was time she started to focus on the present instead of dreaming about an impossible future.

And in that moment Janet knew she had to let go of the past, and to let go of the future, and just be here and now.

"Here and now," she whispered to herself.

As soon as Janet had pressed play on the movie and snuggled into her seat, there was a knock on the door.

The pizza.

She rushed to the door, still holding the bowl of popcorn in her hands. Janet unlatched the lock and swung it open, grinning in anticipation of the cheesy, tomato-y goodness of the Super Pan pizza she'd ordered.

But on the other side of the door was not pizza.

It was something else.

It was some*one* else.

It was someone she never expected to see again, not ever.

The bowl of popcorn slipped from her grip and crashed onto the floor, sending popcorn in all directions through the house and onto the front porch.

She tried to move her mouth, but nothing came out.

"I'm so glad I finally found you," he said, his dark eyes opening like a portal of time, sending her spinning back, erasing the last nineteen years.

And before she knew what was happening, Janet felt herself falling all over again.

Santolsa
 Between Time

Helena stood outside the door to the room in the abbey where they had hidden the permanent circle, the time portal they had created which would allow them to flee if they were ever persecuted again. Helena didn't need to use the permanent circle to travel through time, but it did take less energy which was why she planned to use it today. Helena's magic was powerful. In fact, it was her magic, and her magic alone that had created the permanent circle in the first place. Sister Maria said otherwise, but nothing Helena did was ever good enough for Sister Maria. Not even this. Creating a portal of time that would save all their lives was still not enough to please Sister Maria.

But none of that mattered now. Helena's replacement had been found and she was finally free.

It would have pleased Sister Maria if Helena had done more than leave a letter in the kitchen saying that she had seen a vision of her replacement and knew she would be arriving soon. It wasn't really how things were done. There should have been a ritual when a witch left her coven, but Helena was done with rituals and done with living under Sister Maria's rules.

It had, however, felt appropriate for Helena to wear her habit one last time. She had seen flashes of the future she was going to, and she knew she would look out of place, but as much as she hated to admit it, her habit had protected her in many times and places, and she hoped it would work in the future too.

She took one last look down the hallway of the abbey, towards the kitchen, secretly hoping to get one last glimpse of Sister Catherine. But Sister Catherine was already busy in the garden and Sister Maria was still saying her prayers.

So Helena opened the door and entered the permanent circle.

Peggy was carrying a pile of homework and a fresh cup of coffee and had just managed to open her classroom door with her elbow when she heard a noise coming from the book room. It was still too early for students to be in the building and the school was deserted except for the janitor and Mr. Jenks the Phys Ed teacher who Peggy knew had been sleeping in his office and washing in the school showers since his wife kicked him out. Though neither of those people should have been anywhere near the English Department at this time.

Peggy looked up and down the hallway, but there was no one there. She shrugged and was just about to turn to walk into her classroom when she heard it again.

Peggy's heart began to race. When she had taken this job, she knew it came with a certain amount of… responsibility. But she didn't really expect to ever have to use it. A time portal in the English Department? An oath to keep it safe and protect anyone who came through it? Peggy had time traveled herself, and it still sounded ridiculous.

Taking a few tentative steps forward, Peggy gasped as she saw the door swing open and a girl dressed in a nun's habit appeared. The stack of homework dropped to the floor, papers fanning out in all directions. Just as she was about to spill her coffee the girl came rushing over and slipped a hand under the cup.

"Hello," she smiled. "I'm Helena."

Peggy just stood there, staring.

"I've seen you in my visions. I know you are one of us," the girl went on while Peggy's mouth continued to fall open even wider. "I've come from the past, from when this abbey was first built, I'm one of the…"

"…Nuns of Santolsa," Peggy whispered.

ONE

The Ride Home

Santolsa
1999

Sister Catherine cleared her throat. "That's it for today, detention is over."

David leapt up, sliding his books into his army green backpack in one smooth motion. He gave Janet an impatient look. "Meet you out front?" His shoulder length dark hair fell into his smoldering dark eyes.

Janet wondered how he could make such a simple phrase sound so intense, so *sexy*. She nodded back at him and began to pack up her own books while David and the other few students who were also in detention couldn't get out of there quick enough.

"What did you think?" Sister Catherine asked, giving Janet a kind smile. Janet liked Sister Catherine. She was the only adult in the whole school who talked to the students as if they were equals, as if they were *people*. Janet wasn't religious, but she guessed by the way that Sister Catherine moved and spoke, whatever she believed in, it was something beautiful.

"Of the book?" Janet held up the book Sister Catherine had given her to read during detention. *The Nuns of Santolsa.* "Interesting. Weird." Janet shrugged.

"Weird? How so?" Sister Catherine's eyes glistened, as if she actually cared about Janet's answer to the question.

"I feel like there are bits missing."

"That's usually the way with history books."

"Sure. But it doesn't really explain anything, it just poses ideas."

Sister Catherine nodded. "No one really knows what happened in the past. How can you really know something unless you were there yourself?"

"But it's... intriguing," Janet added, throwing her backpack onto her shoulder, and then pulling her long dark hair out from the straps. "All the history of this place, how it was once an abbey, then a children's boarding school and then a high school. You don't always think about that when you're sitting in Trig, you know?"

Sister Catherine nodded. "We don't always think about the past, most of us are so focused on the future."

Janet nodded. "Three women living out in the middle of nowhere, building this place, with no running water or electricity. I couldn't do it."

"It's amazing what you can do," the nun said. "If you have to."

"The sightings are interesting," Janet continued. "All the times people said they saw the nuns. That's cool. Kind of creepy, but cool. I can't think of anything creepier than a ghost nun. Oh, no offense."

Sister Catherine laughed. "None taken. But yes, it is curious how people thought they have seen the nuns throughout time. Some people think they should be sainted, isn't that something?"

"A bunch of women doing it on their own out in the desert? Make them all saints." Janet handed the book over.

"Keep it." Sister Catherine placed her hand over Janet's and gave a gentle smile.

Janet felt the weight of the key in her pocket. She didn't know why she took it out of the book when she found it, and it felt awkward to mention it now, but she didn't feel right lying to Sister Catherine.

"I… found something. A key. In the book," Janet began.

Sister Catherine nodded. "You'll know when it's time to use it."

"I don't understand…" Janet said.

"You will," Sister Catherine replied with a knowing look. "And you best get going, I think someone is waiting for you."

"What took you so long?" David pushed himself off the wall near the entrance to St. Christopher's high school where he'd been waiting.

"I was just talking to Sister Catherine about the book," Janet said.

"What book?"

"The Nuns of Santolsa. It's actually kind of interesting. Did you know there have been sightings of the nuns who built this school? People say they've seen them in all sorts of places, all at different times. The book was published in the sixties, but people have always seen these nuns. They're like ghosts or something."

"Ghost nuns?" David scoffed as he started walking to the student lot, gesturing for Janet to hurry up.

"Yeah." Janet picked up her pace. "Cool huh?"

"Seriously, Jan?"

"What? It's a cool story."

"I've got a better story." He looked back at her with a suggestive look in his eyes.

"Yeah?"

"It's about this pretty girl who gets on the back of this guy's bike…"

"OK, that sounds kind of terrifying." Janet tried to act cool, even though her heart did a little flip at the idea of him thinking she was *pretty*.

"And then," he went on, "they ride back to his place, where they share a tub of ice-cream and watch a tape of last night's *X-Files*."

"So, ghost nuns are stupid, but aliens are totally fine?" Janet folded her arms in mock protest as they arrived at his motorcycle. It was the only one in the lot.

"Aliens are the coolest." He threw his helmet over to her. "But tell anyone I said that and we're not friends anymore, OK?"

Friends. Janet's heart flipped back the other way.

It was the weirdest friendship ever. They were always flirting with each other. He *knew* she liked him, he would be stupid not to, and he was always talking about how pretty and cool she was, but their whole relationship had always been strictly platonic. David lived in the trailer across from hers and they had been friends since Janet could remember. But these last few months something had changed. David had stopped being the annoying kid next door and had become the hot guy next door who listened to grunge music and rode a motorcycle. At some point he had grown some biceps and a dash of dark stubble and Janet had realized that she didn't just want to hang out with him as *friends*, she wanted something more.

"I won't tell a soul," she said putting the helmet on.

"OK, and I won't tell anyone you're scared of ghosts," he teased as he straddled his bike.

"I'm not scared of ghosts!" She gave him a light thump in his perfectly defined bicep, just above the tattoo which was only partly hidden under his yellow school shirt, before climbing on the bike and wrapping her arms around him. He felt so good.

"Sure, sure," he said, starting the engine and driving off way too fast, spitting up a cloud of orange desert dust behind them.

"So, ice-cream, X-*Files*, are we doing it?" David asked as they dismounted out the front of the trailer he shared with his two brothers and sometimes his dad, if he was around. On paper David lived with his dad, off paper, he only saw him when he was passing through town or doing a job for the Eights, the biker gang his dad was a part of. The biker gang *David* was a part of. He hadn't been formally initiated yet, that wouldn't happen until his seventeenth birthday in a couple of weeks' time, but he was as involved in the gang's business as much as anyone.

Janet wasn't sure what she was thinking. Yes, he was hot, and yes, she found him more attractive than Eddie Vedder, but she knew if she ever got closer to him than she was right now, she'd be tied to the Eights too. And that was something she really didn't want. Even their friendship was dangerous. It was something Gran had been warning her about since she was old enough to understand.

The only thing worse than an unrequited crush was a requited one that would ruin your life.

Janet shook her head. "Raincheck? I have a Biology test this week and I'm this close to flunking."

David frowned, his dark eyebrows drawing together while she imagined putting her fingers between them and smoothing them out. "Do you really think a good grade in Biology is going to matter? You and me, we never stood a chance."

"You know I refuse to believe that," she said. "I'm still going to make something of my life. I'm going to finish this year with good grades, make my final year next year even better and then go to college and get a decent job. And one day," she said, throwing the helmet back at him. "I'm even going to live in a real house." She laughed, as if she was making a joke, but her voice caught and gave her away. While other kids were planning their futures and dreaming of becoming rich and successful, Janet was dreaming about a house with real foundations and bills that got paid on the first notice every month. That was her big dream.

"You need to let that dream go, Jan."

Janet gave him a look.

"It's not that you're not smart enough. You're probably one of the smartest girls in school. Those books you're always carrying around would take me a year to read. But college? Come on, Jan. That's just not going to happen for people like you and me."

"Says who?"

"Everyone. This world. *Money*."

"Gran always says we can do anything, we just have to believe in ourselves. And I do. I don't know how I'm going to do it, but I will. I'm not going to stay in this trailer park for my whole life."

"Are you too good for it?" David's voice turned harsh.

"No." She sighed. "You know that's not what I think."

David rubbed the stubble on his chin. "I believe in you too, you know. If anyone can get out of here it's you. I just don't want you to be disappointed when you wake up here ten years from now, in the arms of some guy who probably doesn't deserve you. Big dreams lead to big disappointment." He gave a casual shrug, as if this is something his dad had been telling him since he was little, but his eyes looked sad, like he really didn't want to believe it himself.

"How about if I study for a few hours and come over after dinner?" she suggested.

"Sure." He gave her a mischievous smile and she knew how easy it would be for her big dreams to disappear into his dark eyes.

TWO

Gran

____

Santolsa
1999

Janet unlocked the door to her trailer and stepped inside. It
wasn't much, but it was home. Gran had been the only
family Janet had ever known, and this trailer the only
home she'd ever had. Beside the door was a small table
covered in her grandmother's things - lipsticks, coupons,
newspapers, big tacky plastic earrings. Janet threw her keys
into a glass dish sitting atop one of the newspapers and
took the three steps from the front door to the couch and
flopped down. Gran was usually playing poker or shooting
pool in the afternoons, so she had a few hours to herself.
She just needed a quick rest before she started her homework. Maybe even a short nap.

Her eyes had just begun to close when a knocking on
the door startled her. *David.* Couldn't he take no for an
answer?

Janet opened the door, a pretend scowl on her face, but

it wasn't David. It was Aunt Lou, not her aunt by blood, but one of Gran's best friends and one of the women who had helped raise her. It was something even stronger than blood. And Aunt Lou had that look on her face. Janet knew that look.

"What's wrong, Lou?"

"It's Gran, she's had a turn."

Janet grabbed her keys from the dish and was out the door in a second. "Where is she?"

"Betty drove her straight to the hospital." Lou gestured out of the trailer park.

"The hospital? You know we can't afford the hospital!"

Lou put a hand on Janet's shoulder. "You'll work it out. Right now we just have to get Gran better."

"Why didn't you come get me?" Janet snapped.

"We didn't know where you were!" Lou snapped back. "School finished hours ago."

Janet's stomach turned. If it wasn't for her talking back and getting detention, she would have been here, she would have been here for Gran. She could have done something. She felt so angry at herself.

David appeared out of nowhere. "Jan, I just heard."

Janet just kept shaking her head. She felt her knees weaken. If anything happened to Gran…

"I… I can't… I don't…"

David gave her a look that felt like her lifeline. "Get on," he said, taking charge and throwing her his helmet.

Lou nodded. "She's at Salt Valley General. *Go*."

Janet got on the bike, Aunt Lou gave her a firm tap on the shoulder and David put his foot down on the gas.

THREE

The Hospital

Salt Valley
1999

The hospital waiting room was hell on earth. The seats were hard, the coffee was disgusting, and the fluorescent lighting kept flickering above them.

It had been four hours and still no one could tell them anything.

David squeezed her hand. He'd hardly let it go since they'd arrived. It was the first time they had held hands, and every time Janet started thinking about how perfectly his hand fit in hers, she felt guilt course through her. She wasn't here to move her relationship with David to the next level, she was here because Gran was sick.

She looked down at their fingers intertwined, at her chipped black nail polish, the hospital lighting making her skin look sick and pale while his hand looked even more tanned than usual.

Janet felt the fingers from his other hand move gently

along her cheek. She hadn't even realized she was crying until he wiped her tears away.

"It's going to be OK," he whispered. Even though neither of them knew if it was true, it still seemed like exactly the right thing for him to say.

David had always had her back, but these last few hours she'd seen another side to him. Instead of his moody, flirtatious self, he'd been strong but gentle. He'd brought her bad coffee and hassled doctors for news, and he'd just sat in silence by her side, holding her hand.

She thought she'd had a crush on him before, but now it felt like the word "crush" just didn't cut it. He was the person who was *here*. Gran was sick and her whole world was crumbling down around her, and David was the one holding her hand through it.

"Miss Bates?" A man with a gray beard, glasses and a clipboard appeared above her.

Finally, a doctor.

Oh God, a doctor.

She glanced at David who gave her a nod and finally let go of her hand. This was something she had to do on her own. She stood up, legs shaking, and followed the Doctor through the waiting room and into a hallway.

"Your grandmother has had a heart attack," the doctor said, stopping outside one of the rooms. He said it just like he was saying "your grandmother has dandruff", like no big deal. Nothing to worry about. "She's not out of the woods yet. At her age…"

Janet didn't really hear the rest, she got the gist. It was bad.

"Can I see her?"

The doctor nodded and opened the door to her room.

Janet stepped in, the smell of disinfectant and bad hospital food overpowering her.

"Gran!" she gasped, running to her bedside.

"Jan-Jan!" Gran reached out and Janet ran into her arms. "Oooof, careful darling, you nearly pulled out my plugs."

Janet gently let go and took a seat on the chair beside the bed. Seeing her Gran like this, all plugged into machines and drips, it was too much. She wanted to stay strong for Gran, but the tears came anyway.

"Oh, don't cry baby girl, I'm feeling just fine." Gran gave her a big smile, but the sparkle in her eyes was gone.

Janet wiped her face. "I can't lose you too," she said, gripping Gran's fingers under hers.

"You think I went through hell and back raising you just to leave now? Right when you're becoming such a beautiful, smart and talented young woman?"

Janet rolled her eyes.

"I wish you could see yourself how I see you. I'm so, so proud of you, honey."

Janet felt the tears falling from her eyes again. Gran was never this sentimental.

"Who's with you?" Gran asked. "Did Aunt Lou bring you?"

Janet shook her head. "David."

Gran gave her a look.

Janet gave a look back. "It's not like that."

"Don't think I haven't seen the way you look at that boy."

"Gran!"

"He's a real looker, but you know he'll get you into all sorts of trouble. Your dad…" Gran stopped herself and put her hand to her lips.

"What about my dad?" Janet frowned. Gran *never* talked about her dad. He was not a topic of conversation in their house. Janet had asked about him a few times over the years, but all Gran would say was that they were better off without him. Janet hardly remembered him. He had dropped her off with Gran when she was just a baby. All she had was a memory of his thick blonde curly hair, her tiny hands holding onto the strands. But she didn't even have a photo of him, so she wasn't sure if it was a memory at all, or just something she'd made up in her head.

Gran took a deep breath. "Your dad wouldn't have wanted you hanging around with anyone involved in any Eights business. Let's leave it at that."

Janet felt the anger rising inside her like a dragon. "Yeah well, my dad's not here, is he? So, he has no right to say who I do or don't hang out with."

Gran's face fell. "I know you never really got over him leaving, and he certainly made some terrible choices in his life. But when he left you with me, he really was doing what he thought was right."

Janet let out a laugh.

"You can't carry your anger at him through your life baby girl. It'll eat you up."

Another tear fell down Janet's cheek. "You carried yours."

"And it did me no good. I should have forgiven him years ago. But maybe I can do it now."

Janet didn't understand. She had always been torn between wanting to know about her dad and not wanting to. If it was bad, she didn't want to know, but something told her it was time for the truth.

"Tell me, Gran, what did he do?"

Gran sighed. "After your mamma went to heaven, he was never the same. I always said Billy was too bright for this world, that it would burn him out, and it did."

Janet had always thought of her dad as a drop out, a loser, a total deadbeat dad who just left her on the doorstep because he didn't want her. She had certainly never thought about him as being too bright for this world.

"He was drinking and hanging around the Eights and I told him to bring you to me until he got his life together."

"But he didn't," Janet guessed.

Gran gave a sad smile. "It was too late. He was so mixed up in it all. But we had a good time through the years, didn't we, Jan-Jan?"

Janet smiled back through her tears and squeezed Gran's hand. "And we still have plenty more years ahead of us, right?"

"You have more than I do. Spend them well."

Janet was choking up. Why did this feel like a goodbye? The doctor said she wasn't out of the woods yet, but that meant she *could* get out of the woods, right?

Gran took Janet's hand and patted it. "You should go home, get some rest."

Janet shook her head. "I don't want to rest, I want to stay here with you. I'll sleep here, I won't leave your side."

"Well, *I* want you to go home and rest. There's nothing to do here. The food is horrible, and the doctors aren't even good looking."

"Gran!" Janet laughed through her tears. Trust Gran to try to make a joke at a time like this.

"Please. I'll sleep better knowing you're sleeping sound back at home."

Janet gave in and gave a little nod.

"And if you're looking for dinner, there's a couple of pizzas in the freezer."

And that was the last thing Gran ever said.

Santolsa
  2018

Helena, or Lena, as she was called then, sat in her usual seat at the back of the English classroom. She hated having to pretend to be a high school student, it was almost as bad as being back in the abbey. This room used to be Sister Maria's chambers. It was now filled with wooden chairs with strange tables protruding from the sides, a board covered in white chalk writing and the smell of modern-day adolescents (strange perfumes that made her head ache, even on the boys), but she still couldn't forget what it used to be and what *she* used to be. Well, what she *still* was.

Lena had traveled to the future looking for a new life, a destiny that held more than washing Sister Catherine's pots and pans and Sister Maria's dinner plates.

Now that she'd seen her replacement was on the way she was finally free, but free to do what? All she was doing now was *studying*.

The motto *Tempore Potior Iure* had been chosen by Sister

Maria when they had first thought of turning the abbey into a school, and it was still here, written above the board made of chalk.

He who is before in time, is preferred in right.

It was usually used in a courtroom and made little sense in the context of being a school motto, but it made perfect sense to time traveling nuns. The nuns had told the first students at the school that it meant don't be late for class, but now it seemed as if no one even knew or cared what it meant.

But still, it reminded Lena of the power she had within her, reminded her that she didn't *really* need to be here. She could choose any time to travel to. If only she had the ability to travel through space as well as time she could leave this hideous desert and go somewhere green! Nevertheless, she had decided to try to fit in with these modern people, and as she really knew of nothing more than God, magic, scrubbing floors and brushing horses, the best way to understand this time and make herself at home here was to attend high school. *Then* she would decide what to do and where to go next.

The people here fascinated her, even though she found most of them detestable. The boys made her skin crawl, especially the one who sat in the seat in front of her in this class. He was what the girls called a "popular boy" - all muscles and blonde hair but no brain, and not even one ounce of chivalry! He was always looking at Lena as if she was a prize pig. He had asked her to attend social outings with him, and each time she said no she could sense his frustration rising. She would no doubt have to work some magic on him at some point, but that was another thing. She had promised herself no magic, not unless absolutely necessary, at least, not until she had graduated and learned the ways of this world. Magic had helped her many times, but when it came to the one thing she really wanted, magic was no use.

There was no spell she knew that could bring Kimana back. She had searched long and hard. She had tried scrying in water, forcing dreams and visions and attempting spells and rituals for lost people and objects. She had even tried going back in time to see Kimana again and to follow her and her people to wherever they had gone, but each time she could not make the magic work, she could not hold it. She could not see where they went. She could not follow them.

"Lena, are you with us?" The voice of her teacher made her jump. Lena liked Mrs. Ruthven. She was a middle-aged woman with long light chestnut colored hair who was always very kind, and she dressed in bright colors which made Lena feel happy after being surrounded by nothing but black habits for so many years.

She also happened to be a time traveler who had taken Lena into her home. Lena was currently living on her teacher's couch which was much more comfortable than the beds in the abbey. It was just until she finished the school year which wasn't long now. Then she would find her own way in this new world.

Mrs. Ruthven looked down at her, peering over her big gold rimmed glasses. "What do you think this means, Lena?"

"Star-crossed lovers, indeed! It's nothing but romantic nonsense." Lena tossed her book to the side. "*Romeo and Juliet* is a tragedy. There is nothing romantic about it."

"OK," Mrs. Ruthven began. "What does star-crossed mean?"

"It means they will both die," Lena said dramatically.

The boy in front of her let out a laugh. "It means it's

fated. Just like you and me, Lena." He turned and gave her what she expected he thought was some kind of flirtatious look. In truth, it was just disgusting.

"Yes, it means fated… *to die.*" Lena glared at him.

The piercing sound of the bell rang out through the classroom signaling it was time to eat. Perhaps high school wasn't so different from living in the abbey after all, it was just that now a loud bell told her what to do instead of Sister Maria's ringing voice.

"Please stay behind after class, Lena," Mrs. Ruthven said.

Lena sighed and looked back down at her notebook as everyone else left the classroom. She was grateful for the few moments of silence before Mrs. Ruthven spoke.

"You're doing so well, I think you should move up into regular classes." Mrs. Ruthven took off her glasses and looked at her warmly.

"Please Mrs. Ruthven, no, I'm not ready." Lena shook her head. She liked being in the remedial classes, what the other students called the "special" classes. She had spent one God-awful day in regular class when she first arrived, and after what the school nurse had told her was an anxiety attack, it had been decided she would stay in the remedial unit until she had settled in. It meant fewer students in the classes, more time with the teacher and less foul bodies to smell.

"I don't know how long I can keep you here," Mrs. Ruthven said. "You are excelling at everything."

"I am gaining confidence with my schoolwork, but I still have some… *anxiety* at the idea of being in those large classes."

Mrs. Ruthven put a hand over hers. "I know this must be so strange for you. It must be so different here. But if you really want to fit in and make a life for yourself in this time, perhaps you could try just one or two regular classes?"

Lena shook her head.

"*One* regular class?"

Lena squished up her face.

"History is your best subject, what if we just started there?"

Lena shook her head. "No, you will not make me!" Tears sprang from her eyes like the Roman fountains she had dreamed about, and she shook her head so fast her curtains of blonde hair got stuck to her tears.

"It's OK, Lena," Mrs. Ruthven said, reaching out to her. "You're OK."

And her teacher pulled her into a warm embrace and Lena let her tears fall. Not really because she was sad, but because she felt safe enough to let it all out.

And not for the first time, even though she'd only known her a few months, she thought that Mrs. Ruthven felt more like a mother to her than any other woman ever had.

FOUR

Rent

____

Santolsa
    1999

Janet woke to a gentle knock on her window.

"Janet!" whispered a low voice.

She pulled her head off the pillow and saw David looking at her intensely through the dusty layer of plexiglass.

"What is it?" She sat up and rubbed her eyes, picking some of yesterday's eyeliner out of her lashes.

"Rent day."

Janet felt like she'd been hit in the chest with a dodgeball. She knew this day was coming, but it felt too soon. She'd been so caught up in the grief of losing Gran she had been focusing on taking one day at a time, putting one foot in front of the other.

But now it was time to face the facts. She had no parents, no family, no one to take her in and she had no money to pay rent.

"I can cover for you, but you need to get out of here," David urged.

Janet grabbed her military boots, slid open the small window and began to jimmy off the fly screen. She threw her boots out the window and David reached his hands through to help pull her though. She toppled forward and landed right on top of him, sending orange dust into his dark hair and up her nose. His dark eyes were like galaxies, and she was falling into them, wondering if she was ever going to come back to earth.

And just when she thought maybe this was it, the moment of their first kiss, he sneezed.

"Oh God, I'm sorry," he said, wiping a little bit of moisture from her forehead.

"Ew," she said, wiping her face with the back of her pajama sleeve. Well, if it had been anyone else it would have been gross, but it was David, and so it really wasn't that bad at all. In fact, she didn't care if he sneezed on her again if it meant he would stay this close to her, their bodies pressed up against each other and…

A loud banging on the door of her trailer broke the spell.

"Go!" He shoved her off him, brushed himself off and then rushed around to the front of the trailer, leaving her sprawled on the ground in her pajamas.

"She's not here," she heard David shout out.

"Hey, kid," came the gruff voice of their landlord - an old cowboy who made little money off his ranch but a lot off the trailer park which sat just on the edge of his property. So many of the tenants could have paid off their trailers in full years ago, but he only did lets. Very cheap lets, which was why no one said anything. They all just kept paying their money each month and spending whatever they had left on drinking or gambling or whatever other vices they had. Even Gran had her vices. She'd lost enough money playing poker to have paid rent for a year. "Just because the old lady died doesn't mean someone doesn't still owe me some money."

Janet felt the anger part of her grief begin to burn inside her.

"You'll get your money," David said calmly. "Just give her some more time."

"Ten days," the landlord ordered. "Or I'm calling social services and the girl goes."

Janet's heart hammered in her chest.

Social services?

Of all the things she had been worried about, it had never occurred to her that she might become a child of the state. That she would be taken away from the only home she had ever known and have to live with complete strangers, probably total creeps, for the next two years until she was legally old enough to be on her own.

"No," she gasped. "No, no!" She yanked her boots on and began to run, weaving through the trailers. She didn't know where she was going to go, or how far she would get. Maybe she could get over state lines, but then what? She had no money, no one, nothing, she hadn't even finished school yet, she was still a year and a few days off getting her high school diploma.

She couldn't stay, she couldn't go. She didn't know what to do.

So, she just ran until she reached the trailers at the end of the lot and looked out at the edge of Santolsa, at a whole lot of nothing. Nothing but the desert, the Joshua trees, the mountains beyond, most of it land owned by the cowboy who wanted to evict her. There was nowhere to hide, and it was too far to run.

She crouched down behind the last trailer in the row, a

TV inside blaring the infomercial channel, and she put her head in her hands and prayed for a miracle.

FIVE

Hungry

Santolsa
1999

"We can work this out, Jan. You just need one month's rent." David was sitting on a bar stool at the tiny kitchen counter in Janet's trailer, his dark eyes full of worry.

Janet turned away from him and opened the freezer. She was feeling hungry for the first time in weeks. There was just one frozen pizza left, but she couldn't bring herself to eat it. It was the last pizza Gran had bought before she went into hospital.

"Maybe you can sell something," he suggested. "Or get an advance from the Burger Barn?"

She shook her head and closed the freezer door. "Gran didn't have anything." She crossed her arms and leaned over the counter across from him. "And I got fired from there like a month ago."

"What? Why didn't you tell me?"

"Why didn't you notice?"

David shook his head. "I guess I've been so caught up with my own work on the weekends to notice you weren't going."

She gave him a look. "You don't have to say it like that, I know what you do."

He looked down and rapped his fingers on the table. "Why did you get fired? Didn't put enough cheese on the burgers?" he joked.

"Too much," she replied with a half-smile. The truth was, her boss had tried to make a pass at her, and when she'd turned around and slapped him in the face, he'd fired her on the spot. It would be his word against hers, and who was going to believe a girl from the trailer park over old Clem who ran the Burger Barn? Maybe she should have just let him do it. At least then she'd still be able to live in her own home.

"I could ask the Eights…"

"No," she cut him off.

"Just one job. We could keep it clean. A one off."

"There are no one-offs with the Eights, *you* know that. You're either an Eight or you're not."

David let out a sigh. "I know it's not an ideal situation, but neither is getting evicted or being sent to live in some foster home somewhere."

Janet felt the hot sting of tears rising behind her eyes. She'd thought she was all out of tears, yet every couple of days there seemed to be a fresh supply. But David had seen enough of her tears - at the hospital, when they got the news, at the funeral. She was done crying in front of him. So, she tried to blink them back.

David's eyes turned into pools of liquid gold as he walked towards her, arms outstretched. And in spite of herself, she fell into them, letting his warmth surround her, letting herself feel safe in this moment. For just this moment she was safe.

The tears broke free, and David pulled her into his shoulder, holding her while she sobbed.

When what felt like hours had passed and the tears had finally run dry, she looked up at him. He wiped her cheeks with his fingertips.

And then, totally out of nowhere, he gently kissed her cheek where the tears had been. His lips were warm and soft, his stubble lightly pressing on her skin and sending a surge of warmth, and something primal, through her whole body.

And the next thing she knew, his lips were on hers, kissing her hungrily. She kissed him back like only they could satiate each other. Suddenly, she felt alive again. Janet didn't know she was ever going to feel anything but sad ever again, but here she was, feeling *everything.*

His hand reached up into her hair, pulling her face closer to his as his hips pushed against her. He spun her around and lifted her onto the kitchen counter, his kisses becoming harder. It was like a fire was raging between them, a fire stoked with grief, pain, passion and fear.

"Is this OK?" he asked, lifting his lips from hers for just a second.

She nodded, and his lips pressed back against hers again.

And for just a few moments she let herself forget about everything else and just let the fire between them consume her.

SIX

Searching

Santolsa
1999

Headlights beamed through the kitchen window and David let out a different kind of groan. One that wasn't like the ones he'd been making just a few moments before when his lips had been on hers and everything in her life had melted away just for a moment. "I think it's my dad," he sighed into her hair.

"Your dad? But he hasn't been in town for ages."

"You know what he's like. He can't turn up for birthdays or when we need him, but he always suddenly appears when there's a job to do. Or when I'm making out with a hottie," he grinned.

Janet wasn't sure what was more exciting, that his lips had just been on hers, or that he'd called her a hottie. "Do you have to go?"

David pulled the kitchen curtains closed. "I should."

He leaned in and kissed her lightly. "But I'm kind of in the middle of something."

Janet smiled up at him and he leaned in and kissed her again.

He pulled back and ran his fingers through his hair. "I don't want you to go," he said softly.

"I don't *want* to go."

"Then we *have* to find a way for you to stay."

Janet nodded, feeling herself landing back in her body after floating on clouds for the last... however long it had been. It had felt like hours but when she looked at the time on the oven clock, it had only been five minutes ago that they had just been friends.

A lot could change in five minutes.

"Are you sure that is nothing here you can sell?" He let her go and looked around the trailer again.

Janet gave him a hopeless look. "You know there isn't."

"Those books on the shelf, are there any dollar bills in the pages?"

"Seriously?"

David gave her a look. "You think I've never had to be resourceful? You'd be amazed how many people store cash money in their books."

"How do you know that?"

He didn't answer but began grabbing books off the shelves, flipping them upside down and throwing them on the floor.

"Hey! Those are Gran's books!" Janet snatched the Danielle Steele novel he'd been holding and clutched it to her chest, remembering Gran sitting in her chair and falling asleep reading it.

A prayer card had fallen out of its pages onto the floor. Janet scooped it up. Saint Christopher. She slid it into the pocket of her jeans. It wasn't worth any money, but it was worth everything to Janet. She didn't remember the last time Gran had gone to church, but this had obviously been important to her for some reason.

"Jan." David put his hands on her shoulders and forced her to look up at him. "We need to work this out. We *need* to fix this."

Janet shook her head and looked down, a solitary tear falling onto the toe of her army boot. She wiped under her eye, her finger coming back black from mascara. "You're right," she said, taking another book of the shelf and flicking through it. "You know, I have this dumb fantasy that something is going to happen that will fix everything. I keep thinking my dad will suddenly show up, or Gran will just walk through the door, like she's coming home from a really long game of Poker. She'll turn on the oven and cook a frozen pizza and we'll eat it while we watch trash TV. She'll fall asleep about half an hour later and I'll turn the volume down and read a book until late." Janet grabbed another book, and old Agatha Christie paperback and flicked through the pages. "But it's not going to happen, is it?"

"Gran and those frozen pizzas." David rolled his eyes.

"I loved those pizzas."

"No, you didn't. You always complained about them. You said you wished you were rich so you could order from Super Pan every night."

"And now all I want is a frozen pizza," she sighed.

"OK, so let's have frozen pizza," he said, moving towards the kitchen.

"It's the last one."

"I think Gran would want you to eat it."

Janet nodded and then watched David make the familiar movements, the ones Gran always used to make -

opening the box, sliding the pizza onto a tray and into the oven.

And while the sweet and salty aroma of Hawaiian pizza slowly filled the trailer, David held her in his arms. And as she closed her eyes, she pretended just for a moment that she was back in time and that Gran was still here.

But she knew she was just waiting for the timer to go off.

———

After they had finished going through the books, eaten the pizza, and kissed again a few more times, David's dad had knocked on the door of her trailer to give his condolences and drag David home for some important "family business", leaving Janet alone with the empty plates and the silence.

Now that she knew how David felt about her it had become even more urgent that she find a way out of this mess. She couldn't lose him too. So she put the radio on, Gran's favorite station - Valley FM, hits of yesterday. Bryan Adams' smooth voice came blaring out of the tinny speaker, singing about dying and going to heaven. If Janet didn't know better, she'd have thought it was a sign from Gran.

Maybe it was.

Maybe Gran was speaking to her through Bryan Adams lyrics, Gran had always been a big fan. Janet had tried to act like she was too cool and grunge for it, but the truth was, she secretly quite liked Bryan Adams too.

She left no pile of papers unturned. She searched the entire trailer for anything that could be worth even just a few cents.

Around midnight she found herself sitting on the floor of Gran's bedroom, her eyes red, face and t-shirt wet with tears, her hair in tangles. It was hopeless. Gran didn't have a dime to her name.

She'd looked through all of Gran's books and magazines but all she'd found were some losing scratch cards and receipts from the corner store. Janet couldn't comprehend how just two weeks ago Gran was buying milk, bread, pizza and tater-tots, and now she was *gone*. Gran was never going to go to the store again. Meanwhile, the world kept turning and right now someone else was probably buying tater-tots, totally unaware that it might be for the last time.

The only place left to look was Gran's closet. It was small, barely big enough to hold the few dresses and skirts Gran owned. Gran's one vice had always been shoes and they were all piled up on the floor of the closet. Janet owned two pairs of shoes - her boots and a pair of second-hand Nike's she wore for gym when she actually participated. But Gran was old school. She always wanted to look her best. Even though she wore the same few blouses and pants over and over, she swore blind that if you changed your shoes and your jewelry, you could change your whole outfit. Whenever they'd gone on their expeditions to Goodwill together, Gran had always found the shiniest, fanciest shoes to add to her collection. She also had an extensive collection of costume jewelry, all secondhand, all someone else's discarded old junk. But Gran wore it with pride. And when Gran did dress up for bingo, or someone's birthday, she really did look like a million bucks.

This was something that Janet, who lived in worn-out jeans and second-hand band t-shirts obviously did not inherit from her.

But costume jewelry purchased for fifty cents at Goodwill wasn't going to get her very far right now.

Reaching into the closet, Janet pulled out a pair of strappy gold sandals and put them on. They were too big, but it was so comforting to have them on her feet. She tried desperately to remember when Gran had worn them, but she couldn't. And it made her feel like Gran was already becoming a fading memory.

Knowing it was hopeless, Janet continued to search through the shoes anyway. Maybe Gran had unknowingly bought a pair of Guccis or Manolo Blahniks for five bucks.

She pulled out a pair of satin green pumps. They were beautiful, but they weren't Gran's style at all. They had a high heel and light wear on the soles. Janet threw the gold sandals to the side and pushed her feet into the green pumps. They were a perfect fit. Gran must have bought them without trying them on first.

Janet was about to stand up and walk around in them when she noticed a shoe box in the back of Gran's closet under the mountain of shoes. Pulling it out, Janet saw the little sticker on the side that said, "Emerald size 8".

The box was heavy. And whatever was inside, it wasn't a pair of shoes.

SEVEN

The Box

____

Santolsa
    1999

Janet lifted the lid off the box.

Her heart thumped in her chest as she realized what this box contained.

It wasn't just a stash of old letters, postcards and photos.

This box contained all that was left of her parents.

A box of matches from some bar, a check from a restaurant in Chinatown, a yellow flier for something called WOM which was praising the benefits of feminism in tidy cursive which looked like it had been photocopied a billion times. Janet smiled at that. She loved the idea of her mom being a raging feminist in the sixties. Maybe she even went to protests!

She pulled out a photo of her mom and dad that took her breath away. She had one photo of her mom, but she had never seen this one before. Her mom's hair was long and dark, just like hers, and she had a patterned scarf around her neck. She was so pretty, and she was looking up at her dad like he was sunshine incarnate. He was grinning up at the camera, his blond curls in a tangle. Those blond curls from her only memory of her dad, it *was* real. And he looked *happy*. Something she never thought her dad had ever been from the way Gran had spoken about him. But there he was, smiling at whoever had snapped this like everything was perfect. Maybe that's what this moment had been. A perfect moment in time, caught on camera.

Janet clutched the photo to her chest for a moment. Why didn't Gran ever show her this? Why didn't Gran ever tell her *anything*? Janet had tried asking many times, but Gran had always deflected, bringing Janet back to the present, to the here and now, always encouraging her to look ahead instead of at the past. To focus on doing well at school and making something of herself.

But this photo made her think there was probably a lot more to know, more questions she should have asked, but now it was too late.

Janet continued looking through the box, looking for the answers to those questions. The contents of this old shoe box were her only connection to her parents. This might be all she would ever know now.

She started sorting through the postcards her dad had sent to Gran from all over. Alaska, Seattle, Vancouver. And one from San Francisco…

Hey Mom,

Greetings from San Francisco!

Forgive me for not writing sooner. It's been wild!

I've been spending the summer working at a coffee house and I met the most amazing girl. She's smart and beautiful and I have no idea what she sees in me, but I'm not going to let her get away! I'm going to ask her to marry me after she graduates.

Start saving for your bus ticket, Mom!

I'll write again soon.

Love you,

Billy

After everything Gran had said about her dad it was hard to imagine him writing this. Was there a time when her dad said things like "love you" to Gran? Was there a time before he put Gran through hell and back by disappearing and leaving baby Janet on the doorstep?

She rifled through the box a little longer until she found a cream envelope which looked like it had once been white. It had her name written on it in the same messy writing that was on the postcard.

Janet frowned. A letter from her dad? For *her*?

She turned it over. It was still sealed.

Her stomach churned as she tried to decide what to do. She had wished her dad had been around so many times when she was younger, that now it was exhausting to even think about him. He'd had sixteen years to find her, even if he showed up now it would be too late. Janet had long ago accepted that if her dad was alive, he didn't care about her, which meant only two things - he either didn't care, or he wasn't alive. Either way, he was gone.

Nevertheless, Janet sat on the edge of Gran's bed, pulling the blanket over her legs and opened the envelope.

Dearest Janet,

My girl, my baby girl.

I am so sorry. There is nothing else I can say.

I don't know what else to do now but leave you here with your grandmother. I know she will raise you right.

She will give you everything I can't.

I wish I could give you everything, Janet. I wish I could give you a good life, but this is the best thing I can do. I really believe that. I have to believe that. And one day I hope you believe that too.

I asked your Gran to give you this letter on your eighteenth birthday. I don't know why. I just thought maybe then you'd be able to understand that I only left because I wanted you to be safe, and my leaving was the only way to know that you'd be protected from all the bad stuff I found myself caught up in.

Everything I touch turns to mud, baby girl. Everything.

I'm in trouble, Jan. I got involved with some bad people, a gang called the Eights. I regret all of it so deeply, but I can't change the past. I can only try to keep you safe from it.

And that means I have to go away.

And you have to promise me you will never get involved with them.

You will probably never see me again. Not because I don't love you, but because I love you too much.

Me and your mom, we had plans to move to Canada with you. To start over, to get a fresh start. But your mom is gone, and I'm not strong enough to do this without her. You would have loved your mom, baby girl. She was the one who should have lived, not me.

Your mom wanted and loved you so much.

And you have to know that I want and love you so much. And that's why I'm leaving you here. I love you too much to pull you into my dark messed up world.

But it's not meant to be in this life, baby girl.

All I can do is hope and pray that you have a good life. That you find your way in this world, and that you always have someone to love you.

I know Gran will love you, and I know she'll try her hardest to keep you on the straight and narrow.

Not a day will go by when I won't think of you.

Love you,

Dad

And Janet curled up in Gran's bed and fell asleep holding the letter to her heart.

Interlude III

Santolsa
   2018

Alexandra stood outside the old building on top of the hill in the middle of the desert.

She sighed and pulled on the collar of her yellow button-up shirt, ruffling up her red pixie cut in the process. She didn't know what she missed more, her L.A. High School where she had friends, knew her teachers and was doing well in her classes or being able to wear whatever she wanted to school.

St. Christopher's was going to be her new school, at least for a while. Her Aunt Patty had been in a motorcycle accident, after buying one during a mid-life crisis that had hit a few months ago. Aunt Patty had always been a pretty normal aunt, doing crafts and dressing in floral print, until one day she suddenly started wearing tight black jeans and slogan tees, demanded that everyone called her Tricia and bought a motorcycle. Uncle Hank was at his wit's end. And then she got into the accident and ended up in hospital with a fractured spine. The only thing for Alex's dad to do was hire some extra management for his chain of wildly successfully plant based diners and pack them all up and move them out to the desert until her aunt got better, whenever that was going to be.

Alex felt for her aunt, she really did, but she also couldn't help but be pissed that one decision in her aunt's stupid mid-life crisis had ripped Alex from the life she loved in L.A. and brought her out here to the middle of nowhere. Her brother Nick had gotten off easily. He was at College in Utah, a school he chose for some lame girl that had broken up with him before his second week, but he was still there, and she was here. In this dusty old town no one had ever heard of.

Alex took a deep breath and walked through the heavy wooden doors and into a sea of lemon-yellow shirts pushing and shoving to get to their lockers and classes.

"Excuse me," she asked a boy with dark hair who was staring at his phone, standing at the doors waiting for someone or something.

His head shot-up and he gave her an annoyed look.

"Can you tell me where the office is? I'm new."

He pointed with his head and she followed his directions, arriving in the office right as the bell for first period went. Great, she was already going to be late for her first class. Being new was bad enough without having to walk into a class halfway through.

Alex didn't like being the center of attention. She liked being behind the scenes, she was more than happy to create the magic while other people stood in the spotlight.

She had a quick conversation with the woman at the office and was soon holding her schedule. No Film Class, no Media Studies, the only creative thing on her schedule was a generic "Art".

Urgh.

But even worse was they'd put her in the special class instead of giving her study hall. Apparently, it was a thing they did for all the new students as a way to help them settle in. Alex thought this was the worst way to settle in ever. Like it wasn't embarrassing enough that the only person she knew in this whole place was her Aunt Peggy. Aunt Peggy was cool. She'd been best friends with her mom and dad since school, but Alex didn't think she was going to get any street cred for being close with one of the teachers.

With her schedule in hand, and a pack for new students which was mostly just fliers for stupid clubs she was never going to join, she walked slowly down the hallway towards where she thought her class was. Her brown Vans (why, oh why did she have to wear brown shoes?) squeaked slightly on the linoleum as old portraits of nuns on the walls between the lockers seemed to be looking down on her, almost as if they were watching her, telling her to hurry up and get to class.

She found her room near the end of the hallway, took a deep breath, and after agonizing over whether or not to knock or just walk in, she gently pushed the door open.

"Alex!" Her Aunt Peggy jumped up to greet her with a warm hug.

"Can you just be my teacher at school?" Alexandra whispered into her ear while she was being squished.

Aunt Peggy shook her head. "Of course, Sorry, I was just so happy to see you after so long. You look so grown up!"

Alex gave her a grin anyway. "You've got a few more gray hairs I see."

"Watch it," Aunt Peggy joked.

And then Alex became painfully aware of all the eyes

that were on her – a boy who looked like he was about to try to devour her, a couple of other boys who looked bored out of their minds, another who had his head on the desk and looked like he was sleeping.

And just one girl. A pretty blonde girl, no, not just pretty, *beautiful.*

The girl caught her eye and then quickly looked down at her books.

"Everyone, this is Alexandra," Peggy said. "Alexandra, this is everyone – Fred, Yuan, Reggie, Ash and Lena."

Lena.

The blonde girl didn't look up.

"Lena," Peggy said. "Would you be so kind as to show Alex around today?"

Lena looked up and frowned. "Sorry to disappoint you, but I don't have time," she said, her gaze moving back to her books.

Aunt Peggy went over to her and had a quiet word, Alex caught small parts of the conversation, something about this being part of a deal, something she could do to get out of something else. Eventually Lena shrugged and gave a nod.

"Take a seat next to Lena, Alex, she'll show you the ropes of St. C's."

And so, Alexandra took her seat, and when Lena finally looked up, and their eyes met, they both felt the magic between them.

And Alex thought maybe Santolsa wasn't going to be so bad after all.

EIGHT

Religious Studies

Santolsa
1999

Janet still had a few days before she was going to be evicted and she thought the best thing to do with those few days was to go back to school and try to pretend none of this was happening. At least at school she could just focus on her studies. If she did find a way to pay her rent, she still wanted to pass her finals next week.

David thought she should be out looking for a job, but even if she found one today, she wouldn't see any cash for two weeks, and no job around here would give her an advance before she'd even started.

She was screwed. And she was sick of hanging around the trailer park waiting for some magical fairy godmother to show up and fix everything.

So instead, she sat up the back of her Religious Studies class passing notes with David.

Even though everything in her life was a mess, and she

should have been using all her brain power for problem solving or studying, she still found her mind mostly just replaying David's lips on hers. Janet wondered if David's dad hadn't turned up that night, that first night they kissed, if maybe he would have stayed the night, and if they would maybe have even gone all the way. She blushed at the memory of him lifting her onto the kitchen counter and...

"Janet?" Sister Catherine stood over her desk, staring down at the note she had been writing which was way too explicit for a nun's eyes.

Janet crumpled up the paper and looked up. "Yes, Sister Catherine?"

"Forty days and nights in the desert."

Janet nodded, trying to look like she knew what had been going on.

"What do you think it means?"

"I... uh, I think it's a metaphor?"

"A metaphor?" Sister Catherine asked curiously. "In the bible, really?" She raised her eyebrows up into her habit.

"Well sure. No one could *really* survive in the desert for that long without food and water."

"Not even the son of God?" Sister Catherine gave Janet a soft smile.

Janet shrugged. "Even if Jesus was the son of God, he was still in a human man's body."

Sister Catherine gave her a nod. "Interesting answer."

Becka Barnes, a very active member of the purity club, piped up from the front of the classroom. "If he *was* just a human man, explain how could he walk on water and turn water into wine? If he could do miracles, he could also like, not eat for a few days."

"Maybe it was magic," Janet said, throwing her a dark look.

Becka gasped. "How dare you! To even suggest that Jesus did *magic*! Magic is the devil's work!"

"Settle down," Sister Catherine said. "Everyone is entitled to their opinion."

"This is a Catholic school, *Sister*," Becka said, slapping a hand on her desk. "And we need to know the difference between opinion and *fact*!"

"You're right, Becka. This *is* a Catholic school, and one of the most important things about being Catholic and following the path of Jesus is compassion and kindness."

Becka harrumphed.

David passed a note that said: "Want to see what other magic a human man's body can do?"

Janet blushed, covering her face with her hands to stop her from letting out a giggle. She scribbled on the note and passed it back.

"Yes."

NINE

David's House

Santolsa
  1999

Janet had been thinking about that note all day. But now, as she got off the back of his bike back at the trailer park, she'd lost all her mojo and wasn't sure she could follow through with any of it. It was easy to talk about sex in a note passed in class. It was a different thing completely to actually *have* sex.

"You OK?" David asked, taking the helmet from her hands and putting it in the storage compartment of his bike.

She nodded. "Uh huh."

"I know what you're thinking."

"You do?"

"This is weird, right?" He mussed up his hair and pulled the keys from the ignition.

"Weird?"

"You and me, it's kinda weird?"

"Why would this be weird?"

"Because you've always been like a sister to me."

Oh God.

"But these last few weeks," he began.

Janet took a breath and looked down at the wheel of his bike sitting in the orangey brown dust.

"But I feel like this is something else now," he finished.

She looked over at him, the snake of his Eight tattoo peeking out from his school shirt, his stubble aging him a good few years. He looked ridiculous in a school uniform. He wasn't a boy, he was a *man.* He was a member of a gang, he was an Eight. He had bad news written all over him, but at the same time, he had been the only thing that had gotten her through these last few weeks. So how could that be so bad, really?

"I don't know why I didn't see it before, but… in a way, you're really pretty." he said.

Janet laughed. "Is that meant to be a compliment?"

"I didn't mean, I just meant…" David sighed. "You're not exactly Claudia Schiffer."

Janet glared at him.

"You're more like… Courtney Cox."

She raised her eyebrows.

"Courtney Cox is hot."

"Right now, you're being a George Costanza."

He let out a laugh. "I know *you* don't see it, but everyone else does. Guys are staring at you all the time and you don't even notice."

"Whatever."

"It's true. When I started to notice other guys checking you out, I felt so protective of you, and then I realized. It wasn't just about being protective, it was because I was *jealous.* I didn't want them looking at you. *I* wanted to look at you."

Janet didn't know what to say to that.

"I guess… I'm kind of into you."

Janet folded her arms. "You sure you don't want to wait for Claudia Schiffer?"

He gave her a gentle shove with his shoulder. "You of all people should know I'm not that good at expressing my… feelings or whatever."

"Make me a mixtape."

"Maybe I will."

"Maybe you should."

He gave her one of his sexy bad boy smiles that she couldn't resist. "Dad isn't going to back until later tonight if you want to come over."

She nodded, probably a little too eagerly. "Sure, I'll just dump my books and get undressed." She blushed and he gave her a smoldering look.

"I mean, get *changed*, not get undressed…" she said, trying to fix the situation but probably making it worse. She took a step back towards her trailer.

"Hey." He reached out and grabbed the bottom of her school shirt and pulled her in close. He kissed her softly, igniting a fire in her belly, and then let her go. "I'll see you soon?"

She nodded and smiled, her brain melting into goo. She'd agree to anything right now. "I'll be right over."

She let herself into her trailer and picked up a note that had been pushed under the door. It was handwritten on the back of an old flier for a circus. It said, "RENT BY THE 10TH OR ELSE". Nice.

She threw the note on the table by the door where it landed on top of Gran's favorite red lipstick. Janet picked it up and opened the lid, looking at the indentation made by Gran's lips. Without thinking twice, she made her way to the mirror in the bathroom and put the lipstick on. It changed her whole face, brightened her eyes, and made her look like she'd actually had a bit of sleep recently. Janet's make-up routine had never consisted of much more than a bit of eyeliner and mascara. But this was different, and she liked it. She felt grown-up, she felt *sexy*. She felt alive.

Janet changed out of her school uniform and into a thrifted Soundgarden t-shirt and a pair of ripped blue jeans. She brushed out her long dark hair and then messed it up a little, just so she didn't look like she cared too much, but she left the lipstick on.

Janet knocked on the door to David's trailer. His older brother Nathan, who hadn't inherited David's same good looks, appeared at the door and pushed past her before looking back. "Janet, wowzers. I should have kissed you first."

She gave him a look. Nathan wasn't her favorite person in the world. "What do you know about it?"

"David's been bragging about it to anyone who'll listen."

Janet couldn't work out whether to be pissed he was kissing and telling or to be flattered that he was bragging about kissing *her*.

"Have a good night," Nathan said with a wink as he walked towards his piece of crap car which started with a chug before he sped off through the trailer park.

"Sorry about him," David said, finally coming to the door and looking her up and down. "You look... different."

David was dressed in a pair of black jeans and a tight burgundy red t-shirt which showed off more of his tattoo than his school uniform ever did. A stark reminder of who he was, and what she was getting into being with him.

"Come in." He ushered her inside.

His trailer was the same lay out as hers, but it was always crammed full of boxes, piles of motorbike and gun magazines and it reeked of cigarette smoke.

"Want something to eat?"

"Sure." She sat down on the couch, nervously bouncing her leg and wondering if this was it. If she going to lose her virginity in a pile of guns and ammo magazines and dirty ashtrays.

He sat down next to her and handed her a box of crackers. She took one and tried to eat it, but her mouth wasn't making enough saliva and she started coughing.

David looked alarmed and grabbed her a glass of water. "Are you OK?"

She nodded. "I'm just… nervous." The relief of admitting it washed over her and she immediately felt better.

"Why?" he asked, like he really didn't know.

She looked down at her hands and scratched at the chipped black nail polish. "I'm not… I haven't…"

"Oh God, Jan, I didn't even think. I just assumed everyone had done it by now and it was no big deal."

She coughed again before reaching for the water and taking a long, slow sip. "Oh, totally. It's no big deal." She waved her hand around, trying to look like she meant it.

"OK, so if it's no big deal…" he reached out and grabbed her hand, pulling her off the couch, through the trailer and into his tiny bedroom which was like a grunge dream. The walls were covered in band posters and every spare surface was covered with piles of old books and tapes. David slid a Nirvana tape into his boombox, which Janet knew for a fact was stolen, and Kurt Cobain's voice filled the room. She watched nervously as he lit a couple of candles that had been shoved into old Jim Beam bottles.

"See, I can do romance," he grinned.

"So I see." Janet looked around the room. She picked up a birthday card and then made a gasp. "I forgot your birthday!"

He shook his head. "You've had other things going on."

"Oh God, I'm so sorry."

"It's no big deal."

Janet's stomach flipped. "Seventeen."

David gave a nod. "Yep."

"That means…"

"Uh huh. I'm fully initiated." He lit one more candle and threw the lighter on a desk that looked like he'd never sat behind, let alone studied at. "We just did it last night."

"What is the initiation?" she asked, putting the card back down.

"You know I can't tell you that, not unless you join us."

She rolled her eyes. "Not now, not ever."

"Good, I don't want you to." He moved closer towards her. "You're too special for this shit." He put a finger through the loop of her jeans and pulled her down onto the bed and into a pile of laundry.

"You could do a lot better than me, Jan," he whispered into her ear, before gently kissing her neck.

"I don't want to do better than you," she said, breathing in the smell of him – cigarettes, unwashed hair and motorbike grease. It should have been disgusting, but it was intoxicating.

And soon they were all arms and legs, hair and lips, crinkled laundry and loud lyrics, and boots and shoes falling to the floor.

He grabbed the hem of her t-shirt and lifted it over her

head. She felt her heart race, partly from the excitement of it all, partly from embarrassment at not owning a sexy bra. But David didn't seem to care. He looked at her ancient gray crop top like it was a birthday cake and he hadn't eaten in three years.

Courage suddenly coursed through her and she grabbed at his shirt and lifted it over his head too, revealing his entire Eight tattoo and another tattoo she didn't even know he had, a black skull with a sword through it on the opposite shoulder.

"I didn't know you had this," she said, tracing the skull with her fingers.

"I had to get the Eight tattoo, but I wanted something just for me too."

"It's… dark."

He gave a little laugh. "I was listening to a lot of Metallica when I got it."

"You know, it's kind of cute."

"Cute?"

She giggled.

"There's nothing cute about me." He grabbed the laundry and threw it all to the floor. "Stupid laundry."

"Sure there is," she grinned, the playful mood helping her finally relax. "Your tattoos are cute, your hair is cute…" She gently curled a finger through one of the long strands of his dark hair.

He let out a growl and moved back in, gently biting her earlobe. "Is that cute?"

"Kinda…"

He found her lips and kissed her hard and fast, sending her heart racing again. "How about that?"

"OK, maybe that's more… sexy than cute…"

"How about this?" He slid his hand down to the top

button of her jeans and unbuttoned it in one quick movement and she gasped.

"David?" A voice rang out, followed by a knock on the
door. A split second later it swung wide open, and his dad
stood staring at them. "Oh, shit, sorry." He closed the door
behind him, but it was too late.

Janet was mortified. "Oh my God," she wailed, grap-
pling around for her shirt.

David jumped off the bed and into the pile of laundry.
"He wasn't meant to be back until later!"

"I need to get out of here." She pulled her shirt and
her boots back on, fumbling to do her jeans back up.

"I'm so sorry Janet, this was supposed to be something
memorable."

"Oh, it will be, trust me."

David turned off the music and blew out the candles.

"Can I go out the window?"

"Don't be stupid, Dad won't care."

"*I* care!"

David put his shirt back on, and when they were both
fully dressed again, he opened the door, gesturing for Janet
to follow him.

"Hey Dad," David said, folding his arms. "You know,
when you knock, you're meant to wait for someone to
answer before you barge in."

His dad looked up from the couch where he was smoking
a cigarette and combing his hands through his own long dark
hair and putting it in a low ponytail while watching *Cops* very
loudly. "Uh huh," he said, not paying any attention.

David gave Janet a look.

"Hey Mr. Stone," Janet said, still pulling on the hem of
her shirt like it would never cover her enough now that
David's dad had seen her in her crop top.

"Come on Janet, I've known you for years. No more Mr. Stone, OK?"

"Sorry… Jonas."

"I heard you were in some trouble," Jonas said, his eyes finally leaving the TV to land on hers.

She gave a shrug.

"I have a job for you. For you both." He threw a stack of cash on the coffee table, just missing the ashtray. It was more cash than Janet had ever seen in one pile. "It's enough for your rent, Janet. For a couple of months at least, plus bills and food."

"No," said David.

"Let her speak for herself."

"No," she said.

"I know you don't want to get involved, but from what I just saw, you're already involved." He took a drag of his cigarette. "You might as well make a buck out of it."

Janet just wanted a regular life with no criminal record, a regular paycheck and more than one pizza in the freezer.

But she also knew that dream was pretty far away right now, and Jonas was probably right. She didn't really have much of a choice.

Gran had always told her she could do anything, but the deck was stacked against her. What else could she do?

It was time to face the truth. There was no other way.

Janet sighed. "What's the job?"

TEN

The Job

―――――――

Santolsa
  1999

In theory, the job should have been simple enough. It was just a "pick up". Jonas hadn't been all that forthcoming with what it was they were supposed to be picking up, but he'd promised it would be straight forward. Janet and David were to wait at the back fence of St. Christopher's High School. A car would pass by and throw the "goods" out the window. They'd wait until the car was out of view and David would say something to Janet like - "Well, that was weird, I wonder what that guy threw out his window?" Just in case someone was watching. He would pick it up, whatever it was, pocket it, get on his bike and drive home.

Jonas had said that if it was the two of them hanging around outside school, they could easily pass for just a couple of kids sneaking out to hook up. If the cops stopped them, they'd just get sent on their way. A couple of older guys on bikes would draw too much attention. It would be safer, less risky for everyone.

So, there they were, two kids, sitting beside a giant cactus by the back fence of St. Christopher's High School. It was just past midnight, the time the drop was meant to take place, and Janet was feeling more and more nervous about the whole thing.

"Hey," David said, putting his hand on the skin of her knee which was poking through her ripped jeans. "It's all good, it's just a simple drop. You'll see. Any minute now, a shitty car will come past blaring some shitty music and a brown paper bag will come flying out the window and then it'll be gone. I'll grab it. We're done. We go home. Rent is paid. Done."

"You seem to know a lot about this."

He raised an eyebrow, the half-moon in the sky above catching the light in his eyes. "This isn't my first job, Jan."

"I know, I just… I wish this wasn't how it was." His hand had slowly made its way a little higher and paused on her thigh where it felt warm, safe, but also just a little scary.

"Well, it is how it is," he said.

They sat for a few moments in silence, both absorbed by their own thoughts until he spoke again.

"What would you want it to be like," he started. "If life could be like anything?"

Janet took a breath. "I just want to be normal. Most kids in our class are thinking about jobs or community college. But you and me, we're thinking about survival you know? I don't want to just struggle to survive. I want a real job, maybe even some kind of career. I want my own home. I want all my bills paid. I want a freezer full of pizza."

"It's one job, Jan. This is just one job for you, to get you back on your feet. You'll pay the landlord, you'll ace all your finals next week, get a summer job, save up some money, finish your last year of school and then you'll get the hell out of Santolsa."

"But what if I don't want to get out of Santolsa? What if I want to stay here… with you?"

David let out a loud laugh and took his hand from her thigh. "Jan, that's sweet, but you know we have no future together."

She didn't want to say out loud she wanted him to be her future. She didn't even know if she was ready to say it to herself. A future with David would be… it would be this. Sitting on the side of the road waiting for someone to throw a bag out a car window. "Maybe, if we were… together, we could help each other get out of this, make something of ourselves," she said.

"It's a nice idea."

"It doesn't have to just be an idea," she turned to face him, her back aching from leaning up against the bars of the fence. "We could really do it. Just like you said. Finals next week, summer jobs, one more year, then we get out of here. Both of us. Together."

"Jan, I'm never going to be able to leave the Eights, you know that. No matter where I go or what I do."

"It could be different."

"You're so naive." He let out a long breath and rested his head against the fence and looked up at the stars above them.

Janet folded her arms. "I'm not naive, I'm just… hopeful."

"Same thing."

She rested her back against the fence again.

"See, this is why it would never work with us. You're smart, you can make it, you can get out. You deserve better."

"If you don't want to be with me, just say so. All this BS about me being too good for you is starting to sound like a line."

He sighed. "I don't want to be the reason your life goes to shit."

"You wouldn't be."

He shook his head and turned towards her, his eyes blazing. "I'm not good enough for you, get it into your head."

"If you're not good enough for me, why are you the only thing I want?"

"You don't really want *me*. We both know that. You're still grieving and I'm just a good distraction." He turned his face away.

"I liked you way before any of this happened," she said quietly.

For a long moment he said nothing. "You did?" he finally asked.

"I did."

"Since when?"

Janet shrugged. "I don't know, a few months, a year."

"A *year*?"

"Maybe."

"Why?" he asked, like liking him was the stupidest thing that someone could do.

"Because you're nice."

"Ha! Nice? I think you're the only girl to ever call me that."

"And you're... kind of good looking."

"*Kind* of? Well, then..."

"Does anyone really know why they like anyone? I just do. You just like someone or you don't."

"I know why I like you," he started, looking back towards her. "I like you because you're smart and you're beautiful, and you make me feel like I could be a better person. But that's also why we can't be together. Because you can do so much better, you *deserve* better. And I don't want to be with someone who feels so out of my league."

"Are you kidding? You're out of *my* league."

"How do you figure?"

"Uh, because you're so fricking cool. You ride a motorcycle, you just got initiated into the most bad-ass gang in the state and you're pretty much the hottest guy at school."

He laughed. "The hottest guy in school, huh?" He leaned into her just a little, like he wanted to hear more about this.

"Oh yeah, you should hear what the girls say about you in the locker room."

"What do they say?" he asked, putting his hand back on her knee.

"They say that you're the most bangable guy in school," she said, trying to keep her cool as he leaned in even closer.

"And what do you say?" he asked, slowly brushing her hair back from her face.

"I agree with them, and maybe one day, if your dad is *definitely* not coming home, I'd like to find out if they are right…"

The side of his mouth curled up slightly and she let out a nervous giggle. He leaned in close and then his lips were on hers. Heat and fire moved from her lips to her stomach and then completely through her.

They were so caught up in each other they almost

didn't notice the car come to a stop right where they were sitting.

They quickly pulled apart.

"They're not meant to stop," David said, jumping up and pulling Janet to her feet.

He was wrong, it wasn't a shitty car, it was a big black SUV, and it was playing some old eighties rock song out of its very nice speakers. And it had stopped.

Everything was wrong.

"Stay behind me," David said, grabbing her hand and walking towards the car.

The driver rolled his window down. "Where is it?" he called out.

"Where's what?" David asked.

"The stuff."

"What stuff?"

"Don't act smart with me kid," the driver said, opening the door and stepping out. He was a big middle-aged guy who looked like some kind of mafia boss dressed in suit pants, a white shirt and shiny black crocodile dress shoes.

"I don't know what you're talking about," David said again. "Me and my girlfriend were just here hanging out." He gestured to Janet, and even though she knew this was a bad time, she still felt a thrill at him calling her his girl-friend, even if it was just for this guy's benefit.

The guy's eyes glazed over and he looked well and truly pissed as he reached at the back of his pants, pulled out a shiny silver gun and pointed it right at them.

"OK, OK," David said, putting up his hands, and Janet did the same. "We were waiting for a drop off, that's why we are here, but we're meant to be the receivers, take it back to HQ. We don't have anything to drop off."

The guy clicked the safety and Janet froze.

Fuck.

This was really happening.

"He's telling the truth," Janet said, adrenaline kicking in. "We are here for the drop off, we were told it would just be thrown out the window. I swear. Please don't hurt us."

"You think I was born yesterday?" The guy asked, still holding the gun at them. "I know what kids like you do. You take the stash for yourselves and come up with some bullshit story. Maybe your little Eights friends put up with that shit, but the Rollers don't. Just give it to me, and no one gets hurt."

The passenger door opened, and a pretty blonde woman popped her head over the top of the car. "Baby," she called out in a high-pitched voice. "Don't hurt them, they're just children!"

The guy looked back at her, annoyed, and suddenly David was flying towards him, knocking the gun out of his hand and shoving him towards the car.

The blonde woman came rushing around. Dressed in a tight red dress and sky-high heels she looked like she belonged in a music video, not in a car with some drug dealer from Salt Valley. "Baby!" she screeched. "Don't hurt my baby!"

"Hurt him?" Janet yelled back. "He was going to kill us!"

"Calm down," David said, taking a step back. "Everyone just calm down. It's all just a misunderstanding, we can work this out."

"Misunderstanding?" The guy was on top of David in a second, grabbing him around the neck and pushing him to the ground. "It might have been a misunderstanding before, but now it's personal." The guy punched David in the face, once, twice, three times, sending blood splattering out of his mouth and nose.

"Get off him!" Janet yelled, running towards them.

The blonde woman grabbed Janet by the hair and started screeching, pushing Janet to the ground also.

The guy looked around for his gun, but David saw it first. He scrambled at the asphalt for it. Janet kicked the woman in the shins and had gotten out of her grip for just long enough to kick the gun closer, thinking maybe David would hit the guy in the face with it, or let off a warning shot, giving them both a scare and they could get away.

But instead, David grabbed the gun, pulled the trigger, and shot the guy in the face, killing him in an instant.

ELEVEN

The Book Room

Santolsa
1999

The man was lying dead on the road and the blonde woman was clutching at her chest and screaming.

"The school!" Janet gasped. "Let's make a run for it."

"We can't hide out there!" David wiped a splatter of blood from his brow. He turned and grabbed her by the shoulders. "We have to get out of Santolsa, cross the state line, get as far away as possible."

"How? On your bike? How long until they are looking for us?"

"Steal a car?"

"You want to add to our list of crimes?"

"My crimes, *my* crimes, Janet." He shook her, a wild look appearing in his eye, like a coyote about to run.

The woman started screaming. "You killed him! You killed him!" she was yelling.

"The gun," David said, holding it out, his hands shaking.

She shook her head. "You can't leave it here, take it."

David nodded and stuffed the gun in the waistband of his jeans.

"Come on!" Janet pushed herself out of his grip and ran back towards the fence. "Give me a boost!"

David shot after her, and in a moment, he had his hands linked together. Janet stomped her boots onto them and launched herself over the fence. David climbed up, hauling himself over the top, his shirt ripping on the way down, leaving him with a gaping hole in the side and a cut that would probably scar. He fell as he landed, and Janet grabbed his hand, slick with sweat and blood, his blood, and the guy's. But she couldn't think about it now. She just had to get out of here. She pulled him up through the scrub and dust on the side of the hill. "In that book I read," she started, puffed from scrambling so fast. "There are secret rooms in the school, secret tunnels."

"What? Why?"

"The school was built by nuns who were on the run."

"Nuns on the run?" David let out a raspy laugh as he continued crawling up the scrub after her.

"They were persecuted for their religion."

"Come on," he said, slipping on the desert earth and nearly falling all the way back down. "As if anyone has ever been persecuted for being Catholic."

"Seriously? Try reading a history book sometime."

It was their same old banter, back and forth, keeping them from falling into total fear and paralyzing panic.

They continued talking, just saying words, any words, scrambling and grabbing at the scrub and the stones to get the top of the hill as fast as they could.

Janet looked back and saw the blonde woman on a cell

phone, looking around in all directions for them. They didn't have long. She dragged him across the dusty parking lot until they reached the back door to the English department.

David kicked the door. "What now?"

She knew it was pointless, but Janet reached out and tried the door handle.

David gasped.

Janet gasped.

"It's open," she said, pushing the door and stepping into the safety of the school building, what was once the old abbey.

"I never thought I'd be so glad to be here," David said.

She slammed the door behind them, turning the lock and bolting the door. "Why would it be unlocked…?"

"Maybe someone is watching over us after all," he joked.

Janet shook her head. "It doesn't matter why, we're safe now."

"For now, but for how long?" David's face had changed. It was as if he'd aged ten years in the last few minutes.

She leaned back against the locked door. "I don't know. Let's just hide out here tonight and then we can make some kind of plan. We just have to regroup. Get our shit together. We can work this out."

"Why are you even doing this? You don't need to help me. You didn't do anything. Just let me take the fall, Jan." He ran his hands through his hair. "We both know how my story is going to go. If I don't get done for this, it will be the next job, or the one after. Sooner or later you know how it's going to turn out for me, maybe it's better if it's now."

"Don't talk like that."

"It's true. We both know my future. You still have a chance."

"You think I have a chance? I can't even pay my rent, I'm getting shipped off to social services and now I'm an accessory to murder. I kicked the gun to you. I'm just as much to blame. You think my future looks any brighter?"

David ran his fingers over his face. "OK, so where are these secret rooms and passages?"

Janet looked down the hallway. She had no idea. She'd never noticed any secret rooms or passages before. She'd only read about them in that book Sister Catherine had given her.

A bang on the door behind them startled them both. Janet leapt back from the door and grabbed onto David's arm.

David swore. "Did someone follow us?" he breathed.

Janet shook her head. "I didn't see anyone…"

Voices carried through the door behind them. Janet couldn't make out what they were saying, but it didn't sound good. She put a finger to her lips, and they stayed dead still until the voices had stopped.

"Probably just security or something," she said quietly.

The door handle started to shake violently, and they made a run for the room closest to the exit, what Janet had always thought was a janitor's closet.

"Locked," said David, trying to wrangle his way in. "It's locked!"

Sister Catherine's voice echoed in Janet's head - *you'll know when it's time to use it.*

And she just knew. She didn't know how, but she knew this was the time.

So she grabbed the key that she had been carrying around in her pocket since that day in detention, the day Gran had died.

And she slid it into the keyhole.

David gasped and Janet let out a high-pitched laugh as she turned the handle and the door opened as if by magic. But they didn't have time to ponder the strangeness of it all, they just needed to hide.

She flung the door open, walked through and reached out for David's hand, pulled him in with her and locked the door behind her.

Interlude IV

Santolsa
  2018

Lena ran her thumb over the back of Alex's hand. Her pale skin was so perfect, the freckles dotted around her wrist reminded her of a constellation of stars. Alex pressed her fingers into Lena's, the feeling of it, of her being so close, felt like it was lighting a fire inside her.

It was lunchtime and the two of them were sitting on a patch of grass by the back of the school, not far from where Kimana used to work the horses. They'd been coming out here most days together for the last few months and it was the best part of Lena's day. At first it had been nothing more than friendship, but over time it had developed into something more. Lena didn't think she would ever feel like this again. She often felt guilty, as if she should still be waiting for Kimana. But with every touch of Alex's hand, or gentle press of her lips, it was as if Kimana was slowly becoming nothing more than a clouded memory. Lena didn't want to lose that memory, but she was also very much enjoying making new memories.

Alex looked over at her and offered half of a sandwich which looked very unappealing.

Lena shook her head and dug her bare feet into the grass.

"Did you have lunch?" Alex asked.

Lena shook her head again. She'd always been unable to eat around Alex, she was too tied up in knots to be able to get any food down, but she also couldn't stop thinking about Kimana. What did it mean to be this close to someone again? What did it say about her? What did it say about her love for Kimana? To have these feelings for Alex, did it mean her feelings for Kimana weren't real? She was consumed with guilt.

"I know Aunt Peggy packs you lunch," Alex said.

Lena shrugged. "I don't like what she gives me. It's always leftover pizza or macaroni noodles or… sausages."

"You could just tell her you don't like it."

"Mr. and Mrs. Ruthven have done so much for me, taking me in and letting me stay in their home, I couldn't tell them I don't like their food." Lena had never had any problem telling Sister Catherine when she didn't like her soups or stews, but she was so happy staying with the Ruthvens. She had her own room now and it was warm and cosy and full of books. There was almost always hot water to bathe in, and the bed was so comfortable. She never wanted to leave. And she never wanted to do anything to give them a reason to ask her to leave.

"Come on, you need to eat." Alex waved the sandwich at her. "Or… I have an apple?"

Lena sighed. "An apple, fine."

"Is something wrong?"

"No… yes. I am not sure."

"Why do you talk like that?" Alex asked, squishing up her adorable, freckled nose.

"Talk like… what?" Lena asked, trying to sound more modern. It had been difficult to become a modern person. She was still making mistakes all the time. She sat up too straight, she spoke too well, she didn't understand their strange technology at all.

"Like… proper," Alex answered.

"I was brought up this way."

"What, like Amish or in a cult or something?"

Lena let out a loud *ha*. She'd heard of this word "cult". It was a word that described a strange religious community. Usually, it was a community people couldn't get out of once they were in it. "Actually, yes."

"Woah," said Alex, passing the apple over.

Lena took a bite, the juices pouring down her chin. She was so hungry she had forgotten how to eat! She tried to look away from Alex as she wiped the juice away. But Alex just laughed and reached out a finger and wiped the drip from her chin.

Lena felt something burst inside of her, and instead of thinking of Kimana, suddenly her thoughts were all of Alex. Of her freckles, her smile, her kindness. And before she really knew what she was doing, she was pressing her lips to Alex's, and Alex was kissing her back and it was the perfect moment of sticky sweet passion.

And Lena felt as if maybe she could finally leave the past behind.

PART TWO

TWELVE

A Dream

____

Santolsa

Between Time

Janet and David sat huddled under a dusty shelf crammed with class sets of novels and plays.

As soon as Janet had closed and locked the door behind them there had been a flash of light so blinding it had knocked them both off their feet. Then, in the pitch black, they had grabbed each other and dropped to the ground, hearts racing in unison.

"What was that?" Janet whispered.

"Faulty wiring or something?" David's voice was hesitant as it came out of the darkness.

Janet nuzzled her head into his shoulder, and he put his arms around her, pulling her closer in a protective gesture. Much good it would do. They were two criminals on the run, no matter how tight he held her, in the morning the sun would rise, and they would have to either turn themselves in or make a run for it.

"What are we going to do?" she asked, knowing there really wasn't much of an answer.

"I don't know Jan, I really don't know." She'd never heard him sound so uncertain. Mr. Cool, the guy who always seemed to know how to handle himself had no idea how to get out of this one.

She pressed herself into him and he held her even tighter. He kissed the top of her head, pushing back her hair with his shaking hands.

Only one thing was certain now – life would never be the same again.

Janet woke with a desperate need to go to the bathroom. For a moment she wasn't sure where she was, or why, until it all came flooding back. She was in David's arms, huddled under a stack of old books in a musty old book room in St. Christopher's High School, hiding out after shooting someone.

David was still fast asleep, his breathing heavy and calm. She gently moved out of his embrace, and he huddled sleepily back into the corner.

Janet slowly opened the door and crept out into the darkness, closing it again behind her. The blinding light returned. Three flashes from under the door.

"David? Are you OK?" she asked through the door.

When he didn't respond she guessed he had somehow managed to sleep through it. She made her way to the girls' bathroom, a sliver of moonlight lighting up the wooden floorboards, showing her the way.

Wooden floorboards?

Janet could have sworn the floor of the hallway was linoleum, but she was exhausted, and her brain wasn't working, and so she just kept walking. That was all she could do now. Just keep walking. One foot in front of the other.

She made it to the bathroom, sacred to turn on a light and alert anyone to her presence, she did what she needed to do in the dark and then slowly made her way back down the hallway. She nearly slipped on a piece of paper and cursed in a whisper before picking it up. She was about to ball it up and throw it in the trash until she saw something curious in the low light of the moon.

Class of 1966 yearbook committee.

Janet blinked and moved towards the notice board from where it must have fallen. She looked through the other notices, squinting in the darkness to read them. Exam dates for an exam which took place in March 1966 and a harsh reminder that anyone with a skirt that showed anything above the knee would have detention for the rest of the school year.

Janet ran her hand over her face.

What was this? A knock on the head? A bad dream? Some senior prank?

She rushed back to the book room, flinging the door open and calling David's name.

But David was gone.

THIRTEEN

Class off 1933

Santolsa
1933

David woke up hunched in a corner with a splitting headache and a stiff neck. It took him a moment to realize where he was. This wasn't his comfy bed in his bedroom in his trailer. This was the book room at *school.* The last place he ever thought he'd wake up in. Janet was gone and he was all alone in the tiny room that had been their safe haven overnight. He knew this was just a temporary hideout. Sooner or later, he'd get caught. Maybe as soon as he walked out that door. Maybe he'd get as far as town. Maybe he'd get over the Nevada state line. Maybe he'd hide out another five, ten, twenty years, but eventually he was going to get done for what he had done.

What he had done.

Images flashed through his mind. The gun, the blood, the look on Janet's face. The look that said she would never be able to look at him the same way again. He wouldn't be able to look at himself the same way again.

He was a murderer.

Even if he did make it out of here, even if he did get to Utah or Alaska or Mexico or anywhere, would he ever really be able to live with this guilt? It wasn't like he did it on purpose, it wasn't planned, but he still did it. In the moment he couldn't see another way, he had done it only to save himself, to save Janet, but he'd still pulled the trigger.

Janet.

And now he had gotten her into this mess. That was the worst part. The idea of her going down for this killed him. She had never wanted anything to do with the Eights. He should have said no. He should have done this alone and given her the money anyway. But if she hadn't been there last night things would have played out differently. He would have been the one who'd been shot. He knew that.

Janet had saved his life by being there.

Janet didn't deserve any of this. She was just broke, and out of options. The same reason most people got involved with the Eights. Necessity. Some joined for the promise of money, some for a family they had never had, and some, like David, were born into it. And when you were born into the Eights, you were an Eight for life. It was like being born into some kind of trailer trash royalty. Your life was never really yours, no matter how much you tried to convince yourself it was. You had no options. You only had duty.

But Janet could've avoided all this if he'd just said no. His dad could have sent one of the others, someone with more experience. Someone with a gun.

He stood up, rolling his neck, trying to get out the

kinks, and then he opened the door and stepped into the light of the hallway.

A young boy raced past, nearly taking David out. "Sorry, sir!" the boy called out, not looking back.

Sir?

David had never been called sir in his life.

A whole hoard of children were following behind the boy, some running and scrapping, some looking on and tutting. There was something about the children that unsettled him. They didn't seem quite… normal. For one, they were dressed strangely. The boys in smart yellow shirts and brown shorts, with their white socks pulled up to their knees. The girls were dressed in brown dresses that looked like sacks.

"What the…?" he whispered to himself as he tried to make sense of what he was seeing in front of him. Maybe it was some kind of kid's camp? Something that happened on the weekends? Just because he'd never heard of it, didn't mean it wasn't a thing.

A nun appeared out of nowhere and before she'd even said a word the kids immediately stopped running, stood up straight and marched into their classrooms, dispersing so quickly it was like they had never been there in the first place.

"Can I help you?" the nun asked, finally noticing David lurking by the entrance to the book room.

"I'm… David," he said. "David Stone." He probably should have given her a fake name, but she was a nun, and lying to a nun didn't feel right, even if he wasn't religious. It was hard to have faith in any kind of higher power when your prayers had never been answered.

The nun just stared at him as if *he* was the ghost in this scenario.

"I'm… just confused. I was…" He tapped at the door behind him.

The nun continued to stare at him, like she was looking straight into his soul, like she somehow knew exactly who he was and why he was here… and what he'd done.

"Look, Lady, I mean, Sister. I'm just… a bit lost. If you could tell me what the hell… I mean heck is happening I'd…"

"You best come with me," she said, before turning on her heel and walking down towards the school office.

David followed after her in a daze, as she led him through the reception area and into the principal's office. David had been in this room only just a few days ago, but now it looked completely different. The desk was old and wooden, covered in scraps and scrapes. There was no computer, just a stack of papers and one of those vintage pen holders that definitely wasn't there last week.

At first it seemed like the nun had disappeared right into the wood paneling wall, giving David one more thing to be confused about, until he realized there was a hidden door in the wall. Again, something he'd never noticed before. In fact, he was pretty sure that there was no wood paneling on that wall before, just bookcases filled with books about best teaching practice and old bibles.

Ghost children, disappearing nuns, what the hell was going on here?

He rubbed his face, feeling the crusty blood from last night on his fingers.

David felt like he was going to be sick. He reached out to the wall to steady himself, placing his hand between a black and white class photo and a Churches of the World calendar showing a black and white picture of some old European Cathedral for the month of July…

July 1933.

David's stomach churned and he had to take a few deep breaths to stop himself from vomiting all over the hardwood floor. He wiped his brow which was sweating profusely, and then fell to the floor as the realization hit him. The words of the initiation repeating through his mind.

I swear to protect the persecuted, to protect them through time, to protect the portals that open and close when needed…

It was an old initiation. Something the Eights had been saying for over a hundred years. No one really knew where it came from, it was just handed down from one Eight to another. Everyone in the Eights thought the words were just about protecting your fellow Eights.

No one took it *literally*.

The nun had reappeared in the wall looking stern, but there was something else in her eyes too. Something that told him maybe this stern nun thing was just an act, and something that felt… familiar. "Follow me," she said.

And so he did.

FOURTEEN

Dee's Diner

Santolsa
1966

"More coffee?" A middle-aged waitress with a dark beehive and a name tag that said Betty looked down at Janet. Betty gave her a look that said she'd rather be anywhere else than having to serve coffee to someone who looked like they'd just been dragged through a bush.

After Janet had found David was missing, she had spent hours searching the school for him. She searched until the sun had come up and teachers and staff started arriving.

But David was gone.

And her shirt was still covered in blood splatter.

She caught a glimpse of herself in a mirror over a sink when she'd been looking for David in the boy's locker rooms. She almost didn't recognize herself. She threw her shirt in the bin and grabbed a yellow *Property of St. Christopher's High School* gym t-shirt from a pile of other discarded clothing and random school items. It didn't smell clean, but at least it wasn't covered in the blood of a dead man.

She thought about taking a shower, but the last thing she wanted was to be naked in a big open space with the potential for anyone to find her. She wasn't exactly sure what was going on, but she knew one thing for sure - this wasn't the St. Christopher's High School *she* went to.

As she checked her reflection again, she noticed the spots of blood on her face and her stomach lurched. She ran her fingers through her hair which was knotted with dried blood and made it to the sink just in time to vomit.

She took a few wobbly breaths and then ran the tap, washing away the vomit and washing her face, scrubbing at the blood as hard as she could with her hands.

There had been a pencil case on the pile where she'd found her shirt. Janet grabbed it and unzipped it, hoping that… yes, a pair of tiny classroom scissors.

She stood in front of the mirror and cut her long dark hair off at chin level. She knew that no matter how much she washed it, it would never feel clean again. The only thing to do was to get rid of it.

And now here she was at Dee's diner, wearing a boy's smelly gym t-shirt, a pair of ripped jeans and a haircut done with school scissors. No wonder Betty was looking at her like that.

Janet nodded. "Yes, more coffee, please." She wondered if you drank a coffee in your dreams if it would wake you up. Because if this was a dream, and she really hoped it was, she would very much like to wake up. "And some toast," Janet added.

Jonas had given them both fifty bucks as an advance. She knew she should probably save as much of it as possi-ble, but her stomach was churning, and she thought if she didn't eat something she was probably going to be sick again. Or at the very least, it would give her something to throw up.

Betty dropped a newspaper on the table, poured the coffee and walked off, leaving Janet alone to stare at the date on the newspaper in front of her - July 1st 1966.

Janet rubbed her eyes and looked out the window as the town of Santolsa began to wake, cowboys picking up supplies, shops beginning to open. But everything was *wrong*. There was no McDonalds, no Mini Mall, just a lot of dust and waitresses with high hair and weird old newspapers.

Janet put her head into her hands and whispered to herself - "wake up, Janet. Wake *up*."

But time kept ticking, and she didn't wake up. Betty kept pouring coffee and strangers kept walking past the window dressed in vintage clothing.

She didn't wake up back in David's arms in the book room. She didn't wake up back in her bed in her trailer, that fated night of the job never having happened. She didn't wake up to the smell of Gran cooking pancakes or pizza.

A man in a suit sat down at the counter, telling Betty all about a great new product, the Power Potato, a potato slicer he was selling door to door to the good people of Santolsa. Betty flirted shamelessly with him, and he lapped it all up. He took out the Power Potato to demonstrate and she went out back to grab some potatoes.

Eventually a different waitress who looked like she was going to stab Betty dropped off the toast which looked like two bits of cardboard. Janet buttered a slice and took a bite. It tasted like cardboard too, but at least it was food.

Two women dressed in almost matching floral dresses sat down in a booth behind her. They were talking in hushed tones, gossiping about all the other housewives of

Santolsa. Janet learned that Judy Ricketts had stopped watering her lawn and it was now starting to turn brown, God forbid. She also found out that Lucy Barnes had made a pass at the postman and Gloria Hancock's husband hadn't been seen going to or from work for a whole week.

It was riveting stuff.

It was only when they began talking about Kay Montgomery, who had been seen reading a book about feminism and how absolutely atrocious it was that anyone would be "into those dangerous ideas" that Janet couldn't help herself.

"Excuse me ladies," Janet said, sticking her head around to their booth.

The two women turned around to face her, both of them looking her up and down.

"There's nothing atrocious about women's empowerment, just so you know. Feminism is for *all* women."

They both looked horrified and then one of them let out a laugh. The other one said, "If being a feminist means letting myself go and looking like something the dog dragged out of the trash, I'd really rather not."

Janet raised an eyebrow.

"Now, now, Grace," the other woman said. "Maybe she's right, us women do need to stick together." She stood up, her kitten heels clicking on the floor as she came towards Janet. She reached inside her purse and took out a lipstick and handed it to her.

Janet turned it around in her hands. "What is this?"

"Frosted nude," the woman said, giving her a bright white smile.

"Riiiight," said Janet, handing it back.

"It's a great color for you," she said. "You know, with a

little mascara, blush and a hairbrush you could almost be pretty."

"Wow, what a sales pitch." Janet continued to hold out the lipstick, but the woman just closed Janet's hand around it.

"Keep it, and if you ever need anything else, just let me know." The woman gave her a card - *Annabelle Gregson, Avon representative.* "I can come to your house and do a whole make-over for you."

Janet rolled her eyes. "No thanks."

"OK, honey, well good luck with this," Annabelle gestured to Janet's outfit and began to walk off back towards her table.

"Wait a sec," Janet called back with a sigh. "Do you have any eye-liner?" She hated the idea of asking this woman for help, but Janet needed something to hold onto. Something to help her remember who she was, even if she didn't know where she was.

Annabelle's own frosted lips parted in a beauty pageant smile. "Grace," she called back to her friend as she scootched into the booth beside Janet. "I might be a while."

FIFTEEN

The Suitcase

____

Santolsa
    1966

Janet woke up to beams of afternoon light hitting her face.

She had been asleep on the couch in David's trailer for most of the afternoon.

But *not* David's trailer.

It was much cleaner and nicer than David's trailer had ever been, but it sat exactly where David's trailer had been... or *would be*.

After she left the diner with the small make-up bag Annabelle had put together for her, Janet had started walking towards the trailer park without even thinking. It was a long way, but she wanted to walk. She wanted to move. She wanted to do *something*. She didn't know what she'd find when she got there, but she didn't know where else to go.

Whether it was real, a dream or some kind of hallucination brought on by what had happened last night -

something her brain was creating so she didn't have to deal with reality, it seemed like going along with the whole 1966 thing was going to be easier than fighting against it.

And if this really was 1966, Gran would still be alive.

Her *mom* would still be alive.

She had been walking almost half an hour before she remembered that Gran didn't move to the trailer park until the late seventies. Before that she'd had a much nicer house somewhere on the other side of Santolsa, the good side. At least, that was before her grandfather had run off with a younger woman and left Gran with nothing. But Janet didn't know where Gran's old house was. She wished she'd paid more attention to Gran's stories.

But what was she going to do if she knew, anyway? Roll up to Gran's house and tell her she was her grand-daughter from the future? Gran was way too practical to buy that story.

When Janet had finally arrived at the trailer park a kid had approached her. He seemed kind of familiar in some way, and when he asked her if she was OK, she'd nearly broken down. This kid who could barely be in seventh grade, asking her if she was OK was sending her off the edge. He took her to his trailer, gave her some pain killers and she'd been out like a light.

And now, here she was, back in the trailer park, back in David's trailer, like nothing had happened, but *everything* had happened.

"Hey," the kid said. He put a glass of water down on the floor next to her and folded his arms over his blue button up shirt as he looked down at her.

"Hey," she said, sitting up and reaching for the drink. "Do you have any more of those painkillers?"

He shook his head.

"Great." She took a gulp of water, but it didn't help.

"I think…" he began, folding and refolding his arms like a nervous habit. "I think I'm supposed to help you."

"I don't think you can help me, kid."

"Someone left something here. I think it's for you."

Janet frowned and watched him go into what should have been David's bedroom. He came back out with a small brown suitcase. One of those old vintage ones you had to carry by the handle.

The boy put it down next to her.

Janet shook her head. "This isn't mine."

"Someone came by, a few days ago. They said a girl would come to pick it up."

"Don't you think if this was for me that I'd know about it?" Janet rubbed her temples. Just when she thought things couldn't get weirder.

"They said you might say that. That you might not know it was for you."

"Who dropped it off?"

"Some old lady."

Janet immediately thought of Gran, before remembering that in 1966 Gran wouldn't have been an old lady yet.

"No old ladies know I'm here, so it can't be for me." Janet gulped down the rest of the water and held the empty glass out to him.

"Look, lady," the kid started, folding his arms again but seeming less nervous now. "All I know is what I was told. Some old lady dropped this off and said some girl would be here in a few days to pick it up. She said you might be acting strange and not remember stuff, that you'd be dressed strangely and to let you have a shower because you'd be dirty, and you really do look dirty."

Janet scowled at him. "What's in it?"

"I don't know, she said not to open it."

"And you didn't? What kid gets given a mysterious suit-case and doesn't open it?"

"I'm not just a *kid*, Lady. I'm an *Eight*, or I will be, real soon. And our word is our honor." He smacked his chest with a small fisted hand.

Janet's stomach dropped. "Do yourself a favor and stay away from the Eights."

He shook his head. "If I help them now, they are going to help me go to college and make something of myself. I'm going to be a dam builder!"

Janet knew there was nothing she could say to stop him. It sounded like he was already in over his head.

"That sounds like a great plan, kid," she said. "I look forward to seeing your dam someday."

The corners of the kid's mouth lifted slightly. "Yeah?"

"Yeah." Janet sighed. She grabbed the suitcase and lay it down on the floor. "You sure this is for me?"

He nodded.

She gave a shrug and unzipped the case, opening it up to reveal what looked like a perfectly packed case for a vacation in the sixties. There were dresses in her size in various patterns and styles, some short some long, a purple velvet purse with a gold chain, a pair of gold knee high boots, underwear and socks. There was even a small beauty case stocked with shampoo, soap, a toothbrush and toothpaste. There was a selection of paperback books Janet hadn't read and tucked into a pocket was an envelope filled with a hundred bucks in cash and a ticket on a Greyhound bus to San Francisco.

San Francisco.

Janet put a hand to her mouth.

That's where they were.

Her mom and dad were both alive and well and living in San Francisco in 1966.

"I told you it was for you," the kid said, grinning.

An hour later and Janet was showered and dressed in a short pink dress and gold knee high boots. It was shorter than she was used to, but it fit perfectly otherwise. She'd even managed to make her hair look half decent by brushing it and tucking it behind her ears.

The kid whistled when she walked out.

She took the key out of the front pocket of her jeans and the photo of her mom and dad and the Saint Christopher prayer card from her back pocket and bundled them into a ball with the phys. Ed. T-shirt. "Can you put these in the trash?" she asked, handing them to him.

He nodded, flinging open the back door and stuffing her clothes into the trashcan out back. "The boots too?" he called back.

"I'm keeping the boots," she said, throwing them into the suitcase with her toiletries.

Janet was standing above the suitcase with the key in her hand, not knowing what to do with it without any pockets, when the kid came back in.

"Here," the kid said, handing her a long piece of yellow ribbon he'd taken from a basket on the counter. "You can wear your key around your neck. It will look groovy."

Janet gave him a look.

"It's what my mom does. She wears her keys around her neck, so she doesn't lose them. She won't mind if you take this."

Janet strung the key onto the ribbon and tied it around her neck, letting the key fall down inside her dress. "Where is your mom?" she asked.

The boy's face fell. "I don't know. She was just here

one day, and then she wasn't. I don't know when she's coming back."

Janet gave him a sad smile. It didn't sound like his mom was coming back. "I don't know where my mom is either, but I'm going to find her."

"Want me to drive you to the bus stop?" the kid asked.

"You can drive?"

The kid nodded.

"Aren't you a little young to be driving?"

"I'm fifteen!"

"Really?"

The boy's face was bright red.

"Sorry," she said. "You just seem… short."

He glared at her.

"It would be great if you could drive me."

"I need to take you now. My aunt will be home soon and it's best she doesn't see you here. She doesn't like all this Eight stuff."

"I don't blame her."

Janet watched from the dusty window of the pick-up truck as Santolsa passed by. A different Santolsa. A pretty, clean, tidy, Santolsa. A town that looked like it was cared for and loved, with perfect green lawns and picket fences and people strolling through town in brightly colored clothes saying hello to each other as they passed.

And even though everything in her was battling this - the idea that this could really be the past, that she had somehow traveled through time, she began to hope with everything in her, that maybe, it was true.

The kid pulled up outside the bus stop at the edge of town. "I know you have a while to wait, will you be alright?"

"I'm going to be fine," she said, giving him a smile, and even after everything, she felt like maybe she would be. She was on her way to San Francisco to find her mom. Maybe this was finally the answer to all her prayers.

"Well, good luck…" he began, holding out his hand for her to shake.

"Janet."

"Good luck, Janet."

"Thank you…" She realized she'd never even asked his name.

"Jonas," he said.

"Jonas?" She asked, not sure whether to laugh or cry or scream.

"Yes mam."

She shook her head and let out a nervous laugh. "Jonas Stone, right?"

The boy's eyes opened wide. "How did you know?"

Janet just stared at him for a moment. This was *Jonas*, David's dad, the man who would send her on the job that would be the reason she was even here in the first place. But he was just a kid. And like David had said, if he was already mixed up with the Eights, what chance did he even have for a better life?

"Are you alright, lady? You look like you might be sick."

She gave a nod and hopped out of the truck. "Thank you, Jonas, for everything."

Santolsa

2018

Peggy felt a wave of nostalgia hit as Sammy pulled the red Mustang up outside Patty and Hank's house and switched off the engine.

The small white house had always been so homey and inviting, but it had always been a little strange coming here as a guest of Patty and Hank's, sitting in their living room and drinking coffee instead of avoiding them and running straight up to Jack's room to watch a movie and eat microwave popcorn.

But this afternoon they would all be there. Patty and Hank, Jack and Lacey. It had been a long time since the whole gang was in one room. Jack stayed true to his word. He'd become successful in L.A. and Santolsa held too many bad memories for him to visit all that often. They still talked on the phone, but it had been a few years since she'd seen Jack and Lacey. She missed them.

"Everything OK?" Sammy asked, gently placing his hand on her knee.

The early evening light caught the gold of his wedding band and she grinned. "Everything is fine," she said, looking up at him.

He held her gaze for a moment and just when Peggy thought he was about to lean in and kiss her, there was a cough from the back seat.

"I'll go in and let them know you're right behind me," offered Lena, opening the back door and disappearing up the steps of the house.

Sammy let out a low laugh and Peggy hid her face in her hands. Sammy gently moved her hands away from her face. "You know, you get more beautiful every day," he said.

Peggy rolled her eyes. "Sure, all these wrinkles are really adding to my looks."

"I love your wrinkles," he said. "Each one is a reminder of our life together." He ran his finger across her cheek. "These ones are from all the times I've made you smile. And these," he started, running a finger across her lips, "these ones are from all times we've kissed…"

And he leaned in and kissed her, and when she closed her eyes, it felt just like it did all those years ago. She was instantly transported back to his bedroom upstairs at his dad's house, electricity flowing through her as they made-out on his bedroom floor.

She slowly peeled away from him, still grinning. "We should go in."

"Lena will be fine," he said, leaning back in for another kiss.

"Are you sure you're OK with her staying with us?" Peggy asked.

Sammy brushed her hair back from her face and nodded. "Of course. She needs us."

"It just feels like we've spent our whole lives looking after everyone else, you know?" Peggy rested her head on the headrest and yawned. "And somewhere in the middle of it all, we never even had kids."

Sammy shrugged. "We pretty much raised Jessie's girls with her after that jerk disappeared."

"And then we looked after your dad."

Sammy nodded. "And now we have Lena."

"Do you sometimes wonder what it would have been like if we had our own kids though? Our own flesh and blood?"

"Do you?"

Peggy took a breath and then shook her head. "I think family can be anything. Janet was always more of a mother to me than my own mother, and I always think of your dad as my dad too."

"Me too."

"I think family can even be taking in one of the Nuns of Santolsa," she laughed. "It's not how I ever thought our lives would turn out, but I've been thinking that maybe I could be like a mother to Lena, too. Like Janet was for me."

"I think if anyone could be a mother to a time-traveling-witch-nun, it's you." And he gave her one of those smoldering smirks that still drove her crazy after all these years.

"I love you, Sammy Ruthven."

"I love you too, Peggy Ruthven." And he leaned over and kissed her again.

SIXTEEN

One Way Ticket

Santolsa
    1966

The sun had long gone down, and Janet was sitting on the bench at the Santolsa bus stop. The bus stop hadn't changed much from her time. The sign would be updated, and the bench would be painted over, but otherwise, sitting here under a dim old streetlight, she could almost forget where she was, *when* she was. She could've easily been back in 1999 watching the headlights flashing by on the main road out of Santolsa.

She said a silent prayer out into the cool night air and thanked God, or whoever was looking out for her that she *wasn't* in 1999. If she was, she'd probably be in the Salt Valley women's prison by now.

It was like a weight had suddenly lifted off her and she could breathe again as she realized she was *safe*.

And then her thoughts spiraled back to David.

Where was he?

Was he back in 1999? Was *he* going to go to prison? Or was he here somewhere? Did he get lost in the school or find another way out? Did he leave her behind while he tried to run? If he did, did he do it to protect her or just to save himself?

She checked her watch, a secondhand trinket she'd found in a thrift store with Gran, for the millionth time since Jonas, *young* Jonas, had dropped her off.

Jonas.

David's *dad.*

She shook her head. It was too weird.

Janet had been way too early to sit at the bus stop all night, so she'd walked around town for a while and then taken herself for a soup dinner at Dee's. She couldn't stomach much else. In fact, she barely ate any of it. She just wanted something to do, something to occupy her time and her mind. She was also secretly hoping to show off her new outfit and washed hair to Betsy, but there was a new shift on, and no one recognized her. It was probably for the best.

"Evening." A voice startled her.

She looked up and into dark deep eyes reflecting the soft glow of the streetlight above them. "Hi," she said, suddenly feeling flustered as she took him in. A young African American man, about eighteen, with broad shoulders, short, cropped hair, and kind eyes. He was dressed in army pants and a plain white t-shirt, an army issue duffel bag slung over his shoulder.

"San Francisco?" he asked, dropping his bag under the sign.

"Uh huh." She nodded and felt herself blush. It was probably too dark for him to see it, but she knew. And she immediately felt guilty. It had only been twenty-four hours since she'd been sitting outside the school with David, hoping he would kiss her and dreaming of their lives together… before her world fell apart.

It had been the longest twenty-four hours of her life. Maybe it was like three months in normal time. Maybe it was perfectly acceptable to find someone else attractive. It's not like she was going to marry him, she just thought he was… the most handsome guy she'd ever seen.

"Do you have the time?" he asked.

She looked at her watch again, completely forgetting what time she'd just seen. "Eleven-thirty," she replied.

He gave her a nod. She felt like maybe he wanted to keep talking, but she didn't know what else to say.

"It should be here soon," she finally said, after a way too long silence.

"I nearly didn't make it." He leaned against the sign pole, looking as comfortable as if he'd been leaning in a doorway in his own home. "Some lady sent me in the wrong direction, said the bus stop was at the *other* end of main street."

"You're not from round here?" Janet asked.

He shook his head. "Just passing through."

"Me too," she said.

"Of all the places to pass through."

"I think we are the only people to ever pass through this town," Janet said. "I've been getting weird looks from everyone all day."

"If they looked at you like that, imagine how they've been looking at *me*."

Janet gave a nod. Racism was still very much alive and well in 1999, but here in 1966 it had only been eleven years since Rosa Parks took her seat.

"San Francisco will be better," she said, hoping it would be true for both of them.

He raised an eyebrow. "I hope so."

"So, what brings you to Santolsa?" she asked.

"I have a brother in Salt Valley. I've been staying with him a while."

"Doesn't this bus go through Salt Valley?"

He shook his head. "Only in the morning. The midnight bus skips right on past it."

"That's weird."

"It is weird."

Another long silence.

"So," he said, "what brings *you* to Santolsa?"

"A wrong turn."

"I don't believe in wrong turns," he said as the bus pulled up, its headlights almost blinding them.

He gestured for her to get on the bus first, and when she stepped onto that bus, for the first time in her life, she knew she was taking the right turn.

Interlude VI

Santolsa
2018

Alex switched the TV off. "So, what did you think?"

Alex and Lena were sitting together on Alex's bed in her Aunt Patty and Uncle Hank's house where she was staying with her parents. It was a cute room, with white slatted wardrobes and a big double bed. It had been her cousin's room before he left for college. Alex had never really known her Cousin Jack. She'd met her aunt and uncle plenty of times, but always in L.A. and her cousin had never been with them. It was weird to have a cousin you didn't really know or know anything about. She'd tried to find him on social media, but her parents had said he was one of those hipster kids who didn't even have a phone. No one had really mentioned it, but Alex was pretty sure that her cousin leaving was the reason her Aunt Patty had bought a motorcycle and crashed it. Her kid leaving home had set off her mid-life crisis and now Alex's whole family had come to pick up the pieces. In a way, it was all her stupid cousin Jack's fault she was even in Santolsa in the first place.

Alex looked over at Lena, her pretty face all squished up as she watched the credits, and she wasn't sure if she should really be mad at her cousin or actually thanking him. She would never have met Lena if she hadn't been forced to come to Santolsa.

Lena made a face. "I... don't really understand TV. And that show was... not really funny."

"Could you *be* any weirder, Lena?" Alex asked giggling.

Lena looked at her blankly.

"Chandler? From the show we just watched?"

"I just don't... get it."

"You girls OK?" her aunt asked, sticking her head in. She was looking tired. Last time Alex had seen her aunt and uncle they had both seemed so much younger and full of life. Now they both seemed a hundred years old, even though they were about the same age as her mom and dad.

"Yes, Aunt Patty," Alex said, quickly releasing Lena's hand and giving Lena an embarrassed look.

"Do you want some snacks?" Her aunt could barely walk, let alone make snacks. It took her about half an hour to get down the stairs.

Alex rolled her eyes. "You should be resting, not making snacks."

"I'll rest when I'm dead." She picked one of her crutches off the floor and waved it around.

Alex frowned at her.

"Bad joke?" Aunt Patty gave her a grin which spread over her pale face.

"The doctors said you will be fine if you just *rest* and if you stop acting like you're seventeen. That motorcycle thing was crazy, even I wouldn't do that!"

Aunt Patty sighed.

"Patty!" came Uncle Hank's voice from down the hall. "Leave the girls alone."

"Alright, dear!" she called back. "Don't do anything I wouldn't do," she added with a wink as she hobbled off.

Alex grabbed Lena's hand again. "I'm so sorry."

Lena shook her head. "What for?"

"That we can't just be together, just the two of us." Alex snuggled her face into Lena's neck and took a deep breath. Lena always smelled like apples and bread, and it was beautiful.

Lena giggled. "That would be nice."

Alex kissed her neck gently. "I wish we could just go somewhere."

"Where?" asked Lena. "If you could go anywhere, where would you want to go?"

"San Francisco," Alex said without hesitation, snuggling back into Lena's shoulder and resting there.

"When?"

"How about right now?" Alex sighed.

Lena gave her a soft smile. "What if... what if you could travel through time? *When* would you want to go?"

"Hmmmmmmmmm..." Alex rolled onto her back and looked up at the ceiling. "The sixties."

Lena rested her head on the pillow and whispered into Alex's ear. "What if I told you, I could take you there?"

Alex laughed. "You want to watch some old sixties movies or something?"

Lena's face was serious. "No, not a movie. The real thing."

"What are you talking about?"

"I haven't been completely honest with you. I wasn't raised in a cult, Alex," Lena's blue eyes shone brighter than Alex had ever seen them, "I'm a time traveling witch."

Alex sat on her aunt's floral couch and stared at a water-color print of roses on the wall.

No, not her *aunt's* couch, her *grandmother's* couch.

Just a half an hour earlier they had been watching re-runs of *Friends* and talking about things all normal teenagers talk about - their dreams and hopes for the future, where they wanted to travel, what decade they'd most like to visit.

When Lena said she was a time traveler Alex wasn't sure if she was just joking or if she truly believed it. Lena *was* weird. She wasn't like anyone Alex had ever met. She thought maybe the cult she'd been a part of really had done something to her brain.

Alex had started to feel more than a little worried when Lena didn't let it go, like maybe she had some serious mental health stuff going on. And maybe falling for a girl who was thoroughly convinced she was a time traveling witch was not such a great idea.

"Maybe you should go home," Alex had said.

Lena had looked like she was about to cry. "If it was real, would you come with me? Would you come to San Francisco? To the sixties?"

Alex nodded. "Uh, sure, Lena," she said, just to try to calm her down.

"Then let's go ask your parents." Lena had grabbed Alex's hand and pulled her downstairs to the living room where her parents were sitting around drinking some weird green drinks with her Aunt Patty, Uncle Hank, Aunt Peggy and Uncle Sammy.

"Can I take Lena to the sixties for the summer?" Lena had blurted out in front of everyone.

Alex was mortified, but at least she knew the truth about Lena. She needed help.

They had all gone stupid, dropping their jaws and her dad nearly dropped his drink.

"You *told* her?" asked her dad who looked like he was about to lose it.

"Told me what?" Alex asked, feeling thoroughly confused.

And that's when her dad told her.

Everything.

That her "Cousin Jack" was actually *him*. Her *dad*. They were the same person. "Cousin Jack" didn't disappear off to college, he went back in time to 1984.

Her Aunt Patty and Uncle Hank were *not* her aunt and uncle, but actually her dad's parents, making them Alex's *grandparents*. Even though they were all the same age.

And Aunt Peggy was a time traveler too.

"I know it's a lot," said her dad, reaching out and patting her leg.

Alex felt like she was going to vomit.

"It does get easier," said her mom, running her hands through the ends of her long red hair. "At first it kind of messes with your head, but…"

Aunt Peggy laughed. "Lacey," she began. "You were the only one who just accepted it!"

"Remember when I found your phone?" Alex's mom laughed. "I thought you were some kind of government spy!"

"That's right," Aunt Peggy laughed.

"That was the day we all went for pancakes together," her mom went on. "You were so stuck on Sammy, then."

Aunt Peggy went bright red. "I was not!"

Uncle Sammy laughed. "You were, but I was stuck on you too." He looked at her like she was the sun itself.

"When Peggy told me she was a time traveler," her dad began. "I didn't believe her for ages. Not until I saw her picture in that yearbook. It was 2016 in our time, but there she was, in the Class of 1983 yearbook."

"If only we had our yearbooks from our time," Aunt Peggy mused. "We could prove it."

"That's an idea." Her dad grabbed his phone from his pocket. He started tapping and a few seconds later he handed it to Alex.

It had come up on an image search. A photo page from a St. Christopher's yearbook dated 2016.

And there was her dad, looking the same age as she was now.

Jack Forrester.

Alex dropped the phone to the floor cracking the screen.

Aunt Patty looked shaken. "The only reason I haven't been handling things so well is because our Jack just left last year."

Uncle Hank took her hand and held it tightly. "You see, Alex," he began. "Your dad was just about your age last year when he traveled back to 1984."

"Mom," said Alex's dad, "I'm still your Jack." Her dad stood up and went to crouch by Aunt Patty, holding onto her other hand just as tightly. "I'm still the same person."

A tear fell from one of Aunt Patty's dark eyes and suddenly her dad, Uncle Hank and Aunt Peggy were all crying too.

"I literally can't process this," Alex said.

"When I was about your age I met my older self," her dad said. "And I vomited on his shoes."

Alex didn't know weather to laugh or vomit herself.

But suddenly Lena's hand was in hers, and she felt better. She felt like no matter how crazy the world got, or how bizarre her own existence was, if she had Lena to hold onto, everything was going to be OK.

"We would just be gone over the summer," Lena said. "I'll have her back before school starts again."

"And if something happened?" her dad asked. "What if she couldn't get back?"

"Nothing will happen. But if it did, she could always go to St. Christopher's and ask Sister Maria for help. Maria and Catherine, and my replacement will be there in the sixties and will able to get her back."

Her dad frowned. "I'm not sure about this."

"Jack, honey," her mom said. "Time travel is practically a rite of passage in this family. We should let her go."

"Is it OK with you Aunt Peggy?" Lena asked, bouncing on her toes.

And Peggy nodded.

SEVENTEEN

The Greyhound

Reno

1966

Janet's eyes flew open with a start as the bus came to a stop. She had been hovering in that space in-between, not quite asleep, not quite awake, for she didn't know how long. She'd tried to use her new velvet purse as a pillow and lean her head against the window, but she just couldn't get comfortable. She might have been able to sleep better if it hadn't been for the two girls sitting a few rows behind her who hadn't stopped giggling since they'd run onto the bus in Santolsa just seconds before the bus driver was about to pull away. They had both been ecstatic, giggling and grinning as the blonde one pulled the redhead aboard and dragged her to the back of the bus.

But she had eventually gotten a little rest anyway, her face squished into the headrest which smelled like cigarette smoke. The whole bus smelled like cigarette smoke. And then she realized it was because the person a few seats in front of her was smoking and she guessed the no smoking on public transport law hadn't come into effect yet.

She was bleary eyed from tiredness and the smoke and tried to squint out the window to see where they were, but all she could see was a thin reflection of her own tired face. It felt like a lifetime since she'd last slept in a bed.

Across the aisle from her was the guy she'd met at the bus stop. He was fast asleep, his head lolled to one side. There was something about watching him sleep that felt so intrusive and intimate. And Janet couldn't help but stare just a bit longer than was probably considered normal.

The giggling started back up again, and Janet shot the girls a look, motioning to the guy who was asleep.

The redhead mouthed "sorry", but she didn't look very sorry.

Janet scowled at them.

"Reno, Nevada," said the bus driver in that gravely monotone bus drivers always have. "We stop here for forty-five minutes if you want to get out and stretch your legs. There's a 24-hour diner across the road for coffee and meals."

The two girls at the back jumped up and rushed down the aisle. Janet was glad to see the back of them. They were way too happy for her liking. After everything that had happened to her in the last twenty-four hours, well, the last few weeks, the last thing she wanted was to be near anyone who was that happy.

Grabbing her purse, Janet was about to go find coffee when she wondered if she should wake the guy across from her. He looked so peaceful, but if he wanted the bathroom or coffee, this might be his last change until San Francisco.

An older woman brushed past her and looked over at him. "You should wake him, dear," she said, as if reading Janet's mind.

Janet reached over and put her hand gently on his arm, the warmth of him filling her fingertips. She moved her hand a little from side to side. "Hey, do you want the truck stop?" she whispered.

His eyes flickered open, landing on hers, where they stayed for just a few moments too long, and in that moment, it felt as if they'd somehow known each other their whole lives. She felt like she could see into the future. A flash of them both in old age, him falling asleep on the couch, her asking him if he wanted to go up to bed.

She shook it off. "We're in Reno," she said.

He gave her a nod, finally averting his gaze. "Thank you for waking me." He rubbed his eyes and gave her a soft smile. "I'm sorry, I didn't get your name earlier."

"Janet," she said, holding her hand out.

"I'm Dale," he said, reaching for her hand.

And they stayed there holding each other's hands, neither one wanting to let go too soon.

EIGHTEEN

The Truck Stop

Reno

1966

Janet was glad to be able to stretch her legs. All the other passengers had gone their separate ways. The two girls had gone into what looked like the kind of toilets you only wanted to use if you were desperate or very brave. Others were milling around smoking cigarettes or walking around just to move again, and to keep warm. It was a cool night and Janet felt stupid in her outfit. Her thighs had never been this cold. She wasn't sure where Dale had gone, and she tried not to think anything of it when she found herself looking around for him.

A flickering neon sign for the 24-hour diner across the road was beckoning her towards it. It made Dee's look like the Ritz. The sign was half falling off the roof and one of the windows had been smashed and taped up. But there would be coffee, and Janet needed something warm in her hands.

She stood by the road, rubbing her arms, and bouncing on her toes trying to get warm while she waited for the cars to go by so she could cross.

An old truck slowed down in front of her and stopped and she was suddenly back in time. The car wasn't a beat-up white truck, it was the black SUV, the driver wasn't an old lady letting her cross, it was the man in the suit, the man they had killed, and he was getting out of the car and pulling his gun… Janet's heart began to race and just as she was about to run, she tripped on her boots and started falling backwards, but she didn't fall, something caught her.

Someone.

"Are you alright?" a voice behind her asked.

And then she was back. The lady in the car shook her head before quickly driving off, and the arms that were holding her gently turned her around.

Dale.

His dark eyes full of concern. "What's wrong?" he asked.

"Nothing, I just, I…" She shook her head. "I just tripped."

"Well, lucky I was there to catch you," he smiled.

"Lucky indeed."

"You must be freezing," he said. "Here." He took off his gray army sweater and handed it to her.

"Oh no, I can't, you'll be cold."

"I'm fine."

"No really," she said, passing it back to him. "I can't."

He put his hands over her hands and passed it back. "You *can.*"

It felt like he didn't just mean the sweater, and she believed him.

"Come on, I'll buy you a coffee," he said, nodding to the diner.

She thanked him and put the sweater on. The soft spicy, sweet smell of him surrounding her and making her feel safe for the first time in a long time.

NINETEEN

Apple and Peach

Reno

1966

He was looking at her across the sticky wooden diner table like she was a butterfly that had just lost a wing. And his deep dark eyes looking at her like that made her feel like she had a thousand one winged butterflies inside of her.

"I'm fine, really," she lied.

"Food will make you feel better." He opened up the menu. The sound of the pages pulling apart made them both laugh.

Perhaps that was really all it was. The dizziness, the butterflies. It was just *hunger*.

"What did you eat today?" His eyes were back on her hers and the longer she stared into them the more lost she felt.

Or was it that she finally felt found?

"Actually," she said, looking down at her own menu.

"Not much. I had some toast at breakfast and a little soup for dinner."

He gave her a frown. "That's not nearly enough food for a whole day."

"No kidding."

"No wonder you fainted."

"I didn't faint."

"Fell into my arms, then." The corners of his mouth twisted upwards, and she wondered if he was flirting with her. He was so handsome and tall, and he had biceps for days. He wasn't the scruffy boy in the trailer next door. He was more like a full-grown *man*. And she was just a girl who couldn't walk properly. What would someone like him be doing flirting with someone like her?

"Sorry about that," she said.

"No need to be sorry. I enjoy being the strong heroic type."

"Is that why you joined the Army?"

He let out a breath. "I don't know if joining the Army is heroic."

A waitress appeared wearing an old blue dress covered in an apron streaked with brown goo. "Whaddaya want?" she asked.

Dale stuck his head in the menu.

"Coffee," Janet said. "And a sandwich?"

"What *kind* of sandwich?" the waitress asked, tapping her pencil on her order pad.

"What do you have?"

"It's all on the menu, that's what menus are for." The waitress clucked her tongue. Janet thought she might offer to give them a minute, but she just stood there, lording over them.

Janet quickly looked around the menu and eventually found the sandwiches. "I'll take a Swiss on Rye." She ran her finger over the prices. "Wait a second, this sandwich is thirty cents?"

"It's a big sandwich," the waitress said. "You can get fries for an extra fifteen."

"*Fifteen* cents. For *fries?*" Janet couldn't believe it. She thought her hundred bucks was going to disappear quick, but that was going to get her a lot of fries.

"It's no problem, I've got it," Dale said in a low voice, mistaking her amazement at how cheap this place was for expense.

"Look, are you kids gonna order, or what?" The waitress seemed like she was about to lose it.

"I'll take the Swiss on Rye and the fries," Janet said.

"I'll get the same, with coffee," he said. "And what's the pie?"

The waitress stared up at the ceiling while she recited a list of fillings.

"Peach, please," he said.

"Oooh, can I get a slice of apple?" Janet added. "And coffee for me too."

"You already said that," the waitress grumbled, scribbling on her pad and then turning her back on them.

"Well, she was pleasant." Janet rolled her eyes.

Dale gave a shrug. "She wasn't that bad, at least she served us." He closed his menu and put it back behind the sauce bottles.

"Why wouldn't she serve us?" Janet asked.

He just gave her a look and she remembered where she was. This was the sixties. This was height of the civil rights movement. Her stomach twisted as she thought about Dale not being served in a place like this.

"I can't believe the prices here!" Janet exclaimed, changing the subject.

"They think they can charge anything they like in these places," he tutted.

"No, I mean, it's so cheap!"

"You think this is cheap?"

"Isn't it?"

"Where are you from?" he asked, looking at her like she'd just beamed down from Mars.

"Santolsa."

"I thought you said you were just passing through there?"

She startled. It was the truth that she was from there, it was also the truth that she wasn't from *that* Santolsa. But what else could she say? "Yeah, passing through for sixteen years," she shrugged.

"I see," he said with a slight hint of a frown.

"I'm sorry I lied," she blurted. "I just… I don't feel like I *am* from there, you know? I kind of hate that place. I never fit in there and I just couldn't wait to get out."

"No, I get it."

A younger, pretty redheaded waitress turned over their cups and poured their coffee. She couldn't take her eyes off Dale and ended up over-pouring his until his saucer was a lake of coffee.

"I'm so, so sorry," she stammered, grabbing a handful of napkins, and trying to clean it up.

"It's alright," he said kindly, reaching out for the napkins and helping out.

"Valerie!" yelled the other waitress.

"Oh, God," the girl said, grabbing the coffee-stained napkins and running off.

"So, how much does a sandwich cost in Santolsa?" he asked, grabbing a few more napkins and finishing the job.

"About five bucks."

He let out a loud Ha! "Five dollars, for a *sandwich*?"

"Look, the truth is…" She didn't know why she was telling him, but there was something about him. Something that felt trustworthy and safe. "I'm not from the Santolsa you know, I'm from… a *different* Santolsa."

"There's a different Santolsa?"

"I'm from the future," she whispered across the table.

He raised an eyebrow. "And how much does a slice of pie cost in future Santolsa, future girl?" he humored her.

"I don't know, like four-fifty?"

He laughed again.

"The lack of food must really be messing with my mind," she said, throwing away the truth she'd just told and taking a sip of the worst coffee she'd ever had in her life.

"It could be the lack of food, or whatever else you've been dealing with," he said gently.

She shook her head. "I don't know what you mean." For some reason she felt like she could tell him about time travel, but being a murderer seemed like too much for a first date. She blushed. Why did she think this was a date? That was ridiculous.

He took a sip of his coffee and made a face. "This coffee is terrible," he said. "Not the best place for a first date."

Her heart flipped. "A date?"

"I'm sorry, I don't know why I said that." He looked down at his coffee and shook his head. "That was stupid."

"No, it wasn't, I was just thinking the same thing," she grinned at him, and he looked up and grinned back.

He had one of those infectious smiles that made you want to laugh along with him, to share the joke, or to just share a little piece of what was left over from it.

"A jukebox!" The redheaded girl from the bus was squealing and trying to work the old jukebox in the corner of the diner.

"How does it work?" asked the blond one.

An old Sonny and Cher song started blaring and the redheaded girl jumped up and down.

"So," he began, leaning forward and resting his arms on the table. "What's in San Francisco? Apart from cheap fries and pie?"

She took another sip of coffee. "Hopefully, some answers."

"Answers to what?"

"Questions."

"What kind of questions?"

"What's the meaning of life? What's the meaning of *my* life?"

"Wow, those sure are some big questions. I hope San Francisco can handle them."

"How about you?" she asked. "What's there for you?"

"Training."

"Why did you join up?"

He looked down at his hands.

"I'm sorry, that's none of my business."

"No, it's alright. It's just a long and complicated story."

"I think we have about five hours before we get there," she shrugged.

The waitress dropped their sandwiches and fries onto the table without saying a word.

"What a bitch," Janet mumbled, just loud enough so she may have been able to hear.

Dale looked at Janet like she'd just set the diner on fire.

"Too far?"

"No, I just… most girls I know don't talk like that, at least not in a public place."

"Well, sometimes it's warranted."

Dale took a bite of his sandwich. "It's actually not bad, definitely worth thirty cents. I wouldn't pay five bucks for it though."

Janet bit into hers too and her mouth went into sensory overload. In that moment, after barely eating all day, it was the best sandwich she'd ever eaten in her life. "I would," she said through a bite. "So, the Army?"

"I didn't really have a choice. I'm an orphan and my aunt raised me, but she recently got married and wanted to go and live with him, so I either had to join the Army or try to find a job and make it on my own. I don't really have any skills or money, so, the Army was really my only option."

"That's not a long and complicated story."

"Well, I didn't want to bore you with all the details."

"I'm an orphan too, in a way," she said. "My mom died and my dad, well, he left us."

"I'm sorry."

"My Gran raised me, but she passed away just recently."

"I'm so sorry."

Janet nodded. She opened up her sandwich and began laying the fries on top. When she was done, she covered the whole thing in ketchup and put the top slice back down again before taking a bite. Her eyes rolled back in her head. "You have to try it like this."

Dale opened up his sandwich and began laying his fries on top, just the way she had. And just as Sonny and Cher were finishing serenading one another on the jukebox, she handed him the ketchup. She brushed his hand and he wished there was no ketchup between them. He wished that she was reaching for his hand instead. And he wished that the beautiful smile spreading across her face was not just because of some over-priced fries on a sandwich, or a cheesy song on the jukebox, but because of him.

124

TWENTY

Late Night Stories
—————————————

Reno
    1966

"That was the best pie I've ever had." Janet wiped her mouth with a napkin and hoped she didn't have food all over her face. She was torn between not wanting Dale to think she was a complete pig and wanting to scoff it all. In the end, scoffing had won out.

"Do you want to try some of the peach?" Dale slid his plate across to her.

She waved it away. "Oh no, it wouldn't be fair, you didn't get any of mine."

"You're the one who hasn't eaten all day. I had a sandwich on the bus already, I don't need to eat all this."

She eyed the last few bites of pie on his plate.

"You need it more than me." He handed her the fork. *His* fork.

And she knew that by taking his fork she was taking more than just his fork. It was such an intimate gesture, one reserved for family members, best friends, *lovers*. But he was none of these. And she could have just used her own fork from her own plate that she'd pushed to the end of the table, but instead, she took his, and she took his pie. And she scooped up the last bite.

She nodded as she chewed. "Thank you," she said when she was done. "That was amazing."

"Worth four-fifty?" he teased, giving her a playful smile as they shared their inside joke.

"Definitely."

"We should get back. Or the bus will go without us."

Janet grabbed her purse, throwing a few dollars on the table.

"No, this is on me," he said, putting his own money down.

"This was the cheapest midnight feast I've ever had, let me."

His face twisted.

"You're not used to girls paying for your dinner, huh?"

He shook his head. "No, not really."

"Want to pay half?"

"OK," he started reluctantly. "How about if you let me pay my half and I'll leave the tip?"

"Don't leave a good one," Janet said, giving the waitress a dark look.

Back on the bus most of the passengers had dozed off already or were staring like zombies through the windows at the darkness outside. Janet and Dale had taken their original seats just a few minutes before they left the stop. But it seemed different now, like they had closed the gap and now it felt like they were too far apart.

She slid over to the seat on the aisle, and he did the

same. She turned her head to face him, and he did the same. And they stayed there for a moment, just looking into each other's eyes by the glow of the truck headlights going by.

"Tell me the rest of the story," she whispered.

"What story?" he whispered back.

"Of how you ended up an orphan, and in the Army."

"That's not a very good story."

"So, tell me another story, then."

"I could tell you the story about a boy who met a girl on a midnight bus to San Francisco."

"Does it have a happy ending? I don't think I could handle it otherwise."

"I don't know the end yet," he whispered. "But I hope so."

"I hope so too."

And Janet fell asleep listening to his voice, and even though she was on a bus in the middle of nowhere, she'd never felt safer or slept better than she did in those few hours of what was left of the night.

TWENTY-ONE

The Arrival

San Francisco
  1966

Lena woke with a start, waking Alex who had been sleeping on her shoulder.

"What is it?" Alex asked.

"A dream." Lena looked down the aisle of the bus which was now softly lit by the light of dawn.

Lena often had these dreams. They were something like visions or prophesies. When she was in one, it was just as real as if it was happening in the here and now. Perhaps even more so.

The girl had looked vaguely familiar when she'd first seen her on the bus, but now she knew for sure.

In her dream she had seen the girl, the one with the dark hair, the awful haircut and skirt that was much too short, the one who had been looking disapprovingly at Lena and Alex earlier. In her dream Lena had seen her enter the book room and step into the time portal.

Lena lowered her eyes at the back of the girls' head. The girl was asleep, her head gentling lolling into the aisle.

"What happened?" Alex asked, closing her eyes and leaning on Lena's shoulder again.

"That girl," Lena said. "She's one of us."

"One of us, like she likes girls?"

Lena rolled her eyes. "No, she's a… she came through the portal," she whispered.

Alex lifted her head up and her pretty hazel eyes widened. "Are you sure?"

Lena nodded.

"What do we do?"

Lena shrugged. Technically she was no longer bound by any responsibility for this. She had as good as left the coven. She was on her own. She could do what she liked.

"Maybe we should ask her to come with us," suggested Alex.

Lena reached for Alex's hand and gently twisted her fingers into Alex's. "I had hoped it would just be the two of us."

"We have all summer, my parents aren't expecting me back for months. We're going to have plenty of time to be alone. Let's make sure she's OK. I'm freaking out enough about all this and I have you. I can't even imagine what it would be like to do this on your own. It's the right thing to do, Lena."

Lena gave a sigh.

Someone was poking Janet in the arm. She swatted them away. Why was it that you always found your way into a deep sleep right before it was time to wake up?

"We're here," a girl's voice said.

Janet opened her eyes. It was the girl with the short red hair, looking down at her with a kind smile.

"San Francisco."

Janet rubbed her eyes with the sleeves of the sweater she was still wearing. She saw eyeliner staining the cuffs and tutted. She was going to have to apologize to Dale about that. She looked over to his seat, but he wasn't there.

"Where's that guy?" Janet demanded, jumping up and grabbing her purse from beside her.

The redhead shrugged. "Most people got off already."

"No, no, no!" Janet rushed off the bus, out into the early morning air, the sounds and sights of the city swirling around her. She looked out in all directions, but he was nowhere to be seen.

Her stomach ached.

It was like every time she fell asleep someone was taken from her one way or another - through death, a time portal or now, getting off the bus.

"Hey, you OK?" asked the redhead who was now standing behind her with a brightly colored backpack thrown over one shoulder.

"I never even got his number," Janet said, more to herself than the girl.

"Are you... do you have somewhere to stay?" the girl asked.

Janet shook her head. "I'll find somewhere."

The girl looked back at the blond girl she'd been traveling with and some knowing look passed between them. "We're going to go stay at the Y if you want to come with us."

"Oh," Janet began. It was only just occurring to her now that she had no plan after this point. "Actually, yeah, that would be great, thank you." Janet felt bad now about everything she had thought about these two girls. This one seemed nice at least.

"I'm Alex," the girl said. "And that's Lena." She gestured behind her at the blonde girl who gave a nod.

"I'm Janet," said Janet.

And Lena gave her a look like she'd just seen a ghost.

But Alex gave her a big grin and she knew they were going to be friends.

And the three time travelers from Santolsa stepped out onto the streets of 1966 San Francisco.

TWENTY-TWO

The YMCA

San Francisco
1966

The three girls had decided to share a triple room at the Y, even though it had been clear to Janet that Alex and Lena would have preferred a double. But they were all trying to make their money go as far as possible and if they went in together their money would last longer.

It was late morning by the time they had finally checked in and made their way to their room. It was what could only be described as "basic". With three single beds covered in white sheets, a gray blanket folded at the bottom, whitewashed walls, and a sink in the corner, it wasn't far off what Janet thought prison would be like. But at least here she had a key.

Janet lay down on the bed next to the window and looked up at the cracks in the plaster on the ceiling. She could hardly keep her eyes open, and just as they were about to close Lena spoke directly to her for the first time.

"We know who you are," she said bluntly.

"Who am I?" Janet asked. She couldn't even open her eyes. She didn't have the energy. She really wanted to know the answer, though. *She* didn't know who she was anymore, maybe this girl could shine a little light on the subject.

"We know you came through the portal in the book room. We know you traveled through time."

Janet let out a laugh. It sounded ridiculous when she said it like that. It sounded like the plot of some movie or TV show, or really bad paperback novel. "That's insane." She laughed as she opened her eyes and rolled onto her side.

"We traveled through time too." Alex perched on the bed next to Janet's, looking at her like she might break.

Maybe she would break.

Janet ran a hand through her clipped hair, before settling it on her forehead. Her head was pounding again.

"We're from the future," Alex continued. "2018."

Janet laughed again, but this time she couldn't stop. She was in hysterics. "2018? *Really*? Do you have flying cars and hoverboards?"

Alex frowned. "No."

"How disappointing."

"When are you from?" Alex asked. "You seem… normal. Like from my time."

"1999," Janet said.

"I bet the nineties were cool," Alex said, grinning.

Janet shrugged. "The music was good. Some of it."

"It was *so* good," said Alex. "Pearl Jam, Nirvana, Foo Fighters."

"And don't forget we have Backstreet Boys, Celine Dion and Bryan Adams," Janet continued.

Alex scoffed. "I guess some of it sucked."

"I hope that wasn't directed at Bryan Adams," Janet

said. "I like grunge, but sometimes everyone just needs a Bryan Adams song, you know?"

"Sure," said Alex, not sounding so sure.

Janet suddenly became aware of Lena sitting on her bed by the door and not joining in the conversation. "When are you from, Lena? What great music did you have in your time?"

"I was born in 1673," Lena said.

Alex gasped.

Janet laughed.

"And the only music we had were terrible hymns and the beautiful singing of the native people... who were sometimes nearby."

"I didn't know you were from that long ago," Alex said, turning to face Lena.

"I was fourteen when my coven and I traveled further ahead in time. We were to be hung as witches, but we used time magic to escape. We then traveled west and began to build the abbey, St. Christopher's."

Janet lifted her head and her eyes widened. "You're one of *them*," she said, pointing a finger. "You're one of the nuns of Santolsa."

Lena nodded. "And please refrain from pointing fingers and saying things like 'you're one of them' if you don't mind," she said.

"Oh, of course, the witch trials and everything, I'm so sorry." Janet couldn't believe what she was hearing. This girl who was sitting with her in this little room in the YMCA was from so long ago, and was tried as a witch, and was now here with her in the sixties...

Alex rubbed her own forehead. Clearly, she was finding this difficult too.

"So then, what are you doing here? In the nineteen sixties?" Janet asked.

"I left my coven. I was done with them. They had not treated me fairly." Lena wrung her hands, clearly this part of the story was upsetting for her. "I can do powerful time magic. I don't need the portal to travel. I am the one who created the portal. The others only added a few drops of their magic to the permanent circle in the school."

"The permanent circle… the book room," Janet mused.

"Yes," said Lena.

"And the other witches, they just let you *leave*?" Janet asked.

"First I had to find a replacement." Lena looked uncomfortable and paused for a moment, again it seemed like there was more to say, but she wasn't going to say it. "But I did. I found a replacement, well, I had a vision that my replacement was coming so I left. Of course, my replacement can't really *do* time magic herself, but she can add her small drops to the magic of the others."

"This is nuts," Janet said, grabbing her purse and her key to the room. "My head is going to explode. I'm going out to find some painkillers and something to eat."

"Is it not also *nuts* that you are here too, Janet?" asked Lena.

And there was something in the way Lena said her name that felt both comforting and terrifying at the same time. This was Lena, *Helena*, one of the Nuns of Santolsa, here in a room in a youth hostel, in the year 1966.

There was so much to ask and so much to say, but Janet just had to get out of there before she puked.

TWENTY-THREE

Pancake Palace

San Francisco
1966

With the painkillers finally beginning to kick in, Janet felt a little better, but she was longing for sleep. Her mind was chaotic with memories and thoughts - David, Gran, Dale, Lena, time travel. She was pretty sure that human brains weren't meant to hold this much. Her brain wasn't big enough for it all.

Janet had never been on a plane, but she felt like she was experiencing some kind of cosmic time travel jet lag. She didn't really know where she was, she was exhausted and confused and had no idea what time or day it was. And then the clothing, the stores, everything was so different here. It felt like she'd wandered onto a movie set, like she was in a 1960s version of *The Truman Show*.

She couldn't face going back to the Y, not yet. She knew she'd have to go back eventually. Everything she owned in the world was in that little room. But Alex and Lena? Time travelers? Time traveling *witches*?

It was too much.

A woman dressed in a pink skirt suit, hat and white gloves nearly knocked her off her feet and she remembered she was a time traveler herself. She looked at her reflection in the window of the Pancake Palace. All the work she'd done at Jonas' trailer showering and dressing and putting on some make-up had worn off, and she once again looked terrible. Her mascara had smudged, her hair was sticking up in all directions. She wiped under her eyes and attempted to flatten her hair, but then the hunger pains gave in, and she found herself walking into the Pancake Palace. It was a big restaurant with wood paneling on the walls and bright orange tablecloths. Frank Sinatra was playing at a volume just low enough to still be heard over the din of the other diners talking and clanking their knives and forks.

"I'm Sadie," beamed a waitress wearing a bright orange dress and her dark hair in a bob cut that was all puffed up at the top and not moving at all. "I'll be your server today, let me show you to a table."

Janet followed her to a small table in the corner, hidden away from the rest of the restaurant. Sadie probably thought she would scare the other customers away. She was probably right.

Sadie handed her a menu. "We have ten types of pancakes and ninety-nine types of pie."

"Then shouldn't this be called the Pie Palace?" Janet asked dryly.

Sadie laughed like she'd heard that before. "The pancake special is walnut maple, and the pie specials are peach and apple."

Janet looked up from her menu. "What did you just say?"

"Walnut maple?"

"No, after that," Janet demanded.

Sadie looked uncomfortable. "Apple and peach?"

"Apple and peach," Janet said, closing the menu and handing it back to her.

"Which one, honey? Apple or peach?"

"Both."

"You sure about that? You know these pies go straight to your hips," Sadie added in a whisper.

Janet glared at her. "You can add ice-cream and cream to them both too."

Sadie raised her eyebrows into her hair. "Of course, mam." And she rushed over to another table and took their plates away before taking Janet's order to the kitchen.

After what felt like a very long time of people watching and trying not to lose her mind about being in the past, her food finally arrived. Janet was thankful she had something to do to take her mind off everything. Eating gave her something to do, something to focus on. A purpose. She could get into a rhythm - cutting into the pie with her fork, layering on the ice-cream, doing it again…

If she had something to focus on, she was OK. Maybe this was the trick to surviving as a time traveler. Focusing on the details, the routine, each bite, each taste.

And so, she ate slowly, thinking of Dale and how much he would love this place, and wondering if by some magical twist of fate, he would be hungry for pie at this exact same moment and find her here.

But he didn't.

Janet walked back slowly, desperate for her bed, but also

not really wanting to have to talk to anyone, especially Lena and Alex. She wished she'd just paid the extra and got her own room.

Back at the Y she stopped by the notice board across from the main desk and took her time searching through the notices. Maybe she could find a place to rent, and she would need a job too if she was going to be able to pay rent. She still had most of the hundred bucks that had been in her suitcase, but she wished whoever had packed it had given her more, and come to think of, *who* had packed it anyway? Who knew she was there? Or rather, who knew she was *going* to be there? At the time it had been like moving through a thick dream-like fog, she just went through the motions, took her bus ticket and the cash, and just followed the path that was set out before her. But who *had* set out the path?

There were a couple of notices for places to rent, but they all sounded terrible. "Looking for quiet girl to share apartment in exchange for cooking and cleaning." Urgh. "Cheap room share with three other tidy girls." Double urgh. She didn't want to be someone's servant, she wanted to pay her own way and have her own space.

The only ads for jobs were for cleaners and nannies, oh, and one for a "pretty receptionist." So much urgh. Janet would rather work at the Pancake Palace.

Then she spotted a yellow flier peeking out from the bottom of the board. "WOM! Join the women's liberation movement!" Janet's heart nearly leapt out of her chest. She had seen a flier just like this before in with her mom's stuff. "We meet on the first Tuesday of every month in the basement of the Y," the rest of the flier said in that same neat, faded cursive.

Just as Janet was about to take the flier off the board a loud tutting came from behind her. "Women's liberation indeed," a voice said. The young woman who worked at the reception desk reached past Janet and ripped the notice off the board. "Complete nonsense." She ripped the paper in two and then started to meticulously go through the other notices, censoring at will.

"You don't think women need to be liberated?" Janet asked.

"Of course not. Women need to know their place. Our job is to look after our husbands and children."

"But you have a job, you work here."

The woman gave a smile. "Of course! It's acceptable for women to work until they *marry*. I'm just waiting until my beloved proposes and then my work will be in the home."

"And if he doesn't propose?"

She glared at Janet. "He *will*." And she walked off, without giving Janet another chance to speak.

She had already made a mental note of it anyway - first Tuesday of every month, that was *this* Tuesday.

Janet had never really believed in signs from the universe, but she didn't know how else to explain it. She knew her mom had been some kind of a part of WOM.

And she found herself once again praying to a God she didn't believe in that her mom would be there.

And then she wondered how many times you had to pray before it was time to admit maybe you did believe.

TWENTY-FOUR

Baguette

San Francisco
   1966

"Do you want to join a women's lib group?" Janet asked.

Alex who was buttering a piece of giant baguette with peanut butter on her middle bed which was strewn with newspapers and magazines looked up. "Women's lib?" Alex's eyes widened as she took a bite. "For sure!"

Janet beamed. "Cool, because there's a meeting here on Tuesday. In the basement. And I think my mom is going to be there." She threw the ripped-up flier on the bed. It was a little covered in mustard.

"Your mom?" Alex screwed up her face at the flier.

"I think she was a part of this group, WOM, in her time. *This* time."

Alex nodded and swallowed her bite. "It's weird, huh? To think about our parents… back in time."

"So weird." Janet pulled a bottle of painkillers out of her purse. "Want one?"

"God, yes."

Janet put two into Alex's hand and took two herself, chasing them down with a cup of the water from their room sink.

"It hurts my head," Janet said.

"You have no idea." Alex held out the baguette. "Want some?"

Janet shook her head. She was still full of pancakes and pie. "I guess you have parents… or *grandparents* in this time?" she asked.

Alex frowned. "It's kind of a long story."

Janet kicked off her boots and lay on her bed. "I think we have time."

"My dad was a time traveler. He was from my time and then he went back to the eighties where he fell in love with my mom."

"You're kidding."

"Nope. I wish I was. I'm struggling to process it all."

"Plus how to process being in 1966?"

Alex took a deep breath. "Exactly."

"Where's Lena?" Janet asked, finally realizing she wasn't here. It was so much easier to just talk to Alex. It was bad enough that Lena was so pretty and blond, the kind of girl that had always intimidated Janet a little anyway, the whole Nuns of Santolsa thing just made it a billion times worse.

"She's taking a long bath. She says the water helps her witch powers or something."

Janet blew air between her teeth. "I can't believe you're dating one of the Nuns of Santolsa."

"I didn't know that when I met her. I just thought she was a cute blond girl who escaped a cult. How was I supposed to know she was a time traveling witch?" Alex peanut-buttered another piece of baguette.

"Who created a time travel portal in our school?"

"She's more than that."

"She seems…" Janet didn't know how to finish that sentence.

"She was born in 1673, it's amazing she's as normal as she is," Alex said, answering the question Janet didn't even know how to ask.

Janet finally sat down on the edge of Alex's bed and broke off a piece of the baguette. "I don't have a lot of experience with relationships, but I'm guessing that's hard."

Alex passed over the peanut butter and a knife. "I really like Lena," she began. "And being here is incredible…"

"But…?" asked Janet as she bit into her bread.

Alex shrugged. "It just feels like a lot."

"It is a lot."

Alex nodded and they both chewed their bread in silence for a few moments.

"So, how are you guys even here? Doesn't the portal only take you back thirty-three years?" Janet finally asked.

Alex shook her head. "Lena can take us anywhere. She used the portal as it's easy for her, for her magic. She did a spell before we went in and it took us back. But I'm pretty sure she doesn't even need the portal. She's really powerful."

"So what happens if you guys break up?" Janet asked.

Alex frowned at her. "If anything happens, I can just find the other nuns. Lena said they would help me. If we got separated or anything."

"Even after she abandoned them?"

"She didn't abandon them, she left because they were horrible to her."

Janet dusted herself off from breadcrumb. She got up

to riffle through her suitcase and pulled out some cute navy-blue satin pajamas to change into, although she already knew she was going to sleep in Dale's Army sweater. "Hey, I have a question."

Alex made a mmmmm? sound.

"How come you guys have no money? If Lena is a witch, can't she just magic us some money?"

"It doesn't work like that."

"Well, that sucks."

"Right?"

"So, how does it work?"

"She can only do selfless magic. It has to come from the heart. It's actually really beautiful. She was only able to bring us here because she did it for me, to make me happy."

"It's selfless if she gives the money to us," Janet said.

Alex let out a soft laugh and shook her head. "I think we're all going to need to get jobs."

Janet sighed. "We're time travelers, can't we use it to make money somehow?"

"I think we're supposed to honor the magic. Be grateful we're here. Integrate. Get on with living."

"Maybe you're right. We want the full sixties experience anyway, right?"

Alex slathered another piece of bread in peanut butter and took a bite. "What about your dad?" she asked through her mouthful. "You said your mom might be at this meeting, but do you know where your dad is?"

"I think my dad worked at some hippie coffee house, but that's pretty much all I know."

"A hippie coffee house? That's so cool!" Alex sprung up on the bed, sending baguette crumbs bouncing around her. "Hey, we should go and check out Haight-Ashbury. That's where those kinds of places were… I mean, *are*. It's pretty straight around here, but if we go out of town, we should start to find the hippie counterculture. That's really what I'm here for. I love the idea of it all, the music, the clothes, the protests."

"I'd love to go to a protest," Janet said, pulling out a paperback and putting it on her pillow.

"Yeah, they were protesting *everything* back then… *now*."

"That's why you should come to this WOM group on Tuesday. Do you think Lena will come?"

"Yeah, maybe." But she didn't sound so convinced. "Lena wants to go sight-seeing tomorrow, but maybe the next day we could go to the Haight together?"

"Sure."

"You are welcome to come out with us tomorrow too, if you want."

Janet shook her head. "You two need some space. It must be weird having me here in your room. I should get out of your hair tomorrow."

"Honestly, it's kind of a relief. I mean, me and Lena have never been alone together like this before and I'm not sure I'm ready to…" Alex blushed. "You're our buffer," she finished.

"Great." Janet reached out and grabbed another piece of bread and took a bite and they both sat in silence for a few moments. Janet chewing and Alex looking at the hunk of bread in her hand.

"How did you know about the portal?" Alex finally took a bite of the baguette, giving Janet plenty of time to answer while she chewed.

"I found the key in a book, and when I was… in trouble, I just somehow knew it would help me. So, when I needed help, I reached for the key in my pocket, and I only ran into the book room to… to hide."

"Lena said they created it especially so that only those

who were being persecuted could use it. No one else would be able to travel through."

"Persecuted?" Janet shook her head. "No, I did something, and I was running away."

Alex frowned. "The way Lena talked, it sounded like only those who were pure of heart would be able to get through."

"Pure of heart?" Janet let out a laugh. "Hardly."

Alex took another bite of bread and chewed for some time before asking - "What happened to your hair?"

"Wow, you really ask a lot of questions."

"Sorry, that was rude." Alex started tidying away the bread and peanut butter.

"No, it's OK, I'm just… on edge. I've hardly slept and so much has happened." Janet reached for the bottle of painkillers and held them in her hand. She had probably had enough for today, but the headache wasn't going away. Maybe she'd have it forever.

"If you want, I could cut it straight for you. I cut my own hair. I learned how on YouTube."

"What's YouTube?"

"Oh," she laughed. "Of course, sorry, it's this online video platform where people just upload videos of anything. It's so weird you don't know this."

"It sounds terrible."

"It's actually great. Really useful. You can learn anything."

"Just normal people making videos? How do they make them?"

"People just use the camera on their phone mostly."

Janet gave her a look. "You have cameras on your phones?"

"Smartphones," Alex said, brushing down her bed and sending crumbs all over the floor. "Well, the offer is there, if you want me to cut your hair," Alex said. "And if you ever want to talk about anything…" The door flew open, and Lena walked in, dressed in a floral dressing gown, slippers and her hair up in a towel. And she was holding… a rubber duck.

"I like this look for you, Lena," Alex giggled. "Very witchy."

Lena threw her a dark look.

"I saved you some bread!" Alex reached out and passed her the last piece of bread.

"Oh," said Lena, softening. "Thank you."

Alex gave her a flirty grin and Lena smiled back.

And Janet went to get showered and changed, and when she finally got into bed, knowing the other two girls were there with her, she slept better than she had in years.

TWENTY-FIVE

The Meeting

San Francisco
  1966

Janet was overcome with the smell of damp walls and old newspapers as the three girls walked into the dimly lit meeting room in the basement of the Y on Tuesday evening. A small light bulb hung loose over a small circle of mismatched chairs in the center. Some looked like they'd been there for centuries, the threadbare cushioned seats probably partly responsible for the stench. Others look liked they'd been dragged down from the dining hall or the dormitories high above them.

Janet was expecting a feminist meet-up in the sixties to be totally happening. She thought there'd be fifty women gathered at least. But there was only one person there.

A woman with blond hair and honey skin who looked like she'd just climbed out of the pages of a vintage Vogue magazine jumped up to greet them. She was dressed in a bright yellow dress, white pumps and her hair and make-up was immaculate. "Are you here for the meeting?" she smiled, hopefully.

Alex nodded and walked straight in, taking the empty seat next to her. "We are. I'm Alex, and this is Lena and Janet." She waved towards them.

"So nice to meet you folks," the blond woman said. "I'm Franny."

Lena took the seat next to Alex and Janet sat on the end, bouncing her leg and wondering if this was just the stupidest idea ever. What were the chances her mom would be one of the few women attending this meeting? WOM was obviously just starting out. It probably didn't have many members yet and her mom was surely not going to be one of them. But Janet's heart kept racing hopefully.

A woman with dark hair and skin who looked like she'd just arrived back from Woodstock walked in and took a seat on the other side of the circle. She lounged on her chair dressed in a crop top and a pair of bell-bottom jeans that didn't look like they'd been washed, ever. She tossed her shoes aside and eyed up the girls. She had a confidence that spoke volumes, an air of power and courage Janet could only ever hope to feel inside herself. She was intimidating for sure, but Janet also knew straight away that she liked her. Janet gave her a smile and the woman nodded her head slightly in response.

A woman with red curls and dressed in what looked like work overalls walked in without making eye contact with anyone and curled up into a ball in one of the chairs. Just after her a younger girl with lank mousy hair and dressed in a baggy t-shirt and brown pants took a seat next to the curly haired ball girl and stared off into the distance. She wouldn't have looked out of place in Janet's time, she could have easily passed for a Pearl Jam fan.

"Nice to see everyone," beamed Franny. "Diamond, did you make it to that rally last weekend?"

An older woman with dark features who looked like she could have been about Gran's age walked in and took a seat, balancing a big purse on her lap.

"It was far out," Diamond, the woman from Woodstock said. "Totally happening. Until the cops came with the tear gas."

"Oh my goodness!" Franny exclaimed, clutching her clipboard to her chest.

Diamond shrugged. "Most of us got out of there OK and just started planning the next one over virgin Martinis. It's going to take more than some tear gas to stop us from protesting this fucked up war."

"Oh, good. I'm so glad," Franny said, moving papers around on her clipboard. She was clearly shaken up by this news.

Janet tried not to laugh. These two women could not have been more different, but here they were, working towards a common cause. It was inspiring.

And while all this was happening, another woman entered the room and took a seat across the circle. Janet's heart was beating so hard and fast she thought she might actually die. She was the most beautiful woman Janet had ever seen. Her long dark hair fell over one shoulder. Big gold earrings dangled against her neck, a silky green dress covered her legs, revealing the toes of a pair of matching green pumps.

The *shoes*.

Her dark eyes flitted over to Janet and Janet swore she saw some recognition in them.

But how would you know if you saw your future child that hadn't even been born yet? How would you recognize her? Especially if she was close to your own age?

Her mother's brow furrowed slightly as Janet did nothing but stare, unable to speak, wave, make any kind of gesture.

"You OK?" Alex asked quietly, over Lena.

Janet turned to Alex and shook her head. "It's my *Mom*," she whispered.

"Take deep breaths," Lena said, reaching out a hand and grabbing Janet's hand in hers.

It seemed like stupid advice, but Janet slowed her breathing, and it did actually help. Or was Lena doing some witchy magic on her? Either way, she was grateful, and she held onto Lena's hand until she felt like she wasn't going to spontaneously combust.

"Thank you," Janet whispered.

Lena gave her a warm look and Janet felt so bad for all the things she'd thought about Lena being creepy and weird and too much to handle. Maybe she was actually nice.

"Should we start?" Franny asked. "I'm so excited to welcome our new joiners!" She clapped her hands together. "Would you like to introduce yourselves?"

Janet still couldn't find any words, she could barely find her next breath, so Alex went first.

"I'm Alex," she started. "Uh, we're new to San Francisco, just arrived a few days ago and we saw, well, Janet saw —" she gestured to Janet, "— your ad on the notice board before the receptionist took it down."

Diamond groaned. "No wonder we can't grow WOM. Why don't we move these things to a cooler part of town, Franny? We keep getting censored here."

"Because, Diamond," Franny said, "there are women who would like to join our group who may not be hippies or druggies."

"Hippies and druggies? *Really*?" Diamond folded her

arms. "It's just too straight to be meeting at the Y. The only people we're going to get here are office girls who are going to leave as soon as they get boyfriends or husbands or bored housewives."

Franny's faced turned red. "And that's *exactly* why we need to meet here. We need to infiltrate the city, not just the places where we feel comfortable. We want all women to be able to access this group. Including bored housewives like myself."

Janet raised an eyebrow. It seemed like Franny had some sass after all.

Diamond gave a nod like she respected the answer but still didn't like it.

"Shall we continue on with the introductions?" Franny gestured to Lena.

"I'm Lena," Lena started, "I'm very much looking forward to meeting with you all and connecting with other powerful women."

Franny grinned at that. "And you?" she asked Janet.

Janet was staring at her mother again and had no idea what was happening. "Sorry, what?"

"Would you like to introduce yourself?"

"I'm… Janet, and… I'm here because… I'm a feminist?" Janet wanted to disappear into the concrete beneath her. She could have sounded so much more confident about being a feminist. These other women would probably think she was weak. But as she looked around no one seemed to care or notice. In fact, the girl in the ball was nodding at Janet like she got it.

"Perhaps we should all introduce ourselves too ladies?" Franny suggested, giving the new girls a big grin. "I'll start. As you know, I'm Franny. I work as a typist by day, I'm a wife and a mom to two girls and I want them to grow up in a world where they can be anything they want. Oh, I'm also the secretary of WOM. That stands for Women's Em-*pow*-erment Movement. We were going to call it WEM but it sounded too much like men, so we went for WOM."

"I still think we need a new name," Diamond said. "Or just say it means WOM short for WOMen."

"Or how about women's freed-om?" suggested the mousy haired girl.

"We'll get round to that." Franny said, waving their concerns away as she gestured to the next woman in the circle.

"I'm Grace," said the woman with the mass of red curls, uncurling herself from her seat and sitting up a little straighter. "I'm a scientist, or at least, I'm trying to be. I'm in college. It's tough being the only women in my class. I want women scientists and women in any job to be taken seriously, treated with respect *and* get equal pay."

"You might be waiting a while," Alex said under her breath.

Grace shot her a look. "I want to see women in science, in all careers. I believe change is coming, and I'm here to be a part of that change." And then, after that display of strength, she curled up into a ball again.

Franny nodded and raised a fist. It was almost comical, this woman dressed so perfectly, looking like some kind of 1960s Barbie, raising her fist in solidarity. Janet didn't know whether to laugh or cry. It really was kind of beautiful.

"I'm Lu," said the grungy mousy girl. "I don't belong in this world. This group is the only place I feel safe."

Janet could relate, to the first bit at least.

"Diamond Jones," said Diamond. "When you put enough pressure on a rock, it turns to diamond." And that was all she said about herself. Nothing. Or maybe it was everything.

"My name is Maria," said the older woman with a

thick Hispanic accent. "I've been fighting for women's rights since before you were all born. My wish is one day we don't have to fight so hard."

Janet's heart nearly shot out of her chest as her mother took a breath to speak. She had never heard her own mother's voice before.

"I'm Mayumi, or May," she said. Her low soft voice was like a lullaby, soothing Janet's broken heart, telling her everything was going to be OK. "I'm studying Arts and Literature at Berkley, and I'm passionate about any movement or group that cares about social justice."

Janet's cheeks were suddenly wet with tears. This was her *mother*. Her mother was *here*. Her mother was *alive*. And her mother was articulate and smart and passionate about important causes… and she was so very beautiful.

"Thank you everyone," Franny said. "Our next order of business is to come up with some ideas about how to grow our little group."

"We have three new members," said Grace, anxiously toying with one of her curls. "The notice must have worked."

Diamond Jones scoffed. "Before it got taken down. We need to do something more than just put up fliers. We need to take to the streets, do something *big*…"

Diamond's words began to dissolve into the stagnant air around them and Janet stopped listening. All she could focus on was her mother. Her head was pounding as she tried to make sense of it all. How could she be here with her *mother*? How could she be sitting here across the room from her very own mother, when her mother was *dead*? How could this be happening?

But it *was* happening.

Janet studied her, trying to squeeze each word she said

or mannerism she had like a sponge, like she was trying to rinse out everything about her and put it in a jar to keep forever…

"Well, if there isn't anything else to discuss, we can end our meeting there," Franny said.

Janet started. It was over already?

"We will meet back here next month," Franny continued. "Everyone is to take that time to come up with some ideas of how we can grow our group."

And everyone started chatting quietly and scraping back their chairs.

Diamond Jones put her hand on Janet's shoulder. "You OK, kid?"

Janet bolted up out of her chair. "Yes, I'm fine, I just…" She turned to go and find her mother, but she was already gone. How could she have left so fast? "I need to go!" Janet ducked out of Diamond's grip and ran out of the room and down the hallway to find her. She ran all the way to the stairs, up to the lobby and out into the street, but it was no good.

Her mother was gone.

"Hey. Janet, isn't it?"

Janet looked up from where she had been standing, staring out at the street in front of her, hoping to catch a glimpse of her mother somewhere, somehow, even though it was useless. She was gone. *Again.*

"Is everything OK?" Diamond Jones asked her, worry hidden behind her dark lashes.

Janet shook her head as tears began to fall. Tears of

grief. It was like losing her all over again. She'd grieved her whole life for someone she'd never met, and now she had met her, and it was so much worse. Like being constantly punched in the gut.

"Hey, come on." Diamond Jones pulled her in gently and gave her a motherly embrace. It was the first time since her Gran had died that she had felt that kind of comfort.

It just made her cry harder.

"Your friends are worried about you."

Janet pulled back and wiped her tears. "Do you know Mayumi?"

Diamond Jones gave a little shrug. "I know her from the group."

"Do you know where she lives, or where I can find her?"

Diamond Jones gave her a look. "I know she'll be back in the basement of the Y next month for our meeting."

"That's all?"

"And that she studies at Berkley."

"Maybe I could find her there…" Janet started making a plan to hang around the campus grounds, the Arts school.

"Berkley is a big place," Diamond Jones said.

"It can't be that big."

"It's also summer vacation."

"She's probably enrolled in summer school, I bet that's something she would do."

"What's all this about?" Diamond Jones asked, lowering her eyes. "Why do you need to speak to Mayumi so bad?"

"Well, she's my…" Janet tried to think of something quickly. "Half-sister."

"Ah, I see. And she doesn't know?"

Janet shook her head. "No, she doesn't know about me. I was hoping to talk to her at the meeting."

"How did you know she'd be at the meeting?"

"I didn't, it was really just a total coincidence."

"I don't believe in coincidence," Diamond Jones said.

TWENTY-SIX

The Pegasus
____

San Francisco
   1966

Janet got off the bus at the corner of Haight and Ashbury and as soon as the soles of her knee-high boots hit the pavement, she felt like she had come home. She was dressed in a short flowing dress in a shade of vomit green with pink flowers splashed haphazardly all over, and although most people here weren't even wearing shoes, she felt like she somehow belonged.

The streets were busy with all kinds of people – middle-aged men on their way back to work after lunch, older women standing on the street talking, but it was the young people who owned these streets. All along the road people were sitting or standing around, like they had no place else to go, and nothing to do but just be here, now. And everyone was happy, like *really* happy. It was like nothing Janet had ever experienced before. It was like some kind of Utopia.

As she began to walk, just picking a direction at random, she had no idea where the coffee houses were, people were smiling at her and saying hello. Some guy offered her a joint and a girl with a guitar called her over to sing with her. Janet shook her head but smiled back.

She didn't even know a place like this could exist.

And then she wondered what had happened, why this way of life was lost. Would all these people end up getting real jobs and buy homes in the suburbs? At some point they were all going to pack up and go home, but right here, right now, this vibe was magic.

Alex had promised to come along, but once again, she'd been spirited away by Lena to go on yet another romantic sightseeing trip. Janet got it, she knew what it was like to want to be with that one person... Dale's face flashed through her mind, his warm eyes, the smile that lit up his face, and hers in response. Then David's face appeared, his dark eyes smoldering before he leaned in to kiss her, and then suddenly his face was splattered with blood and Janet had to reach out for a wall to steady herself.

"Hey, flowerchild." A girl with big fluffy blond hair was looking up at her from the pavement. "Stay steady, baby."

Janet righted herself. She was OK. The flashbacks were getting less, easier to deal with. She had found a method of redirecting her thoughts which was relatively successful. Whenever she thought about David, about that night, she whispered to herself - *apple and peach, apple and peach, apple and peach*. And she immediately transported herself from that moment when the gun went off to the night in the diner with Dale. She felt his arms around her, catching her, she thought of his smile, and she felt safe and sound again. She had tried with some other memories, memories of Gran, memories from home, but nothing worked as well as thinking of apple and peach pies.

Nothing worked to clear her mind of David and everything that had happened that night but thinking about Dale.

"Apple and peach," she mumbled to herself.

"Apple and peace!" The girl called back. "Right on!" She gave a peace sign.

Janet gave a peace sign back, forcing a smile.

"I dig these boots…" And suddenly the girl had her hand on one of Janet's legs, running her hand up and down her long boot.

Janet shook her off gently. "Thanks."

"Where'd you get 'em?"

"You know, I actually don't know."

"Did you find them?"

"Kind of, yeah."

"Cool! Magic boots!" The girl's eyes were starting to glaze over.

"Hey, do you know any coffee houses around here?" asked Janet.

"Coffee houses?" a guy sitting next to the girl turned towards Janet. He had long dark hair and a beard. He kind of reminded her of a stoned sixties Jesus. On his other side was a pretty dark-haired girl with flowers in her hair. "You're not from 'round here, huh?" the guy asked.

Janet shook her head.

"Well then, welcome to the neighborhood." He opened up his arms like he was delivering a sermon. "What brings you here? Love? Peace? Looking for pieces of your lost soul?"

Janet let out a laugh, but it wasn't far from the truth. "Actually, maybe you could help me," she started, reaching for the photo in her purse.

"Help you?" he asked. "The only person who can help you… is you."

"That's so deep," said the dark-haired girl nodding.

"I was just wondering if you knew these people?" She held the photo out to him, and he took it from her. Her heart leapt. What if he dropped it, or ripped it or accidentally burned it with his joint? What if he didn't give it back?

Janet stood anxiously waiting while the guy examined the photo for what seemed like a very long time. Surely he either recognized them or not. She wasn't sure what was taking so long.

The guy kept staring at it. The two girls stared at it with him, and it was like they all entered a hypnotic trance for a few moments.

It felt like ten minutes had passed when he finally said. "Oh, yeah! That's Hog!" and handed the photo back.

Janet took it back, relieved it was still in one piece and shook her head. "That's not his name."

The guy nodded. "I swear to you, this is Hog." He poked at the photo. "I know Hog!" He seemed very sure for someone who had taken so long to recognize him.

"Everyone knows everyone in the neighborhood," the blond girl said. "We're like family here."

"Not *like* family, we *are* family," said the dark-haired girl.

"His name is Billy Bates," Janet said.

The guy just stared at her intensely. "Hog is his spiritual name."

Janet raised an eyebrow. "Hog doesn't sound very spiritual."

"It's his power animal. A hog came to him in a vision. I'm telling you, this really happened. I was there. The guy comes out of the trip *completely* changed."

"OK," Janet said, feeling stupid for even thinking these people might be able to help her find her dad.

The guy continued, "we all had these mind-bending spiritual awakenings, man. That night we all changed our names."

The girls nodded.

"So, what's your spiritual name?" Janet asked, playing along.

"Cheese." He said it like he'd just told her the meaning of life.

Janet had to try not to laugh. "*Cheese*?"

"And that's Bow," he pointed to the blond. "And this is Lamb," he said, putting an arm around the brunette.

Janet wasn't really sure what to say next.

"What's your name?" Cheese asked.

"Janet."

"That's cool," said Lamb.

"Pretty," said Bow.

"Thanks. So, do you know where I can find him?"

"Find who?" he asked.

Janet was losing her patience. Whatever time zone these people were on, it was totally different than hers. "Billy… *Hog*, or whatever you think his name is."

The guy shook his head.

Great. Janet fought the urge to throw her hands in the air.

Bow nodded. "Hog's just in there." She pointed just a few doors up from where they were sitting.

"Yeah, I totally forgot he worked there." The guy let out a loud laugh. "Which is weird, because I was just there yesterday, or was it the day before?"

"Time is now," Bow said, giving Janet an eerie look.

"Yes, babe, yes. Time *is* now." And Cheese leaned over and started kissing her.

"OK, well thanks for your help." But Cheese was already turning around and now kissing Lamb, completely oblivious to her standing over them. So *that's* how that was.

Janet really did like a lot of things about the sixties so far, but she wasn't sure free love was ever really going to be her thing.

She wiped the photo on her dress, removing whatever the film of dirt was that Cheese had put onto it and then walked towards the coffee house, butterflies exploding in her stomach.

Now that she was here, she wasn't sure she really wanted to meet her dad. But she knew she wanted to find her mom again and he was probably the best way to find her, assuming they had even already met by now. And maybe, just maybe, he wasn't as bad as she'd always thought he was. Reading that letter had really changed something, and now she felt like maybe she did want a relationship with him after all, even if he wasn't really her dad yet. Maybe there really was more to Billy Bates than just ditching his first born and running off with the Eights.

Her head began to pound, and she opened her purse and took two painkillers dry.

The Pegasus had a big sign above the window painted in bright purple which made it look like it was about to burst off the wood. It looked vibrant and cheerful, and the door was open, so she just walked right in. It was a small place, but it was crammed with people. It stank like marijuana, summer sweat, and cigarette smoke and the walls were covered in psychedelic art and band posters. There was a brown couch by a big bay window that looked out onto the street, occupied by a group of three girls who had their legs sprawled all over each other and were giggling uncontrollably. There was a splattering of mis-matched tables and odd chairs, all in different colors and styles.

People were everywhere, sitting in chairs, perched on tables and standing around in-between in any space available.

And behind the counter, was her dad.

TWENTY-SEVEN

Honey Cake

San Francisco
    1966

Once again, Janet's heart was racing.

This was her *dad*.

Janet had spent her whole life being angry at him. Thinking he had abandoned her, she had shut down that part of her heart and shut him out. While she often felt sad about losing her mom, she had never really felt that way about her dad. It was easier to hate him, to believe he was just a deadbeat dad who didn't want to stick around, than it was to feel sad about any of it.

And while the letter had made her wonder what the truth about him really was, she wasn't expecting to see him and feel like *this*.

He looked like he was in his early twenties. A blond beard hid much of his face, his hair was a shaggy mess of dark blond curls, and he was dressed in a purple paisley shirt which looked like it had never been ironed and cut off denim shorts.

He looked up at her and grinned. It was one of those grins that lit up rooms, that made everyone around them feel at ease.

And she knew if she let herself, she would break the dam she'd built around her dad so long ago and burst into tears, right here in the coffee house.

"Everything alright?" A soft expression crossed his face, like he really did care, he wasn't just asking to be polite.

And then, instead of crying, she started laughing. Something needed to come out, and since she wasn't letting it be tears, it came out in a kind of crazed cackle. "I'm sorry." She covered her mouth with her hands.

"Never be sorry for laughing." He took a slice of yellow cake from the stand next to the register and put it on a floral-patterned plate. "For you," he said, holding it out to her.

She took a step towards the counter, a step towards her *dad*. "What is it?" she asked.

"Honey cake." She was about to take a bite when he added in a stage whisper, "laced with a little acid."

Janet dropped the plate onto the floor, smashing it in two and sending bits of cake in all directions. She looked up expecting him to be upset.

"Not usually the way people react to honey cake," he told her.

"You always give people drugs without telling them?"

"What did you think you were going to get here, coffee?" He let out a warm laugh. "I'm just kidding, we do coffee too."

Janet dropped to her knees and began picking up the pieces of the plate and some chunks of cake.

"You're new to the neighborhood, huh?" He looked at

her curiously as she continued to pick up the mess she'd made.

She nodded. "I just moved here."

"From the mid-west?" He looked down at the pieces of plate as Janet stacked them on the counter, dropping the cake which was now covered in dust and hairs onto the top.

"Santolsa," she said.

His eyebrows disappeared into his curls, and he let out something that sounded like part laugh part sigh.

"Do you know it?" she asked.

He shook his head. "Never heard of it."

Janet gave him a look. Of course he'd heard of it, he was *from* there, but the door on that topic seemed closed for now. She thought of Dale asking her if she was from Santolsa and how she'd denied it too.

"I'm sorry about your plate," she said. "Do you have something to clean the floor with?"

He handed her a dustpan and broom, and she began to sweep, catching all the crumbs and tiny shards of the plate.

"I can pay for the plate, and the cake." She passed back the dustpan.

"You're good with a broom. Do you want a job?"

She shrugged and then nodded. She did want a job. And working here with her dad would be the perfect way to find her mom again, and maybe even get to know her dad too.

"You can start now, and I'll take the plate and the cake out of your first week's wages," he winked.

And that's how Janet found herself working at the Pegasus coffee house in 1966 with her dad.

TWENTY-EIGHT

Moving In

San Francisco
   1966

"Should we put this here?" Alex was standing on the bright orange couch, holding a huge psychedelic art print. The scratchy vinyl sounds of the Rolling Stones blared from the speakers of the record player Alex had found on the street earlier that morning.

"Perfect!" Janet jumped on the couch beside her and helped her to stick it to the wall.

Lena stood back squinting. "A little to the left."

It had only been a few weeks since Janet had arrived in 1966 and yet it sometimes felt as if she had already lived a whole life here.

She was settling into her job at the Pegasus and getting used to emptying ashtrays and slowly getting to know her dad. He was a real ladies' man and could charm the pants off any girl who walked into the shop. It was disturbing to watch, really. From one look at him there was nothing about him that was that special, he was just another bearded hippie working in a coffee house, but there was a charisma that he exuded. He was like hot caramel fudge and totally irresistible to most people.

And even Janet had found that she wasn't immune to his charms. She was still trying to keep him at arm's length. Getting to know him from a distance, but each time she saw him at work, she felt like she wanted to be his friend, to open up to him, to have him open up to her. But for now, they were friendly co-workers, and that was exactly how she wanted it. No use in getting too close was there? He was only going to run off and leave her at some point. That was his pattern. His past… his future, whatever.

She hadn't seen her mom again yet, although she was taking a double look at every woman with long straight black hair as she passed on the street or came into the coffee house, and she was counting the days until the next meeting of WOM. She didn't know what she was going to say to her, and she didn't have any kind of plan for how they were going to become friends, but she knew she couldn't just let her go. She also knew at some point soon her mom and dad were going to meet, if they hadn't already, but her dad was definitely not acting like he'd met the love of his life the way he was flirting with the attractive customers!

While Janet had been pouring coffee and slicing cake, Alex had found a job just a few streets over from the Pegasus at a little Italian restaurant called Mario's. It turned out Mario had an apartment above the restaurant that was empty. He said that people kept moving out because of the smell of pizza. If anything, that was a plus for Janet, and the other girls didn't mind at all. It was cheap rent since Alex worked downstairs and it was the perfect size for the three of them. Alex and Lena had moved into the large master bedroom and Janet had taken the smaller one.

Although her room was small, to Janet it was like a palace. She had a large window facing out over the park, high ceilings and the room had already come furnished with a double bed, which Janet had covered in a red chenille bedspread she'd found at the flea market. It had also come with a dresser and an old dressing table which was now covered in the few bits of make-up Janet had bought from Annabelle in Dee's Diner. She had borrowed a few secondhand books from the store Lena was now working in and was having a love affair with the modern classics that weren't really that old here. She was currently reading *Catcher in the Rye* and carrying it with her wherever she went. It even had some jam smeared on the cover from work. She hoped no one would notice when she returned it. Janet had stuck the photo of her parents into the mirror of her dressing table, along with the Saint Christopher prayer card she had found that day searching through Gran's books. It was the only thing she had left of Gran. It was one of the only things she owned at all.

The girls were trying their best to make it feel like home, but since none of them really had that much money, their decorating was limited. A few fringed blankets and throws thrown around in the living room, some posters on the walls, but it didn't really matter. What mattered was that they had their own place. They all had jobs and a bit of money and it was summer in the sixties in San Francisco. What more could they really need?

And then Janet thought again of Dale.

When the poster was finally stuck to the wall, they both stepped down from the couch and looked up at it.

"I love it," Janet said.

Lena returned from the kitchen with three glasses of

lemonade, put them on the glass coffee table and then squished her mouth up. "It's very…"

"Loud?" offered Alex. "Over the top? Bright?"

"Vibrant?" suggested Janet.

"Ugly," Lena finished.

"Oh, come on, Len. It's beautiful in its own way," Alex said.

Janet rolled her eyes. "I've heard that line before."

"Who said that to you?" Alex sat down on the couch and patted a space for Janet to sit down next to her, leaving Lena to take the egg-shaped chair opposite them.

Janet tried to push the memories of David away. *Apple and peach, apple and peach*, she thought, conjuring up Dale's bright smile in her mind's eye. "Just this guy I used to know. Back home."

"Well, he sounds like a jerk," Alex scoffed.

Janet shrugged. "He wasn't that bad, he was just… involved in some bad stuff."

"Like what?"

"He was an Eight. It's this gang…"

"I know what an Eight is." Alex reached for her glass of lemonade. "My dad was an Eight."

Janet's heart leapt into her mouth. *Her* dad was an Eight. At least, he would get involved with them at some point in the future.

"I'm not really supposed to talk about it," Alex started. "But… anyway, he only got in by mistake. He was dating some girl who made him do it or something. He was never fully initiated so they let him out on the condition that he get his tattoo covered up or removed. He got the snake turned into this massive tattoo of this cat he used to have called Tux. He said he loved that cat more than anything until me and my brother came along." She smiled at the memory of it.

"Do you miss him? Your dad?" Janet asked, reaching for her glass.

Alex nodded and looked thoughtful. "Yeah, I do, and my mom. But being here is amazing," she smiled and looked over at Lena who was sinking further into the egg chair.

"My dad was an Eight too," Janet said. "Not yet, not now, but later on he will be. He ended up having to disappear. I thought he had abandoned me, but I think now that he was maybe just trying to protect me from all that Eight stuff."

Lena let out a sigh. "Those darn Eights," she said. She smacked her empty glass on the side table next to her which was piled high with books she had also borrowed from the bookstore.

"Right?" Alex nodded.

Lena's eyes turned stormy. "They have caused nothing but trouble."

"We know," Janet said.

"No, you don't know." Lena leaned forward in the egg chair. "Do you know that they were originally recruited to be the *protectors* of the portal and all those who traveled through it? But the traditions and rituals and rules got so mixed up over the years. What was once a sacred society of men who would do anything to protect the persecuted turned into a gang of criminals. My heart aches." She pressed her hands to her heart as if she was physically in pain.

"What?" Janet put her drink back down. "The Eights were…?"

"Our protectors."

Alex let out a whistle.

"We tried many times to find the point in time where it all went wrong so we could somehow go back and fix it.

But it was little things, small changes over a long time. It wasn't just one thing that we could go back in time and change. We have been unable to change it. At least, we have been up to now." Lena picked up her glass and slid back in the egg chair as if she was finished with her story.

"So, you can change things? *We* can change things?" Janet asked. "Think of all the good we could do!"

"What would you change?" asked Alex.

"I would stop my dad getting messed up with the Eights, so I didn't have to grow up in a trailer park. So I wouldn't be alone when Gran died. So I wouldn't be…"

"So you wouldn't be here and now?" asked Lena. "This is how it gets complicated. If we did go back in time and somehow manage to change it…. if your father had never left, you wouldn't have moved in with your grandmother, she wouldn't have left you, you wouldn't have needed to escape, and you wouldn't be here. You would never have met us and you would never have met Dale and you…"

"How do you know about Dale?"

Lena gave her a look. "I have eyes."

"Who's Dale?" asked Alex.

"He's her destiny," said Lena.

TWENTY-NINE

The Protest

San Francisco
1966

"The glue stings!" Janet squealed.

"Just keep your eyes closed for a little bit longer." Alex blew hot air on her face and Janet cringed. It was already warm enough in her small room in their apartment.

"Why are we doing this again?"

"So we can fit in at the protest."

"I don't think this is going to make me fit in."

"You have to stand out to fit in here, didn't you know?"

Alex had been working on Janet's make-up for over an hour, while Lena had been spread out under the ceiling fan in the living room with a stack of books on Yoga and Buddhism. While Alex had been trying to live the sixties experience to the full, Lena had spent most of her time at the bookstore or curled up in the egg chair reading.

"Are you sure you don't want to come along, Lena?"

Alex called out while she waved her hands over Janet's eyes in an attempt to dry the lash glue quicker.

Janet slowly opened one eye to see Lena appear in the doorway. She was dressed in loose fitted flared jeans and a blue and white striped t-shirt. With her long blond hair falling over her shoulders she was the perfect image of the sixties. No one would have ever thought she had nearly been hung as a witch.

"Close your eyes!" Alex demanded.

Lena shook her head. "I have work. Sandra wanted to go to the protest, so I swapped with her."

"I wish you could come," Alex pouted.

"You know I don't like crowds."

"Maybe you could come to the next one," Janet suggested. "If you feel up to it."

"Maybe," Lena shrugged. "You both look nice," she added, before disappearing back to the living room.

"Do you think your mom will be there?" Alex asked as she put the finishing touches on Janet's eye make-up.

"I don't know, I hope so. I'm still really bummed she wasn't at the last meeting. But Franny said *everyone* would be there today, and that has to mean my mom, right?"

"If *everyone* is going to be there, do you think that means Dale, too?"

Janet scoffed. "At a peace rally? He's in the Army, remember?"

"So? Not everyone in the Army is pro-war. Most of them want peace as much as we do."

"You know, when Lena said he was my destiny I really wanted to believe her. But I can't help but feel like it's just all bullshit and I'm going to die alone," Janet sighed.

"Why? Because of one guy who didn't leave his number?"

Janet hadn't told them about David. She hadn't told

them what happened. She hadn't told them that the reason she constantly whispered *apple and peach* under her breath was so that she didn't have to think about him, or the guy he shot. She slowed her breathing like she'd read about in one of the books on meditation Lena had brought home and tried to bring herself back.

"No, because my love life has always sucked."

"You're sixteen, Janet. You have plenty of time to find your person."

"Maybe I already found my person, and they left me on the bus and didn't leave their number."

"That's not your person. Your person *always* leaves a number. That's how you know. They leave their number."

Janet half laughed and half sighed.

"If Dale is your destiny, nothing can get in the way of that, you'll find him again."

"And if I don't?"

"Then someone else or *something* else is your destiny."

But Janet didn't want anyone else to be her destiny, and even though he hadn't left a number, somewhere in her heart, buried deep under all the angst and fear and anger, she really did believe he was it.

But maybe your destiny wasn't always about being with that one person forever. Maybe sometimes your destiny was just to meet on a midnight bus and eat pie together, and that was all you got.

Maybe sometimes that was so special it was enough.

"OK, you can open your eyes," Alex announced.

Janet blinked her eyes open. They felt gooey and heavy, like her eyelashes were made of sticky crusty tree branches.

Alex leaned back on Janet's bed to admire her handiwork and have a nod. "You look like love and peace in human form."

"Ha! Now *that* is something no one has ever said to me before."

"I'm sure it won't be the last time." Alex gave a wink and then gestured for Janet to look in the dressing table mirror.

She almost didn't even recognize herself. Janet had finally given in and let Alex cut her hair into a "Twiggy" - a short cut with a long fringe swept to the side. Alex had also given her the classic sixties make-up look - pale lipstick, a little blush and huge eyes, not only was she wearing the biggest false lashes ever known to mankind, Alex had also drawn long eyelashes under her eyes.

"I look like a doll!"

"But such a *cute* doll!" Alex grabbed a pot of liquid liner off the dressing table. "One more thing." She leaned in close and began to paint on Janet's cheeks.

"What are you doing?"

"Just hold on… OK, there. Now you're perfect." On one cheek she had painted a peace sign, on the other she had drawn a heart.

"Love and peace, man." Alex made a peace sign with her fingers.

"Love and peace." Janet returned the gesture.

They rode the bus with a group of other protesters on their way into town. They really did fit in well. Janet was wearing a short brown and purple dress with her knee-high boots, even though it was eighty degrees, and Alex was wearing a long flowing chiffon dress covered in tiny blue flowers. People were carrying placards saying things like "NOT OUR WAR!" and "BRING OUR TROOPS HOME!" and "PEACE NOW!" Everyone smiled at each other, a common cause connecting them all without having to say a word.

Janet felt a wave of emotion pass over her. This was beautiful.

"Lena would have hated this," Alex said looking out the window as they approached the square where the protest was being held. It was absolutely heaving with people.

They got off the bus and made their way to the front of the drugstore where they had arranged to meet Diamond Jones, but she was nowhere to be seen.

"Janet!" Hog nearly bowled her over with a big warm embrace. He'd never hugged her before and it took her back. There was something about being in her dad's arms that made her want to just stay there for as long as possible. She had to blink fast to keep the tears from falling down Alex's artwork on her cheek. Janet couldn't remember any of his hugs from her childhood, from before he'd left, but this felt as familiar as holding Gran's hand. She shook her head, this was not the time to think about any of that. *Here and now*. Another mantra that had been helpful for the times when her head felt like it was going to explode from the effects of time travel.

"Alex!" He turned and gave Alex a hug too, even though he'd only met her a couple of times when she'd gone in for coffee.

Alex raised an eyebrow. "Hey, Hog."

He threw a big bunch of purple flowers which looked like they were plucked from someone's garden into Janet's hands. "Can you hand these out around the protesters? So they can give them to the cops in an act of peace? Everyone is doing it!"

"Sure, but we're just waiting for someone," Janet began.

And there was Diamond Jones, dressed like an absolute queen in her big, flared jeans, a tank top and platform clogs that made her taller than most of the guys here. She was drenched in beads and wearing an oversized pair of sunglasses. She looked like she had fallen straight out of a documentary on the Vietnam War protests.

"Ladies," she said giving them each a kiss on the cheek. "And who's this?"

"Hog, Diamond, Diamond, Hog." Janet flailed her arm between them.

"Well, well, Janet has been holding out on me." Diamond looked like she was about to devour him.

"Likewise." Hog grinned at her.

"Oh, no, *this* is not happening." Janet gave Hog a playful shove.

"It's *all* happening." Diamond lowered her glasses. "Free love, baby."

"Diamond!" And thankfully, before Diamond Jones and her dad could get it on, Franny and all the other women from WOM arrived, and there, right at the back of the group was her mom.

The relief Janet felt over seeing her again made her feel like she'd been holding her breath since that night so many weeks ago when they first met. Well, when they first sat in a room together.

And Hog was feeling something too, because his gaze had moved past Diamond and he all of a sudden only had eyes for Mayumi.

"May!" Janet heard herself say. "Have you met Hog?" And she reached out for her mom's arm which was covered in painted words - NO MORE WAR. Janet smudged the corner of the R and threw her in front of Hog.

"Oh." Mayumi looked up at Hog and Janet felt everything click into place.

Janet wondered for a moment what she had just done. Was she the one who introduced her own parents? Would they ever have met if she hadn't traveled back in time? Was everything just one cosmic wheel of destiny that you couldn't stop? Was it her destiny to be here, to introduce them so that *she* could exist?

She questioned everything. She could have stopped it. She could *still* stop it. She could save her mom. She wouldn't be born, but maybe that was OK if it meant her mom got to live.

But she *had* been born.

Janet felt the headache kick in, but she didn't have enough painkillers in her purse for an existential crisis right now.

Here and now, here and now, here and now.

"Everyone, huddle in!" Franny shouted, waving around a small camera. "I want to get a photo for our next newsletter!"

Everyone crowded around, Franny yelled "smile!" and the moment was captured forever.

"Give me the camera," said Janet. "I'll get one of you and the women from WOM."

Franny smiled and handed it over, squishing herself in between Mayumi and Diamond, the other women squeezing into the frame.

Janet took the photo, and then, while Franny was busy giving instructions, Janet saw her dad looking at her mom like she had just fallen from heaven, and she snapped a photo.

The photo.

Janet was overcome with emotion and was about to burst into tears when Franny took the camera out of her hands and Hog shoved the flowers at her, not taking his eyes of Mayumi the whole time. She passed half the flowers to Alex, and they began to move through the crowd.

Janet couldn't stop smiling as she passed out the flowers, slowly moving through the packed crowd, giving each person a flower, saying "peace, sister," or "peace brother" as she did. People smiled back at her, strangers embraced her, one rather attractive young man even placed his hands on the side of her face and gave her a gentle kiss. She blushed and then she saw him turn to the pretty dark-skinned girl next to him and kiss her too. She giggled and continued to pass out flowers and join in the chants – "NO MORE WAR" and "WHAT IS IT GOOD FOR?"

She felt like she was gliding through a sea of love and hope, everyone was here to try to stop the war, everyone doing their small part to make a big statement, to be part of this change. There was so much love here and Janet could feel it moving through her entire being. She'd never been high, but she imagined it felt something like this.

But all good things come to an end, and in a flash the mood changed.

One of the protesters, a young man with a dark hair and beard accidentally bumped into one of the cops standing around the edges of the group and all hell broke loose. A group of police pushed through the crowd, pushing and shoving people away and down onto the ground with the ends of their rifles. They started yelling at everyone to go home, shoving the boy who'd kissed Janet and the girl next to him to the ground, her knee exploding with blood as she fell, her eyes filling with tears. The man rushed to her side and one of the cops kicked him in the stomach.

Just seconds ago, this had been the most beautiful

moment of Janet's life and it was now turning into a complete nightmare.

"You assholes!" Janet shouted, the brief euphoria of sixties love and peace gone in an instant and her nineties fuck the man feminism bursting to the surface. She regretted it as soon as it happened. A cop shoved her into a group of people. She apologized to them and righted herself, only to come face to face with the end of a rifle. She gasped and the girl on the ground near her screamed, but nothing could stop the butt of the rifle knocking into her forehead, sending her spinning and falling to what should have been the ground.

But instead, she landed in a pair of arms. A pair of arms she'd fallen into before.

And then she fainted.

THIRTY

Another Dream

San Francisco
1966

Janet felt like she was in a dream. Strange black clouds danced across her vision as she tried to make out the voices around her.

"Janet, Janet, you have to stay awake."

Someone was shaking her. She didn't know who and she didn't know how to open her eyes to find out.

"You could have a concussion, you can't go to sleep."

"What happens if she goes to sleep with a concussion?"

"I don't know, I just know you're not supposed to let people sleep with a concussion."

"She could go into a coma, or even die."

Die?

"That's just a myth, it's **OK** if she sleeps as long as we keep an eye on her."

Janet felt a little relief at hearing that voice, it sounded like…

"Are you sure, Alex?"

Yes, *Alex*.

"This is *exactly* why I didn't want to go to that protest, it's too dangerous! I don't want you going to something like this again, Alex!"

Lena.

"Before the cops got involved it was really peaceful and beautiful!"

"Pigs."

Diamond Jones?

"I'll get her some water."

"I'll sit with her until she wakes up."

That voice was familiar too…

"Apple and peace," Janet whispered.

"See, she's fine."

"Dad?" Janet asked.

"She's OK! Oh, thank God!" And that was her mom. "Maybe a little out of it, but she's OK."

"I need a mocktail. Let's go make a pitcher of virgin margaritas and let her rest."

"Diamond Jones," Janet mumbled into the pillow.

"Yes, honey, it's me. Everything is OK."

"You sure you're OK to sit with her, Dale?"

"Of course."

Dale.

"Apple and peace," Janet said. "I mean… apple and *peach*."

And then she was asleep.

THIRTY-ONE

The Day After

___

San Francisco
  1966

Janet once again woke up with a splitting headache and no idea where she was.

For a moment She could have sworn she was back in Gran's trailer. The scent of Hawaiian pizza on the air while she obsessed about her unrequited crush on the boy in the trailer across the gravel.

But those days were gone.

Gran was gone.

David was gone.

And she was *here*, in 1966, in her apartment in San Francisco, lying on the bright orange couch underneath the psychedelic poster she'd bought at the flea market with Lena, a time traveling witch from the 1600s and Alex, Lena's time traveling girlfriend from the future.

She slowly sat up, rubbing her forehead, and realizing

there was a big bump on her face. So it wasn't just another time travel headache after all.

Flashes of yesterday's protest moved through her inner vision. Alex sticking false eyelashes on her and painting peace signs on her cheeks. Sitting on the bus, Hog passing her the purple flowers, the smiles on everyone's faces, the amazing vibe, and then the police. The police officer coming towards her and shoving her down… and just as she was about to hit the ground someone catching her…

"She's awake!" cried Lena as everyone rushed into the living room.

"Are you OK?" Hog leaned over her with worry in his deep blue eyes.

"She needs water," demanded Mayumi. Her mom was here!

"That bump looks bad, those asshole cops!" fumed Alex.

"Maybe we should just let her rest," came a kind but strong voice from the doorway. Janet looked up and there he was. *Dale.*

"Dale?" Janet ran her hands through her hair in an attempt to make herself look slightly less like she'd been sleeping off a police beating.

Mayumi handed her a glass of water. "Let's give her some space."

Everyone nodded and began to move out of the room again.

Everyone except Dale. The corners of his mouth moved up into a smile. "I'm glad you're alright."

"You saved me."

He let out a light laugh. "Not really, I just caught you."

"How did you, why did you…" she trailed off, not really knowing what she was trying to ask anyway.

He sat down on the edge of the couch, tucking the

multicolored crochet blanket in around her feet but keeping a slight distance.

"How are you feeling?"

"My head feels like it has an entire drill team running through it."

"I can't believe they did that to you." His dark eyes examined her bump.

"I probably deserved it."

"That's a strange thing to say."

Janet bit her lip. In a weird way she did feel like this was her karma for what she did. For what she didn't do. For what happened. She was knocked down by a gun, *they* knocked someone down with a gun… they did a lot worse than knocking him down. This wasn't even close to paying off her karma for what they did to that man.

"No one deserves something like this," Dale said. "The police are supposed to keep us safe, not be the reason we aren't safe."

"Well, I guess we don't live in that world."

"I guess we don't."

Janet took a sip of the water Mayumi had left for her. Until that moment she didn't know that water tasted different when your own mother poured it. But it really did.

"What were you doing at a protest for the war, anyway? Aren't you in the Army?"

He gave a nod. "That doesn't mean I want to go to war."

"But you would go, if you got called up?"

He looked down at the rug. "I would have to. I wouldn't have a choice."

"You could run away."

"And go where?"

"Anywhere."

He paused for a moment before answering her question. "I didn't know the protest was even happening. I was just out in town to run some errands. But when I saw what was happening, I was curious. And then your friend, Alex, gave me a flower. I remembered her, from the bus."

"The bus."

"Yes. And then I thought… if she was there, that maybe you were there too."

"So… you were looking for me?" Janet looked up at him and his dark eyes held hers.

"Yes. I was looking for you."

"And you found me."

"And I found you."

"You know something, Dale. I've been looking for you too." She reached over and shoved him.

"What was that for?" He rubbed his arm, a curious smile spreading over his face.

"For not leaving your number, or any way I could find you!"

"I didn't want to complicate things."

"You made them complicated when you didn't leave a number." She folded her arms.

He let out a sigh. "Look, that night at the diner, with the pie, and then talking to you on the bus until we fell asleep, that was…"

"Nice? Fun? Pretty great?"

"*Really* great," he replied.

"So, what's the problem?"

He looked up at the ceiling. "I bet you didn't even notice. You probably didn't even see them."

"See who?"

"When we were at the diner. The looks we were getting - the way the waitress said enjoy your meal mam, and then just put my plate down without acknowledging me. The way those guys at the counter were staring at us like I'd kidnapped you…"

She cut him off. "You're right, I didn't notice. All I noticed was you."

"That's kind… but you probably didn't notice because you've never *had* to notice."

Janet frowned. "So, you thought you were doing me a favor by never seeing me again?"

"Exactly."

"Maybe you could have let me decide that." Janet re-folded her arms. "And it's not like that here, in the Haight. People aren't like that here."

He gave her a look. "People are like that everywhere."

"I'm sorry that you've experienced… whatever you have experienced. I'm sorry this world is how it is. And I'm sorry that you think it's not a good idea… but I do."

"You do what??"

"I do think it's a good idea for us to… see each other again. If you want to."

"You don't even know me."

She reached for his hand and ran her fingers across the back of it until her fingers were gently folding into his. "I know you," she whispered, her heart racing as he folded his fingers into hers in return.

"You should get some more rest," he said.

"Will you stay?"

"Yes, I'll stay."

"Will you see me again?"

"Yes, I'll see you again."

"Will you leave your number?"

He let out a light laugh. "Yes. I'll leave my number."

And Janet fell asleep in his arms, and she'd never felt more at home.

Pancake Palace II

San Francisco
1966

"I don't get it. Why is it called the Pancake Palace if they have more pie than pancakes?"

Janet grinned across the table. "I knew you'd love this place."

Dale grinned back at her. "One hundred types of pie..." he let out a low whistle. "This could be the best date I've ever been on."

"Date?" Janet gave him a hopeful look.

He rolled his eyes playfully. "Of *course* this is a date. Do you think I watch just any girl sleep for almost two days straight?"

"I don't know what you do in your spare time."

"Spare time, what's that?" he asked, staring down at the menu, and running his fingers across the sticky laminate of the pie section.

"You're free now."

"Exactly." He looked up at her. "All the free time I've had, I've spent with you."

She beamed at him and rested her elbows on the dark wood of the table, holding her head in her hands. She felt like she was looking at him like a cartoon character with hearts beaming out of her eyes. Probably because she was.

By the time Janet had finally woken up and felt semi-normal again it was Sunday night and Lena was serving a dinner of lentil curry and fresh bread. Dale was still there, true to his word, he had stayed. The food, followed by a hot shower had helped, but what she really craved was sugar. Dale was getting the bus back into the city anyway, so she jumped on a bus with him, and they stopped off at the Pancake Palace for a late evening slice of pie.

"Everything alright?" he asked. "You seem a little…"

"I just can't believe I found you," she replied. She went to tuck her hair behind her ears and remembered it wasn't there anymore.

"You cut your hair."

"You noticed."

"Yes, I noticed. I like it. Short hair suits you."

"What can I get you kids?" asked a waitress in an orange dress who was barely older than them but already had that middle-aged attitude.

"Pie," said Janet.

"One peach, one apple?" Dale suggested.

Janet nodded.

"Cream or ice-cream?" The waitress asked.

"Both," they said at the same time.

"What, both on each slice? Or… what?"

"Both on each slice sounds wonderful." Dale put his menu back in the holder and Janet did the same.

"Crazy," Janet said. "Both on each slice, that's so… decadent."

"Only the best for my late-night pie date."

"What time do you have to be back?" Janet sat back while the waitress turned over their cups and poured black coffee for them both before bringing a tiny jug of milk.

Dale rubbed at the watch on his wrist. "Ten."

"Ten? That's so soon. We don't have much time," she pouted.

He looked down at the table for a moment. "I have next weekend off again. I'm a free man for a whole 24 hours."

"So, I should book you in, before some other girl passes out and you have to stare at her all weekend."

"I'd like to think that maybe we could do something else next time if that's alright with you." He pushed the jug of milk and sugar bowl towards her.

"Oh yeah, like what?" Janet asked flirtatiously. She didn't even know she could flirt.

"Like spend time with you while you're awake?"

"I'd like that too," she said, grinning over her coffee cup.

"Apple and peach," the waitress announced putting the plates down on the table, both smothered in cream and ice-cream. "Enjoy mam, sir," she said.

Janet raised an eyebrow. "Maybe we can leave a tip this time."

Dale smiled and picked up his fork, stabbing gently at the ice-cream. "What is that about?"

"Hmmm?" Janet had already taken a bite.

"Apple and peach. You were saying it in your sleep."

Janet shook her head and wished for a moment that she could dive into the sea of cream in front of her. If she told him her secrets, if she told him about apple and peach and the Eights and David, and *God*, if she tried to tell him about time travel again, he'd run a mile. So she just replied, "I don't know."

And then she went for her other mantra - *here and now, here and now, here and now.*

And then everything was OK again… at least for now.

THIRTY-THREE

Blast from the Past

San Francisco
1966

Janet was sweeping the floor of the Pegasus when she became aware of someone watching her from the bay window that looked out onto the street. They had just closed up for the night. Usually, they were open all hours of the day and night, it was all a little free flowing - their opening hours were mostly based on whenever Hog could be there. Tonight though, he had left the keys with Janet to lock up and gone to a party on the other side of town. Janet wasn't in a hurry to go back home, Alex and Lena were going through a phase of extremes - fighting or making up, and neither was that appealing to be around. She loved living with Lena and Alex, but she was like a permanent third wheel. She was always in some way going to be the sad lonely girl they picked up at a bus station and took pity on. She was becoming close with Alex, but she still didn't feel like she really knew Lena, but then as nice as

Lena could be, she also freaked Janet out a little. She was one of the Nuns of Santolsa! How on earth was Janet supposed to feel comfortable around someone who was born in the 1600s and had magic powers?

A knocking on the window broke her thoughts and she looked out at the street.

She dropped her broom.

What she was seeing made absolutely no sense.

But there he was.

David.

He gave her the biggest grin she'd ever seen on his face, his eyes all lit up. He looked… *happy*. She wasn't sure she'd ever even seen him happy before. Of course she'd seen him smile plenty of times, but had he ever really been *happy*? Without stopping to think, she rushed to the door, unlocked it, and pulled it open.

"David?" she gasped. "It's *you.*"

"It's me," he grinned, before sweeping her up in his arms.

Her heart felt like it was going to burst into his. She closed her eyes, and she was immediately back in 1999, in his bedroom, in his arms. It felt like she'd just gone back home. But *that* wasn't her home anymore, *he* wasn't her home anymore.

"How did you know where to find me?" she asked, finally breaking free of his embrace.

"I… I met this… nun. It was wild."

"A *nun*?"

He nodded. "She explained everything – where you were, how we ended up back in time, how time travel works and…"

Janet shushed him. "Come inside if you're going to talk about time travel!"

"Oh sure, like anyone out here is going to look at us

twice. I just saw two guys talking about how sunflowers were brought to earth by an alien civilization in the Middle Ages."

Janet gave a little laugh. "I guess you're right. But still, come in!" She ushered him in, but he stopped short.

"Uh, hold on a sec." He disappeared for a moment and returned with a pretty petite girl with blond hair in pin curls.

Janet's stomach dropped as she watched him interlace his fingers with hers. She stood slightly behind him, her eyes flickering around the coffee house, avoiding Janet's gaze.

"This is Abigail," David announced.

Abigail finally looked up and made eye-contact with Janet for just a split second before looking away again. The girl was a mouse.

"Hi." Janet hadn't intended her voice to sound so unfriendly, but what the heck was going on? It had been just over a month since David had disappeared from the book room. And now he was at the Pegasus in 1966 with a *girl?* A very pretty girl no less. Definitely prettier than Janet was. Abigail reminded Janet of a varsity cheerleader, classic All-American, blond, big boobs, petite. Janet was... none of those things.

"She doesn't speak English. Abigail is from..." David glanced at Abigail and then back to Janet, "1933."

"1933? What? How?" Janet pulled up two chairs for them to sit down, and then reluctantly pulled up a third. She gestured for them to sit and then picked up the broom, leaning it against a Grateful Dead concert poster on the wall before taking a seat opposite them both.

"When you left the book room that night, you closed the door behind you, remember?"

Janet nodded.

"It reset the time portal and sent me back *another* thirty-three years to 1933."

"Oh my god," Janet gasped, jumping up from her chair.

David nodded.

She went to the fridge and grabbed three ginger beers, cracking open the tops. She handed one to David and one to Abigail who looked at it like it was the devil himself trapped in a brown glass bottle.

"That's where I've been, in 1933. It's been crazy, let me tell you."

"What have you been doing all this time?" she asked, sitting back down again.

"I was helping the nuns with some things that needed doing around the abbey. In exchange for room and board."

"So, wait a second, you were going to *stay* there? Why not just go back to 1966 when the portal reset, and then back to 1999 the next day? You could have been home in two days."

"I can't *go* home, *remember?*" He said through gritted teeth. Abigail clearly didn't know anything about that.

"Well, why not stay there then, why come here?"

"There was some trouble." He looked sideways at Abigail who was staring soullessly at the Grateful Dead poster.

"What kind of trouble?" Janet took a swig of her ginger beer.

"1933 isn't the greatest time."

"No?"

"Abigail is… *German.*"

Not so All-American then.

Abigail startled and looked up at him. He gently rubbed her arm, and she went back to staring at the poster and ignoring the drink in her hand.

"Her family left when Hitler came into power. They were lucky to get out. But not so lucky to be in America at a time when people… didn't really like Germans." He grimaced.

"So… wait a second, you didn't come here for me, you came here to help *her*." Janet didn't like what she was saying or how it sounded coming out of her mouth. She didn't like that she was jealous as hell of some mini Claudia Schiffer David had picked up from the thirties. She didn't like that she was angry at David for not just trying to get to her as quick as he could. She didn't like that she was feeling anything about him at all. And she *really* didn't like that she was fighting her old feelings for him while knowing that she was meeting Dale this weekend. Nothing physical had happened with Dale, nothing more than handholding anyway, but it had still been the best handholding of her life and she didn't want anything to mess that up.

But everything that happened with Dale was when she thought David was lost in time and she thought she was never going to see him again.

Now she just felt everything, and it hurt so damn much. All of it felt like it was about to explode out of her head, out of her mouth, out of her eyes.

But no, this wasn't going to be the thing that would make her cry. Not this.

He had moved on, *fine*. So had she.

But if she had moved on, why was she so damn angry?

David's dark eyes flickered around the coffee house. "I wanted to come back for you," he said softly. "But then, things got weird."

"Uh huh."

"I wanted to get back to you. But I didn't even know

where you would *be.* I didn't know how to find you in 1966."

"Well, you found me now somehow." Janet threw her hands in the air.

"One of the nuns… said she had a dream and saw you here."

"Sure."

"It was the strangest thing about that nun… I felt like I knew her. Did you ever feel like you knew someone when you couldn't possibly know them?"

"Yes."

"But then… I met Abigail."

Janet looked over at the girl. She looked like she was about to vomit. Janet felt like she was about to vomit too. How could David go from falling asleep tangled in her arms, covered in blood, with them promising to look after each other, to hooking up with some blond girl from 1933? And what was he thinking, bringing her *here?*

"Well, good luck." Janet pushed back her chair and stood up. Being angry was the right choice. David and Abigail could go off on their merry way and she could just pretend *this* had been some bad dream.

"What do you mean, good luck?" His eyebrows knotted.

"I don't know why you came here. You're not here for *me,* so what do you want?" She folded her arms and looked down at them both.

"I came here for your help," he pleaded.

She laughed. "Are you kidding? You come here with some new girl, sorry Abigail, all acting like whatever it was *we* had was nothing or had never even happened at all. And you expect me to *help* you? That night in your room, before your dad offered us the job… did *that* completely escape your mind?"

"I have nowhere else to go," he said, pityingly.

"Fuck you, David."

Abigail finally looked up. Maybe she couldn't understand English, but she could understand fuck you.

"I don't have any money, I don't know what else to do." He ran his hands through his hair, something she had seen him do over and over in their time. But this wasn't their time, and the gesture didn't warm her heart, it just pissed her off.

Janet wanted to scream.

"Fine, you can stay here tonight. Sleep on the couch. Do whatever you want. Just make sure you keep yourselves locked in. You can't lock the door behind you, so I'll come in early and let you out."

"Thank you," he said, standing up and following after her as if to give her a hug but she backed away. "I really did miss you. I missed you so much, Janet." His hand reached out for her, but she pushed it away.

"Obviously not that much."

She quickly finished sweeping, locked the cash register, grabbed a bag full of nearly stale angel cake to take home to the girls and left without saying another word.

THIRTY-FOUR

Bagels

San Francisco
1966

"Thank you, Janet, really." David leaned forward on the couch, looking like he hadn't slept at all. His dark hair was sticking up at the back and his eyes were bloodshot. Abigail was still asleep, curled up in a ball at the other end of the couch. Janet was standing above them, her arms folded over a dark blue dress covered in tiny bright pink flowers which she was wearing with her military boots. She decided to get ready for her day with Dale before she left the apartment, just in case she didn't have time to get back later. She had accessorized with a strand of white and gold beads, the key to her past on the yellow ribbon tucked into her dress as always, a pair of big brass teardrop earrings and Gran's red lipstick.

It was still early, the sun just getting comfortable over the rooftops of the old Victorian houses. There were a few people wandering around the streets, but it was still quiet.

The neighborhood was in that dozy space of being awake but not quite having its eyes open yet.

Janet had worried she would find them in a tangle of limbs on the couch, in some romantic embrace, but he wasn't even close enough to touch her. She tried to remember that Abigail was from 1933 and was probably horrified at the idea of sleeping on a couch with a man she wasn't married to. David on the other hand, was probably totally up for it, but she didn't want to think about that.

Seeing him now, in the light of day, though, things felt different than they had last night.

Last night she'd been angry and confused about her feelings and pissed off at how he had treated her.

It wasn't like her feelings for him had just disappeared overnight. David was important to her, he was her only link to home, and apart from Gran, he was the only person who ever had her back in her whole life. That wasn't something that just went away in twelve hours.

The idea of him and Abigail being together still made her want to hurl or throw a chair through the window or punch him in the face. But when she thought about apple and peach pies, when she thought about Dale, and how she would soon be seeing him again in a few hours, she wanted to do those things a little less.

"Coffee?" Janet threw an old copy of *Wuthering Heights* down on the counter and grabbed a coffee pot.

"God, yes."

"Coffee?" David gave Abigail a gentle nudge.

She looked up at him and then over at Janet, confusion all over her face. Janet almost felt sorry for her.

Janet held up a bag of coffee. "Coffee?"

"Kaffee, ja!" Her eyes lit up, like she was finally thankful she could understand something.

"Coffee, yes," Janet explained.

"Coffee, yes," Abigail repeated, nodding and giving Janet a weak smile.

"Jeez, David. What have you been teaching her? The poor girl must be so lost. She doesn't speak English *and* she's suddenly thirty-three years in the future? I'm surprised she isn't totally freaked."

"Oh, she's freaked." David stood up and walked over to join Janet behind the counter. He grabbed three coffee cups from the side and put them out on the counter.

"You should be teaching her the basics at least."

"We've been getting by and communicating through… well." He didn't finish.

Janet clanked the coffee pot into the machine.

"How am I meant to teach her a whole language? I don't even know where my next meal is coming from. I don't have any money or anywhere to live. I don't have anything."

Janet leaned on the counter, willing the coffee to percolate faster. "Maybe you should have thought about all this before you just turned up here. Maybe there is somewhere else you can go."

"You're the only person I have." His eyes filled with sadness, or maybe remorse.

Janet sighed. "Look, you can stay with us in the apartment for a few nights, but that's it. Just until you work things out. And you'll both have to sleep on the couch. I'm not giving up my room."

David moved towards her and gently placed his hand on her shoulder, his dark eyes drawing her in. "Thank you, Janet."

"Janet?" Dale had appeared and was standing on the other side of the counter, looking handsome as ever, dressed in dark blue pants and a white button up shirt. But his expression wasn't so bright, and he clearly wasn't sure about what he had walked in on.

"Dale!" Janet stepped back from David's embrace. "What are you doing here?"

"I went by your place and Alex said you were here. She said you had to drop the keys off for Hog?"

"I did…" Janet was about to make up some elaborate lie about why she would be here with David, about why there was a German girl sleeping on the couch, but she didn't want to lie to him, and while there were things she probably would need to omit from the story, she went with as close to the truth as possible. "These are my friends, David and Abigail."

Dale gave a curt nod to David and looked over at Abigail who was still bundled up on the couch with a blanket.

"They were in a tight spot last night. They've been…"

"Evicted," David finished, saving her from having to lie. "We got evicted from our place and we had nowhere else to go, so Janet let us stay here last night." David stretched out his hand. "I'm David."

Dale, ever the gentleman, shook his hand. "Dale."

Janet wondered if this was going to create some kind of space-time paradox, her kind-of-ex from 1999 meeting what she hoped was her current from 1966. Talk about worlds colliding.

"You a friend of Janet's too?" David asked.

Dale raised an eyebrow.

"Dale is my…" Janet began, not knowing how to finish. It was all so new, and she didn't know if the word "boyfriend" was too much. But at the same time, it felt like it wasn't even close to enough.

"Oh!" David gave a slow nod and his eyebrows shot up as it dawned on him. "I see."

"Coffee, Dale?" Janet asked, grabbing another cup from the shelf.

Dale gave a nod.

"Have you been here all night, Janet?" Hog walked in, looking like he hadn't been home yet. His paisley shirt was open, showing his fluffy blond chest hairs and he stunk of cigarettes and marijuana.

Abigail looked horrified.

Janet shook her head. "No, I was just returning the keys from last night and then I saw some friends and brought them in for coffee. I hope that's OK." Lying to Hog didn't seem like a big deal. After all, he still abandoned her as a baby. A little lie about this was nothing compared to that.

"As long as they're paying."

"Of course."

"I'm kidding, Jan." He gave her a wink and dropped onto the couch beside Abigail. "It's fine with me as long as you pour me one first." He pulled a packet of cigarettes out of his pocket and lit one.

Abigail moved over and away from him on the couch, but Hog just used the space to spread out more. "Hey, I'm Hog," he said, giving her one of his flirtatious smiles.

"She doesn't speak English," Janet explained.

"No comprehende?" he asked her.

"She's German."

"No Deutsch, sorry. But the language of love is universal, right?" He leaned in a little closer to her and she made a squealing sound.

"She's with *me*." David grabbed Abigail's hand and yanked her off the couch, wrapping the blanket around her and pointing to a chair at one of the tables close by.

Hog raised his hands. "Take it easy, man. All this owning of each other, it's so Piscean."

"Piscean?" David frowned at him.

"This is the age of Aquarius, man. Free love is the future." Hog gave him a wink.

"Not for us." David looked over at Abigail with so much concern for her that it made Janet's stomach ache. That was the same look he had given her when Gran had passed away. That protective look that told her he would always be there and keep her safe. So much for that.

"Is everything OK, Janet?" And there was Dale, giving her a similar look of concern.

"It's a really long story, and you wouldn't believe it even if I told you."

"Maybe you could try me, let me decide what I believe."

"You're right." And she reached over and put her hand on his. "I'll tell you later, though, OK?"

"I hope you know you can tell me anything." And even though it was still so new, she really did know she could tell him anything. Whether or not he believed it was another thing.

"Bagels!" Hog slapped his hands on his thighs and stood up. "I'm going to make us all some bagels."

Hog dropped a platter of bagels on the table with a tub of butter, a jar of peanut butter and a jar of jelly.

"Sorry we don't have any lox," he said. "But the Pegasus is just not that kind of place."

Janet topped up their coffee cups, and then took her place next to Dale at the two small tables they had pushed together.

"Thanks so much for this Hog," said David. "Things have been a little tough, so a free breakfast is really appreciated."

"Who said it was free?" Hog took a sip of coffee.

David's face fell.

"Lighten up, man. Eat as much as you want."

David's shoulders relaxed and he reached for a bagel, putting one on Abigail's plate first. Janet wasn't sure if the gesture was sweet or kind of controlling, but Abigail didn't seem to mind, in fact she gave him a soft smile, the first smile Janet had seen on her face. But as soon as Abigail looked over at Dale her smile disappeared again.

"Why don't you ask the Eights for a job?" Hog suggested.

David nearly spat out his bagel. "Excuse me?"

"The tattoo, you're an Eight, right?"

Dale gave Janet a look.

"Uh, yeah, but I'm trying to get out," David explained.

"Ha! If you got out, you'd be the only Eight ever to do it. Let the rest of them know how!" He let out a guffaw as he took another bite of a bagel that was more peanut butter than bread.

"How would I... uh, how would I get in touch with them?" David asked.

"You don't know?"

"We're not from here," David said. "We were evicted from our place in... Santolsa."

Now it was Hog's turn to almost choke on his bagel. When he'd finished chewing, he said, "Why did you come all this way from Santolsa?"

"No jobs in Santolsa."

"But you're an Eight, the Eights always have jobs. Even in Santolsa."

Janet put her bagel covered in jelly back down on her plate. She was no longer hungry.

"Trying to get out, I told you," David said, reaching for the butter.

Hog took another bite, chewing, examining him.

"There are some Eights in my unit," Dale said. "I could get you in touch if you wanted."

Janet shook her head and grabbed his arm. "I don't want you, or anyone else at this table *ever* having anything to do with the Eights."

Hog gave Janet a look. "OK, *mom*," he said with a laugh.

Dale nodded. "I understand, but if it's his only option and he needs to get in touch with them…"

"I know a guy. I can give you his number." Hog wiped his fingers on his shirt.

"No one is contacting any Eights. *No one*," Janet said, glaring at Hog.

"Look, babe," Hog started. "You clearly have some issue with the Eights, but they aren't all bad. I did a couple jobs with them myself a few years back when I needed the cash."

"What?" That wasn't the story. The story was that he got involved with the Eights later. "You're an *Eight*?"

Hog shook his head. "I never initiated."

"You just said no one gets out," said David.

"Once you're *in* you can't get out, but if you're never really *in* you never really have to get *out*."

"You were either an Eight or you weren't," David said.

Hog shrugged. "Look, whatever man. I don't believe in all this owning you, initiation bullshit. No one owns me but me. I can either give you the number or not. Just be cool though, alright?"

"I don't understand," Janet shook her head. "How did you do jobs for them but not join them?"

Hog sighed and grabbed another bagel. "My brother was an Eight."

Janet gasped. "You have a *brother*?"

"*Had* a brother."

Why hadn't Gran ever mentioned she'd had an *uncle*?

"I'm sorry," said Dale.

Hog shrugged. "We didn't grow up together, he was my half-brother. Dad's side. The messed-up side."

Janet stared down at the bagel she'd hardly touched.

"What happened to him?" asked David.

Hog glared across the table at him. "That's none of your business, kid," he said, his tone and the mood turning dark.

David just glared back at him.

Janet looked over to see Abigail was still staring at Dale, and with everything she'd just found out and now this, Janet had had enough. "What?" Janet demanded, slamming down her coffee cup and nearly smashing it on the table.

Everyone went silent.

"Why are you staring at him?" She looked at David. "Why is she staring at him?"

Hog waved a bagel in her direction, the storm in his eyes clearing back their usual calm blue. "You'd be stupid to think that everyone approved of that."

Her chest tightened. "Of *what*?"

"Oh, not me. I don't care what you do, or *who* you do."

Janet's face went bright red, she could not believe her father had just said that to her. "We're not even... we haven't... urgh!"

"Hey, what you do in the bedroom is up to you. But out on the streets, especially if you go out of this neighborhood, not everyone thinks it should just be your business. And *that* girl," he said, pointing his peanut butter covered knife at her, "thinks it's her business what you do and who you spend time with."

"Are you saying what I think you're saying?" David put

his bagel down and stared across the table at Hog, at her *dad.*

Hog shrugged. "I just call it like I see it."

Dale sighed and put his folded-up napkin on the table. "Maybe I should just go."

"No way. If anyone goes, it should be *her.*" Janet fumed.

"Not everyone gets it," Hog said wistfully. "Not everyone is cool. Not everyone understands free love. Free love isn't just sex, it's a whole belief system. It's the belief that love is love. That's my belief, anyway. But some people don't get it. They think love should have rules."

No one said anything.

"What I'm saying, is that some people," Hog waved another bagel in Abigail's direction, "Don't dig the interracial thing," he finished before taking a bite.

"Are you calling my girlfriend a racist?" David's face was burning now.

"Like I said, I call it like I see it." Hog took another bite, completely un-phased.

Dale looked over at Janet, and she grabbed his hand and held onto it, tight, and put it on the table for everyone to see. "Dale is with me, and if anyone here isn't OK with that, they can leave."

Hog gave a whoop.

"I'm fine with it." David said, not sounding very fine with it.

Hog raised his eyebrows.

"Abigail is fine with it," David added.

Silence thick as raspberry jelly fell over the table.

"Well, as long as everyone is fine with it," began Hog. "I'm guessing you will both be at lunch later?"

"Lunch?" asked David.

"We're all going to this place Mayumi knows in Chinatown for lunch," Hog said. "Kind of like a triple date. You could come and make it a quad."

"Mayumi?" David asked, throwing a glance Janet's way. She hadn't even had time to explain to him that Hog was her dad, let alone that she'd found her mom.

"How are things going with you two?" Janet asked. "You're dating now, right?" She looked over at David, hoping he would get it now, but David was too busy staring at Abigail.

Hog grinned. "Where do you think I was all night?" He wiggled his eyebrows.

Janet didn't know whether to laugh or cry or vomit.

"And I think she's the most beautiful woman I've ever met," he sighed. "She might even be the one. And I don't give a damn who doesn't like it that I'm hooking up with a gorgeous Japanese woman, and trust me, there are many people out there with their outdated ideas about love. But love is bigger than culture or race. You kids do your thing, I'll do my thing, and fuck anyone who has a problem with it." And he took another bite of his bagel.

"I thought you didn't believe in the whole one-woman one-man thing?" David said, giving him a look.

"The only thing better than free love is true love, man," said Hog.

THIRTY-FIVE

The Bookstore

San Francisco
1966

Lena wasn't really sure how she felt about San Francisco in 1966. The people here were strange, and not just strange like she was, not time traveling nun strange, more like completely out of it strange. Like they had lost all touch with reality.

It was a very important part of being a witch to stay grounded. When you had magic, it was easy to lose yourself. Lena had nearly lost herself on a few occasions. But she had found some ways to stay connected to the here and now - putting her bare feet in the grass whenever she could was one of them. And kissing Alex had made her feel very human too.

She blushed at the thought of it and picked up a box of new age books that needed to be shelved. Lena loved working at Bill's Books. It was a small secondhand bookstore that was cozy and quaint and although it got busy at times, it never felt as scary or out of control as the city outside did. Lena had barely gone further than the half a block between the bookstore and the apartment since they'd arrived in San Francisco.

Alex was different. Alex loved the noise and chaos of this time and place, and Lena was glad she was able to give it to her. But a strange realization had been dawning on Lena.

She missed Santolsa.

Not old Santolsa, not building the abbey with Sister Maria and Sister Catherine. But New Santolsa. Where her little bedroom was waiting for her in Peggy and Sammy's house. Where she felt safe. Where she felt loved. Not that she didn't feel safe and loved with Alex, but it always felt like she was one wrong step away from losing her. She could give Alex 1966, but Alex also wanted things Lena couldn't give to her – like parties and protests and a normal modern teenage experience.

When Lena had first arrived in 2018, she had been so relieved to be free from the coven and out on her own, she had not expected to be sad or lost or confused. It was all she'd ever wanted. Peggy had found her sitting in a heap outside the book room. Lena had recognized Peggy from her visions, she knew they were both time travelers.

When Lena had told Peggy who she was and where she'd come from, the teacher helped her up and drove her home, putting her to sleep on the couch and then making her a dinner of macaroni cheese. It wasn't the sort of food Lena usually liked, but because Peggy had been so kind, she ate it all and made no fuss. And even though she didn't even really like the creamy sludge, now she felt herself craving it.

Sammy had been just as kind, offering her anything to read from his bookshelf of paperback novels and books about cars and growing vegetables in the desert and making her cups of tea.

Lena sighed. She could stick it out until the end of summer, but eventually she knew she was going to have to go home to Santolsa. And what did that mean for her and Alex? After summer was over Alex would go back to Los Angeles and then what? Lena would not go to the city with Alex, and she couldn't ask Alex to stay in Santolsa, could she?

But just because their future was uncertain, did that mean they didn't deserve a present?

Lena kneeled down and opened the box of old books, sliding them into their right places alphabetically onto the shelves. She picked up a book on bi-locating and frowned. She didn't know this word. She turned to the back cover and read – *"Bi-location is the art of sending your energy and awareness out into time and space. Activate your powers of bi-location and you really can be in two places at once!"*

How curious, Lena thought. She had mastered the magic of time travel, but she couldn't travel to different *places*. She could only move through time and arrive in the same physical location in which she left. If she was able to travel through time *and* space, that would *really* be something…

"Lena?"

She looked up and her heart lurched. There was always something about seeing an old woman dressed in a nun's habit that gave her a fright, as if she was expecting it to be Sister Maria shouting at her and ruining her life.

But she knew this woman, and it was not Sister Maria, it was the replacement Lena had seen in her vision.

Lena frowned. "What's wrong? Why have you come here?"

"I need your help," the old woman said.

Lena shook her head. "I'm not in the coven anymore.

Please don't ask anything of me. Just go back and let me be."

"I just need one small favor," the woman pleaded. "It's something you must do for me so I can take your place."

Lena stood up, still gripping the book on bi-location. "What is it?"

And the old nun told her, and Lena understood exactly what she needed to do.

THIRTY-SIX

The Park

San Francisco
   1966

Janet stared up at the bright blue sky above her, wishing more than anything that Dale would sit a little closer to her, that he would forget about stupid Abigail. That he would forget about the rest of the world and just put his arm around her.

Instead, he just looked broodingly out at the Golden Gate Bridge peering through the trees.

She gave him a gentle nudge. "You OK?"

He nodded.

"You don't seem OK."

He shook his head. "You're right. It's just, this is what I was talking about."

"What *are* you talking about?"

"When I said I didn't think it was a good idea for us to see each other."

"You're going to let stupid Abigail stop us from…

spending time together?" Janet still didn't even know what to call this. They clearly had feelings for each other. At least, she clearly had feelings for him. But still nothing had really happened between them, and it was driving her to distraction. She couldn't look at his arms without wanting them around her. She couldn't look at his lips moving when he spoke without wanting them on her. She felt like she had to concentrate twice as hard as usual just to stay on track with the conversation.

And it was taking all she had not to just ask him straight out when he was going to kiss her!

He gave a shrug. "If it was just Abigail, I could deal with that. But it's the whole damn world, Janet."

Janet put a hand on his knee and he gently picked it up and dropped it back into her own lap.

"Do you know what they think when they see us walking down the street together?" he asked. "It's bad enough if they think we are just in each other's company, if they saw us holding hands, or…"

"Or…?" Janet leaned in a little closer.

Dale took a breath. "It's not safe for you."

"It's safer for us to… be seen together than it's ever been, and it's getting safer all the time."

"I don't want to put you through it," he said, like that was the end of it and he was about to get up and just walk out of her life.

But Janet wasn't going to let this be the end of it.

"I *want* to be a part of this," she said, taking his hand in hers. "There are protests happening all over the country and things are changing."

"People don't want change. They want to keep us all in our place."

"People *do* want change. I want change and I want to be a part of the change."

Dale shook his head. "You have no idea what you'd be getting yourself into."

But Janet did know. She'd studied the Civil Rights Movement in history class, she knew it wasn't going to be a walk in the park. But she also knew that she wanted to do something that mattered, and be with someone that mattered more to her than anyone.

"I know it's going to be hard," she started. "But I think that maybe what we have is worth fighting for."

He let out a laugh. "You're crazy."

"Crazy about you," she grinned at him.

He smiled back for a moment before his lips pressed together again and he returned to looking at the view over the bay.

Janet inched a little closer towards him, letting her knee bump up against his. "I don't care about stupid Abigail. And I don't care about the stupid rest of the world."

Dale frowned out at the perfect view. "It's not just that."

"I told you I don't care about the entire world, what else is there?"

He picked a piece of grass out of the ground and threw it. "David."

"*David?*" Janet ran her hand over the back of her short hair. "What's he got to do with anything?"

Dale looked at her, his eyes searching for answers. "I'm not an idiot, Janet."

"I never said you were."

"Just be honest with me, then. About you and him."

Janet blew out a sigh. "OK, fine. So back home we… kind of dated. You could hardly call it that really, we just… well, you probably don't want details."

"Not really."

"But he left, or I left. I don't know, we split up. We went

our separate ways."

Dale pulled out another tuft of grass.

"And then I met you and I…"

"Am I just second choice for you?" he asked, still looking out over the bay.

Janet moved around and sat in front of him, obscuring his view. "Are you kidding me?"

"I don't know how you feel about me, Janet, but since that night on the bus, I haven't been able to stop thinking about you."

Janet's heart skipped a beat.

"I was kicking myself that whole time for not leaving my number, even though I was terrified you wouldn't call. Because that's the real reason I didn't leave it. I thought maybe, if I didn't see you again, I could hold onto this idea of you, this idea of *us* that could never be real, not once the sun came up. If I didn't leave my number, I could just hold onto the apple and peach pies. I could remember watching you fall asleep in my sweater on that bus, knowing that I'd had this one perfect night with this amazing woman, and I could forever just think about what might have been. In a different place and time."

Janet tucked her hands into her lap and looked up at him. "Do you know I slept in your sweater every single night? I haven't even washed it yet."

He let out a low laugh. "You really should wash it. It wasn't even that clean when I gave it to you."

"I know. That's why I didn't wash it. I wanted to keep you with me."

He reached out and gently brushed her cheek. "I want to keep you with me, too."

"Do you know what I think?" she said into the palm of his hand which was still resting on her face.

"What?"

She reached up and put her hand over his. "I think that if we want the world to change, *we* have to change it. I want to be a part of the change. I would sit through a hundred breakfasts with stupid Abigail for you. I will fight waitresses and defend your honor every chance I get."

He brushed his thumb gently over her cheek. "You're beautiful, do you know that?"

She shook her head. "Nope."

"You're a beautiful person."

"Is that a nice way of saying I'm not that pretty?" She squished up her face.

He pushed her bangs out of her eyes. "You are so pretty I can't even stand it."

"Well, you're so handsome it hurts to look at you."

He let out a laugh. "You're so pretty I want to look at you forever."

"Forever, huh?"

"Am I getting ahead of myself? We hardly even know each other, and yet I feel like I can say forever to you and it's alright."

She shook her head and smiled. "I'm good with forever. More time to get to know each other."

Dale's heart was racing like it was about to take off as he slowly began to lean in towards her. And when his lips found hers, nothing mattered but this moment. It didn't matter who saw them or what anyone else thought. All that mattered was being here with her, being here like this.

And he thanked his lucky stars for her, for missing the morning bus and ending up in Santolsa. For being there to catch her when she fell, and for knowing she would be there to catch him when he fell too.

And he really wished they could have forever.

THIRTY-SEVEN

Chinatown

San Francisco
1966

After their afternoon in the park, and the most romantic kiss of both of their lives, Janet and Dale were in that wonderful, but very annoying for anyone around them, phase of new love. They had spent the afternoon lying in each other's arms on the grass, searching for shapes in clouds, talking about their hopes and dreams and sharing stupid stories from their past. Janet had to slightly alter some of hers of course. She would tell him about the time travel thing when the time was right. There had also been a lot more kissing.

By the time they got to the restaurant to meet everyone for dinner they were both so happy that even seeing David and Abigail outside the restaurant didn't faze them. They just held hands and smiled at anyone on the street who looked their way. They smiled extra hard at the people who looked like they didn't approve of their love.

And when Mayumi, dressed in an emerald green dress and the matching shoes, and Hog dressed in a floral shirt that had actually been ironed for once, turned up together, tangled in each other's arms, Janet's heart felt like it was going to burst. The sun was just setting, shining down rays of light over them all and everyone was in love! Even Lena and Alex were giggling like they had that first day Janet had seen them on the bus.

Mayumi had chosen the restaurant - The Dragon Inn. Janet was expecting it to be something fancy, but it was just a simple place with shiny wooden tables, delicious smells and friendly smiles.

They were given a booth by the window and all piled in together - Hog, Mayumi, Janet and Dale on one side, Lena, Alex, David and Abigail on the other.

Janet's heart raced as Dale squished her in closer to her mom. "Oh, sorry," Janet said, trying to make some space.

"Oh, it's fine," Mayumi said. "It's always a little squishy in here, but it's worth it!" She gave Janet a bright smile. It was the closest she had ever been to her mom, and it felt weirdly normal and nice.

Hog reached out and put his hand on her mom's knee. "What do you call a double double date?"

"A quartet date, or octuple for eight people." Mayumi said as she reached for a menu.

"You're so smart." Hog reached for her hand and drew it up to her lips. "Tell them how smart you are."

She blushed. "Oh, I'm not that smart."

"I bet you were the only one here who knew about octumble."

"Octuple."

"Exactly. See? You're a genius."

Mayumi shook her head and laughed, her long dark hair brushing Janet's shoulder. "What about you, Janet?"

she asked. "Do you have any plans for college? Hog says you're always carrying around a book."

"Oh, I don't know." Janet shook her head. "I actually haven't even got my high school diploma yet."

"You don't have your diploma?"

Janet shook her head. "I had a… situation and I didn't get to finish high school."

"You should finish," Mayumi said, suddenly sounding very mom-like. "Get your GED, go to college, you can be anything you want you know. Women don't have to just stay at home in the kitchen anymore."

Janet pushed back the emotion rising within her. Her mom would never even get to have the choice. She'd be gone as soon as Janet was born. Janet fought back the tears and nodded. "I definitely don't want that," she managed to say.

"What about you, Alex?" Mayumi asked. "And it's Lena, isn't it?"

Alex started talking about her plans to take a few years off and travel through Southeast Asia while Lena sat quietly beside her looking like this was the first she'd heard of it. Dale shared about signing up to the armed forces and Hog was talking about the war and how messed up it was, and David started talking about getting a job… and Janet was just running her mantra again.

Here and now, here and now, here and now.

Janet had never had a sip of alcohol in her life, Gran had always been teetotal, but when the waiter brought wine for the table and poured glasses for them all she found herself taking a sip. Just a small one. And when the wine hit her, making her feel all warm and fuzzy and relaxed, she suddenly felt OK. Like she *could* handle this dinner with her parents and her ex and his new girlfriend.

And *Dale*. The most wonderful man to ever exist.

And by the time the lychee ice-cream parfait bowls were being cleared from the table Janet had realized two things. One - even though her parents were here and now, they wouldn't be here and now forever. And two - neither would Dale.

And three - this wine was really good.

But still, it would be sixteen years until she was going to be born, so worrying about what happened to her parents was pointless, she could try to change things later. In sixteen years' time she could be there to help get her mom better medical care, she could help her dad get away from the Eights. She could be there to change things, to help them. It was all going to be OK.

Lena had said something about being able to change things. She could talk to Lena, she could work this all out.

And maybe Lena could use her time space magic to keep Dale here too.

Janet squeezed Dale's hand even tighter under the table and prayed to whoever was listening that she wouldn't lose him too.

THIRTY-EIGHT

The Dive

San Francisco
1966

"I thought you meant it was *a* dive, not *the* Dive." Mayumi let out a laugh.

"Oh, it's still a dive, don't you worry." Hog gave her one of his winning winks.

The Dive did not look like a nice place. It was in a sketchy part of town and barely even looked like a bar. It looked more like a hole in a derelict building. If it wasn't for the neon bar sign in the window no one would even know it existed.

"It's nicer on the inside," Hog promised.

Mayumi gave a shrug and followed him in.

Lena and Alex had made their excuses and had gone straight home after dinner. Janet suspected they were looking forward to having the whole apartment to themselves. They'd been giggling and carrying on all evening and Janet thought maybe tonight would be the night they took their relationship to the next level. She was happy for them. In fact, after all that wine at dinner, she felt happy for everyone right now.

She was even almost happy for David and Abigail, although the expression on Abigail's face as she stared at the dingy dark entrance to the bar suggested *she* wasn't very happy.

"Is this really how you want to spend our Saturday night together?" asked Dale looking up at the winking neon sign.

"It'll be fun," Janet said grinning up at him.

He reached out to catch her as she stumbled slightly into him. "Did you have a little too much wine at dinner?"

"I saw you have some," she said, poking him in the chest with a finger.

"I only had one glass, and I'm twice as big as you."

Janet laughed. "I'm fine. Better than fine." She grabbed his hand and started pulling him towards the bar before looking back over her shoulder towards David and Abigail. "You guys coming?" she called out.

David shook his head. "I don't think so. I guess I'll see you back at the apartment."

"Take your time going back. I think Lena and Alex want some *alone* time!" Janet called back.

David gave her a wave and Abigail looked relieved and then Janet dragged Dale into The Dive.

Hog was right, it was nicer inside, but not by much. The tables were dark wood and had benches around them instead of chairs, giving the whole place a medieval church feeling. A band of guys with long hair and clothes which looked like they'd never been washed was playing in one corner. It was a song that sounded vaguely familiar. The neon lights behind the bar gave the barman a kind of halo, and a string of multicolored party lights strung haphazardly around the rest of the big open room gave the whole thing a festive kind of feeling.

Hog and Mayumi were already at the bar ordering their drinks.

"Back at the apartment?" asked Dale over the music.

Janet shrugged. "They have nowhere to go, I said they could stay with us for a few days."

Dale didn't look pleased, but he gave a nod. "Drink?" he asked.

"More wine?" she grinned.

He gave her a look. "Do you think maybe you should switch to soda?"

Janet pouted. "You're no fun."

"I thought you didn't drink."

"Well, I didn't, and now I do. What about it?"

Dale put his hands in the air. "I'm just trying to look out for you."

"Well maybe I don't need looking out for."

"Everyone needs looking out for," he said. He ordered two sodas and handed her one.

She looked at it and frowned and then took a sip. "I don't want to fight," she said, looking up into his warm eyes.

"Me neither. But I also don't want to have to carry you home. And I don't want you to forget this night because you're too drunk to remember."

"What do you mean?"

Dale nodded towards a table, and they slid into the pew-like seats. He took her hand across the table and between their sodas. "You've probably already worked this out, but I'm not going to be in town forever."

Janet looked down at their hands. His strong fingers gently gripping hers in a way that felt like he never wanted to let go. She shook her head. "I don't want to talk about that," she said.

"Me neither. I just want to enjoy our time together. Sober."

"Of course." She twisted her fingers into his and held on tight.

"Janet!" Diamond Jones had appeared out of nowhere and had slid onto the bench next to Dale. She was clutching a pink drink that smelled like candy.

"Diamond! Hi! You remember Dale?"

Diamond gave a nod. "The handsome man who saved your life, of course I do."

Dale let out a laugh.

"Are you doing OK? You know, after..." She pointed to Janet's forehead.

Janet nodded. "It was nothing." She didn't know why she'd said that. It wasn't nothing.

"You're here with Mayumi! And Hog!" Diamond swung herself around and waved over at the bar where Mayumi and Hog were waiting for their drinks. "Are Lena and Alex here too?"

"No, they bailed after dinner. I think they wanted some... alone time."

"I see." Diamond's eyes lowered and her voice took a serious tone. "Did you tell her yet?"

"Huh?"

"Did you tell Mayumi that she's your sister?"

Mayumi and Hog had appeared at the perfect moment with their drinks.

"Your *sister?*" Mayumi asked, her perfect eyebrows furrowed together.

Diamond Jones put her hand to her mouth. "Oh, shit. You *didn't* tell her yet."

Mayumi stared down at Janet. "What is this about,

Janet?" She wondered if this is what it would've felt like, being told off as a child.

"Nothing," Janet said, just like she was a kid trying to get away with something.

Mayumi lowered her eyes.

Diamond pointed towards the dance floor and slowly walked away, leaving the mess behind her.

Mayumi folded her arms. "What is going on, Janet?"

Hog sat down and whacked his beer on the table. "You two are sisters? Cool!"

Mayumi shot him a look that Janet suspected he would see often in their relationship.

"Janet, why did you tell Diamond that I was your *sister*?"

Janet took a long slow sip of soda while she tried to work out how to get out of this. "I, uh…"

"You, uh, what?" Mayumi asked, sliding her glass of white wine in small circles on the table.

"So, I thought you were, but it turns out, I was mistaken."

Everyone just stared at her like they were expecting her to say something else, or something more.

Janet took another sip. "I've been looking for my… half-sister. We both had the same mother, but different fathers. I knew she was in San Francisco, I'm part Japanese and I knew she was Japanese so…"

"So, you thought I was your sister because I'm part Japanese?" Mayumi was pissed.

"No, there were other things too, but I…"

Mayumi frowned at her.

"That's so sad," Hog said. "That you have a sister out there somewhere that you don't even know."

Mayumi's expression softened slightly hearing Hog's perspective.

"I knew she was involved in women's rights and that she was a student, and I thought maybe... but I was wrong."

"Maybe you are her sister," suggested Hog.

Mayumi shook her head. "I don't think so."

"Maybe you could ask your parents?" suggested Dale.

"They are both gone," Mayumi said, just stating a fact.

Janet met her mom's gaze. "I'm sorry, I didn't think it mattered. At first I wanted to get to know you because I thought you might be... but now I'm just glad we became friends."

"You should have told me."

"I realized pretty quickly it wasn't you, so I didn't think there was any point."

"Looks like David got Abigail to come in after all," Hog said, looking over at the two of them as they made their way to the bar.

David was ordering them drinks, Janet had no idea how they were paying for them or why they were even in here in the first place. She did not need her ex and his racist girlfriend harshing her vibe.

"We're the Un-grateful Living!" the lead singer of the band announced into the scratchy microphone. "We're back at midnight, until then, please pour all your quarters into the music machine in the corner!"

"C'mon," Dale said, tugging gently on Janet's bright floral sleeve. "Let's choose a song."

Janet grabbed her soda and followed Dale to the jukebox.

"The Four Tops?" he suggested.

"Hmmmm, maybe?" Janet leaned in next to him and watched as he flipped through the pages of song titles. "Oh, this one! Number 83! Sonny and Cher!"

He gave her a grin brighter than the neon lights behind him. "This was playing that night…"

"At the 24-hour diner," she finished, grinning back at him. "It's our song."

Janet put her drink to the side and grabbed his hand, and he spun her around on the dance floor. They sang along to the parts of the lyrics they knew and mumbled and made up the rest.

And for three minutes time stood still. Nothing else mattered but being here with Dale, hand in hand, arm in arm, singing and laughing and holding each other tight.

And at the end, he dipped her and was just about to lean in for a kiss when someone whooped and changed the song to James Brown. Dale lifted her up and gave her a kiss on the hand instead.

"You can kiss me, you know."

"With everyone watching?"

"Sure, why not?"

Dale grabbed her and leaned in close, sending goose-bumps down her back and arms. He pressed his lips to hers and gave her a warm, slow kiss. "Like that?" he asked a few seconds later.

"Exactly like that," she grinned. "You can do it again if you like."

He grinned back at her and took her hand again, spinning her around in circles, while he pulled out the most incredible dance moves Janet had ever seen anyone do.

"You've seen a lot of James Brown music videos huh?"

Dale gave her a weird look. "This is just how we dance back home. Come on, I'll teach you some moves."

Janet wasn't very good at the moves, but she tried, and a bunch of people, including Diamond Jones came to dance with them and cheered for Janet, even though she was messing it up. No one cared, everyone was just having fun.

In fact, it was the most fun Janet had ever had in her life. The wine had worn off and she was just high on the music and the laughter and being here with people she cared about.

"Janet!" David had shoved through the crowd and was grabbing her arm. "I need to talk to you."

And suddenly she was back down on the dirty wooden floorboards of earth again.

"No, not now, we can talk later." She pushed him off her, but he just grabbed her again, the bourbon in his other hand sloshing around in the glass.

"There might not be a later."

"You're being dramatic, let me go!"

"Hey." Dale stepped in. "She asked you to let her go."

David lowered his eyes. "I know her better than you do."

"It doesn't matter how well you know her, she asked you to let her go and you need to respect that."

David took a step towards him. "I've known her since we were kids, since we were *born*, you've known her for five minutes and you think you can tell *me* how to talk to her?" He threw back the drink and smacked the glass on the closest table.

Dale took a step back, but he wasn't retreating. "It doesn't matter how long you've known someone, what matters is how you treat them."

David laughed. "You want to talk to me about respect? You stole her right out from under my nose!"

Janet gasped.

"As far as I was aware, she wasn't yours to steal, and you have a girl." Dale nodded towards the bar where Abigail was standing looking absolutely terrified.

"David, you are being crazy," Janet said, trying to get in the middle of them.

"I want *you*, Janet," David said. "It's always been you. Abigail isn't the one, *you* are."

"It's too late!" Janet shook her head. "We can't go back. I don't *want* to go back!"

Someone put the Yardbirds on the jukebox and David looked back at Dale and shoved him, hard, pushing him into the spectators behind him. Dale righted himself and turned around to apologize, but it was too late. Suddenly the two barmen were on either side of Dale, dragging him out the door.

Janet ran after them. "He didn't do anything!" she yelled. "If you are going to kick anyone out, kick David out! He started it!"

"Don't wanna see you back in here," said the barman giving Dale an extra shove.

"You assholes!" Janet yelled at them.

"Or you," the guy said, spitting on the ground next to her before reciting a bunch of racial slurs directed at them both.

Janet was in shock.

Dale sighed and brushed himself down. He looked up at her, his eyes thoughtful, sad. "Well, now you know what it's going to be like. I understand if you want to walk away right now. You *should* walk away right now."

Janet was fuming. She yelled out some more expletives at the closed door of the bar.

Dale just put his hands in his pockets.

"How can you just stand there and do nothing?" Janet asked. "Why aren't you angry? Why aren't you fighting back?"

"Are you kidding? I'm angry as hell. My anger is generations deep and I've had to work hard as hell to keep it in place."

"And you're just going to take this?"

Dale raised an eyebrow. "What exactly do you think will happen if I fight back?"

"I don't know, *something*, anything!"

"I know what happens when we fight back. We don't always make it out alive."

Janet took a deep breath. Her pulse was still racing. "You mean…?"

He stared into her eyes, and she could see a type of pain and suffering that she knew she could never under-stand. She didn't know what to say so she just threw her arms around him, holding him tight and breathing him in.

"There are times to fight and times to just leave the bar," he said.

Janet pulled back from him. "Fuck them," she said, kicking a can at the door.

Dale's eyebrows shot up.

Janet shrugged. "Fuck them all," she said. "Fuck those bar guys!" she yelled as David, Abigail, Hog and Mayumi all piled out of the bar.

"Let's just go," Dale said, taking Janet's arm and guiding her away from the bar.

"And fuck you, David!" Janet called out.

"I'm sorry, I'm sorry!" David kept repeating. Abigail reached for his hand, and he took it, pulling her along with him as he walked off down the street in the other direction.

THIRTY-NINE

Sleepover

San Francisco
   1966

If the night had made one thing clear, she now knew without a doubt where her heart was. Seeing David put it on the line like that and hearing herself say *no* without a second thought really hit it home that she was done. She was done with David. She didn't want him. Not here, not now, not ever. She wanted what she already had. She didn't want the boy next door who was caught up in a life of crime and lies and chaos, the boy who was resigned to his lot in life. She wanted Dale. She wanted the boy who was trying to find a different way, a boy who had made a different choice. As much as Janet hated the war, she could see he had tried to make something of himself. Dale had probably had the choice to go in another direction too, he had contacts with the Eights, he could have chosen that life, but he'd at least tried to choose what he thought was right.

After they'd gotten kicked out of the bar, the mood had dampened, and it was clear the night was over. Hog had taken Mayumi home, to her place or his, Janet wasn't sure, and although Dale had at first said he should get back home too, Janet had convinced him to stay the night at theirs - it was closer after all.

And they had fallen asleep on Janet's bed still in their clothes, safely tangled up in each other's limbs.

It was dark when they both woke to a loud bang. Janet's heart raced, it was like it was happening all over again and she was back there. Back on the road outside the school, the car slowing down, the gunshot, the blood…

"Hey." And suddenly strong arms were around her, rocking her gently. "You're shaking."

She let him hold her for a few moments as she gasped for breath and tried to find her way back to the present.

Dale reached over and flipped on the lamp.

"Why are you looking at me like that?" she asked, pulling the blanket around herself.

He shook his head. "It's like you're… shellshocked or something." He pushed a strand of her bangs back from her face and she shook him off.

"I'm fine."

They heard shouting from the living room. Dale jumped off the bed and opened the door an inch to see what was going on before opening it all the way and rushing out. Janet threw a blanket over her shoulders and followed slowly behind him.

Abigail was shouting in German and David was shaking his head at her. "I have no idea what you are saying!" he was shouting back.

"What's going on?" Janet asked, pulling the blanket tighter around herself.

David glared at her.

Abigail screamed.

Alex and Lena appeared from their room, Lena in a long white nightdress and Alex in nothing but a striped t-shirt and her underwear.

"For God's sake!" Alex rubbed her eyes. "It's three in the morning!"

Abigail continued to shout in German, her arms flailing towards David. She made vroom vroom noises and mimed getting on a bike and then pointed to her own arm, before grabbing David's arm, pulling up his shirt and pointing to his tattoo.

Janet took a deep breath. "You found the Eights."

David nodded.

Abigail kept speaking in German until Lena grabbed her wrist and pulled her out of the apartment. Alex shook her head and retreated back into her room, leaving Janet standing in the hallway between Dale and David.

Dale put his arm on her shoulder. "I'll give you a minute," he said. "I'll be right here if you need me."

She couldn't have been more grateful. It wasn't that she didn't want him here, she wanted him here more than anything. But it was the first time she had been alone with David since he'd arrived and even though she knew he wasn't her future, there were still things that needed to be said about the past.

Dale's hand slid down her arm and into her hand, his fingers locking into hers. He lifted her hand to his lips and gave it a gentle kiss before letting go and stepping back, giving her time, giving her space, giving her everything she could have ever asked of him and knowing he was right there. Knowing that after this, she would be able to crawl right back into his arms.

"Thank you," she whispered, watching him step back into her room, and there was something about that, about watching him walk into *her* room, that made her heart so at peace, so happy.

She turned to face David who was not making anyone's heart very happy right now. She gestured to the living room and took the egg chair, curling up with the blanket covering her. "So," she began.

"What, Janet? What do you want from me?" he asked, sitting on the edge of the couch and leaning forwards.

Janet was taken aback. "I don't want anything from you."

"Well, that's obvious."

"What are you talking about?"

"You and… *Dale*."

"What about it?"

"When I found you at the Pegasus, all you could do was bitch about me running off with Abigail and not waiting for you, but you did exactly the same thing."

"It was *not* the same."

"Yes, it was."

Janet felt her blood about to boil over. "You and me were never even *together*," she said. "You never even committed to me in any way. I was going to…" she lowered her voice. "I was going to *sleep* with you, and you weren't even going to call me your girlfriend. I'd liked you for so long David. And I was going to completely give myself to you and then you turned up with some pretty blond girl you'd know for five minutes and *had* fully committed to. How do you think I would feel about that?"

David just sat and stared into his hands.

"You *never* really wanted me," Janet finished.

"That's not true," he said looking up at her, his eyes pleading. "I do *want* you, Janet."

"Why?" She shook her head.

"Because I realized something. I realized that it was always supposed to be you and me Janet. We got this amazing clean slate, this fresh start. We can do this together. We can start again here and now. We can do things differently."

Janet shook her head. "No. It's not you and me David. It's you and Abigail, and you can't put her through all the same Eight bullshit you put me through."

"That's hardly fair," he said. "You took that job too."

Janet felt a chill go through her and she tried to push it back down. "I had no choice."

"*I* have no choice."

"There has to be something. You can both stay here as long as you need to, OK? Just don't go down this road again."

"I just don't think there's any other way for me, not even here."

"I can ask Hog if he can give you a job, or you could take my job, I can try to find something else."

"Janet." He was sitting on his knees in front of her now. He reached up and took her hand. "There's nothing else for me, not without you." His eyes were glistening with tears she knew he would never let fall. "You're right. I need to get out of your life, once and for all. I'm only ever going to hold you back. I just thought if there was a chance… I had to try, you know. Janet, Is there a chance? Is there a chance for us, for you and me?"

He sat there for a while, holding her hand, just staring at her, waiting for her to respond.

"I keep thinking about that night," she said softly. "I keep seeing it happening."

"Me too."

"I can't forget. I'm a… murderer," she whispered.

"Janet, no." He squeezed her hand. "Look at me." She did. "What happened was nothing to do with you. It was *my* fault. *I* pulled the trigger."

"*I* kicked you the gun."

"*I* pulled the trigger."

"You had to."

"*You* had to. If you hadn't kicked me the gun, do you know where we'd be right now?"

She shrugged. "Dead?"

He nodded. "Exactly. It was self-defense, and it was me who pulled the trigger. Just remember that when you have the flashbacks, OK? You didn't pull the trigger, it was self-defense. Tell yourself that. Tell yourself it was self-defense. It was David who pulled the trigger. He had to. We had to."

She nodded and he nodded, a mutual understanding, a way for both of them to live with it.

"You're not coming with me, are you Janet?"

She shook her head.

"I… I'm sorry Janet. For all of it. For getting you kicked out of that bar, for Abigail. For not seeing you all that time. But most of all, I'm sorry I can't be the man you deserve."

Janet felt the familiar sting at the back of her eyes and gave a nod.

Abigail and Lena burst through the door, Abigail was still speaking fast, and Lena was holding a book and trying to get her to slow down. Abigail stormed over to David with a fiery look in her eyes.

He let go of Janet's hands and stood up. "We're just friends," he said.

"Show her in the book." Lena handed David a book. "It's an English/German dictionary."

She handed the book to David, and he began to flip through. "Uh, Freun… din," he said finally, pointing the word.

Abigail lowered her eyes. "I swear." He put his hand up like he was going to give evidence in court.

Lena gave a nod. "I think my work is done here, goodnight everyone."

Janet stood up to leave also, and when she looked back, to wave or say goodnight, David was already huddled up on the couch beside Abigail, pointing to another word in the dictionary, a big smile spreading across her face as he leaned into her and smiled.

And the next morning, Abigail and David were gone.

FORTY

Scrabble

San Francisco
1966

Janet was sitting in the egg chair drinking an iced tea through a paper straw. She'd just finished the last slice of an olive and cheese pizza Alex had brought home from work and it was her turn to make her move. "I can't make anything with these letters," she moaned, as she put down the word *dog*.

"Dog? Is that the best you can do?" Alex laughed before pondering her own letters, sliding them around in the wooden holder. "And you got sauce on the G!" she laughed.

Janet picked up the G and licked it. "Better?"

"Ewwwww!" Alex hid her face in her hands and Janet let out a laugh.

Lena ignored the whole thing, concentrating on her own letters before putting down the word *qi* on a triple letter score and Alex groaned. "Lena!"

"It's all I could do," Lena shrugged. "I can help you if you let me look at your letters."

"Nooooo!" Alex pulled away from her on the couch and her letters went flying around the room.

Janet laughed and nearly spit her iced tea out.

Alex sighed and began crawling around on the shag rug looking for all the pieces.

"What is Qi?" Janet asked.

"Energy, life force," Lena replied.

"You've really been reading a lot of those weird new age books from the bookstore, huh?" Alex picked up a couple of letters and gave Lena a look.

Lena shrugged. "I like reading about this… stuff. There was only so much the sisters taught me. Pure talent is wonderful, but with all this knowledge in all these books, almost anyone could be a witch if they just worked on it. I mean, it would still take someone very powerful to open up a time portal, but you could still do quite a lot with all this information."

Janet scoffed. "Really?"

Lena nodded and raised an eyebrow. "Even you, Janet."

Janet rolled her eyes. "Oh sure, the three of us could be the witches of Haight-Ashbury!"

"Now that has a ring to it!" Alex laughed.

Lena shook her head and smiled.

"Found them all!" Alex cheered as she put her letters back on the holder. "Oh, no wait, I only have six." She went back to searching the rug.

"Where do you think David and Abigail went?" Lena asked as she took two more letters from the pile.

It had been a week since David and Abigail had disappeared and it was the first time anyone had mentioned it.

Janet said nothing. She'd been thinking about David,

of course she had, but she had been trying not to. He was not her problem anymore.

Alex was still scrounging around on the floor. "What happened at the bar that night… it was… intense."

"No kidding," said Janet.

"Are you OK?" Alex asked.

Janet shook her head. "I think it's time for us both to move on. So, him leaving, it's for the best. For all of us"

"You'll see him again," Lena said.

"Lena," Alex warned. "Stop doing that."

"Doing what?"

"Being creepy like that. Telling people what will happen."

"I don't really know what will happen, I just see visions, threads."

"But they're not always accurate," Alex said.

Lena gave a shrug. "No, not always. I can be wrong, but only if the timeline shifts."

"What does it take to shift a timeline?" Janet asked.

"It's difficult, extremely complex magic. I only know of one that has shifted."

"But you could shift one, right, Lena?" asked Alex.

Lena made a face. "It takes great will. The person would have to want it very badly. But even then… Well, even then, it is no guarantee. Some destinies are mailable, most are like stones."

Janet slurped the bottom of her ice-tea.

"I found my z!" Alex held it up from the carpet like she'd struck gold.

"Good, now you can take your turn," Lena said.

But just as Alex was about to make her move, there was a knock at the door.

The three girls looked at each other, no one wanting to

move, until eventually Janet sighed and pulled herself out of the egg chair and made her way to the front door.

And as soon as she opened the door, she knew.

She knew that her whole wonderful world she had found here was about to come crashing down around her.

"Janet." Dale's eyes were dark. "I've been called up."

FORTY-ONE

The Last Night

San Francisco
    1966

"When?" Janet didn't want the answer, she didn't want this to be happening at all. But maybe if she knew when, maybe they had time to stop it, to do something…

"Tomorrow morning."

"*Tomorrow?*" Janet felt her knees give way and had to hold onto the door frame. Dale reached out and took her in his arms. She beat her fists at his chest. "No, no, I won't let you go," she said, tears flooding out without her ever giving them permission.

He didn't say anything, he just stood in the doorway, holding her tighter until she had stopped sobbing.

"Let's sit down," he said.

She nodded, taking his hand, and holding it like she would never let it go. She somehow made it into the room which a few minutes ago was full of laughter over Alex's terrible Scrabble playing which all seemed so stupid and pointless now.

"What is it?" Alex asked, moving to the egg chair to give them space to sit together on the couch. Lena sat on the floor by Alex.

"I leave tomorrow," Dale said.

Janet shoved Lena's pile of books on bi-locating and astral travel to the floor and curled up into him on the couch. She didn't care how much she cried, she didn't care how sad she looked, or how much of a public display of affection this was. She needed every single second to be holding him.

Alex gasped, but Lena didn't look surprised.

"Did you know about this, Lena?" Janet asked, fury rising within her.

Lena wiggled her head as if to say no, but not fully commit to it.

"You *knew*?" shouted Janet.

"Janet," Alex started. "Dale is in the Army and in case you didn't notice, we are in the middle of a war." Her tone softened. "You knew this was going to happen eventually, you both did."

Janet shook her head. She had known, but she had also been totally in denial. It was the only way to cope. "There has to be something we can do."

Lena gave Janet a shrug. "You'll see each other again."

"Not this again," Janet tucked her head into Dale's shoulder.

"What's this about?" Dale asked, giving Lena a strange look.

"Lena has… a gift," Alex explained.

Dale gave a slow nod. "I see."

"Except it's not always accurate," Alex added.

"Do something!" Janet yelled between her sobs. "Lena, *do* something!"

Dale pulled her in tighter and tried to shush her and calm her down, but it was no use.

"I'm not losing you too!" she cried. "Lena, help us!"

"What do you expect me to do?" Lena asked, showing no emotion at all.

"Do *something, anything*. Cast a circle, open a portal, take us all back! We don't belong here, we can take Dale with us."

"Dale does belong here, and so do you."

"Me and Dale belong *together*, it doesn't matter where… or *when!*"

"I can't do that," Lena said firmly.

"Oh, so you could do it to impress Alex and take her on a summer vacation to 1966 but not to save someone *I* love?"

"That's not…" Lena shook her head. "You need to stop talking about this while he's here." Lena gestured to Dale.

"I'm done with secrets," Janet said.

"It's not just *your* secret," Alex said quietly.

"I think someone needs to tell me what's going on," said Dale.

Suddenly Janet had the terrible thought that if she kept going, if she told him everything, he might leave her anyway. It might be too much, he might think she was crazy. He might leave tomorrow and never want to talk to her again.

"I'm a murderer," she said, hoping she could swap one truth for another. It was only after she said it out-loud that she thought maybe time traveler was better than murderer after all.

Dale shook his head. "What do you mean?"

"I killed someone." And saying it out loud suddenly made it real, and even though David had told her it wasn't her fault, that he pulled the trigger, that it was self-defense, she still felt like her words were true. She began to shake.

Dale put his arm around her. "What happened?"

"It was…" she began.

"It was self-defense," said Alex. "And it was David who pulled the trigger."

"How do you know…?" Janet asked.

"I heard you talking… the other night."

"You're on the run," said Dale.

Janet nodded. It was the simplest way to explain everything.

"And you're not from… here."

Janet shook her head.

"Tell me everything."

And she did, well, she told him a version of everything that didn't include time travel. She told him about the job with the Eights. The car, the gun, the shooting, the running and the midnight bus.

"I'm glad you told me," he said perched on the corner of her bed.

"I'm glad you don't hate me." She sat down next to him.

"Janet," he said, taking her hand. "I never want any secrets between us, you can tell me anything, nothing can change how I feel about you. And from what you told me, it wasn't your fault. You did what you needed to do. I'm about to go to war and there are going to be things I'm going to have to do. It's how we survive. It's how you survived. You need to let it go. Promise me you'll let this go. Don't let it consume you."

She nodded.

"I'll write you, all the time."

She squeezed his hand. "I'm scared I'm going to lose you."

"I want to tell you that I'll come home safe, and everything will be fine… but the truth is I'm scared too."

"So don't go. Run away. Hide."

He shook his head. "I'm not going to pretend I haven't thought about it, but I can't. I have to do this."

"You don't have to."

"I need to. I *want* to."

"You want to fight a war for this country? For a country that treats you like it does? For those guys in the bar?"

He shook his head. "It's not like that."

"So what is it like? Help me to understand."

"It's not them I'll be fighting for. It's for you."

Janet felt another tear fall down her cheek. "I want you to fight for me *here*."

"It's just something I know I have to do. I can't explain it. I just know it's my destiny."

"What about being here with me? Isn't that something you have to do? Isn't that your destiny?"

"Being with you has been one of the most amazing things that's ever happened in my life." He ran his thumb over the back of her hand. "I have never met anyone who made me feel like you do."

She wiped another tear from her face. She didn't want their last night together to be full of her tears and anger.

"I'm not going to ask you to wait for me," he said.

She let out a sad laugh. "I *want* to wait for you."

He shook his head. "I don't know when I'll be back… I don't know *if*…"

She grabbed his hands and cut him off. "You *will* come back, and when you do, I'll be right here waiting."

"I won't expect you to."

"Are you just saying this so you can have a free pass over there? So you can find some woman over there and..."

"Don't be crazy. You are the only woman I want," he said, brushing her bangs back from her eyes. "But I don't want you to wait. I'd like you to write, but don't wait. If someone else comes along, or if David comes back..."

"Now *you're* the one being crazy."

"Janet, this has been the best time of my life."

"Mine too."

"And maybe if you don't meet anyone else, and you're still single when I come back, maybe you and me, maybe we could really do this."

"Do this?"

"I'd want to make an honest woman out of you." His fingers tangled in the hair at her neck.

"Now who's making promises they can't keep?"

"Would you marry me?" he asked, twirling his fingers around her hair. "If I came back."

"*When* you come back, yes, I'll marry you."

He gave her a sad grin.

"Yes!" she said again, kissing his face all over. "I'll marry you!"

He laughed and playfully brushed her away. "Would you take my name?" he asked, leaning into her.

"I'd have to seriously think about that," she started. "I mean, you know I'm a raging feminist, right? Card carrying member of WOM?"

Smiling he leaned into her. "Maybe I'll take yours, *really* give them something to talk about."

She laughed. "You'd do that?"

"I'd do anything for you."

"I'd do anything for you too," she said.

He shook his head and leaned in close. "If I come back… if you'll have me, I'll be yours forever."

"I'm already yours forever."

He leaned in and kissed her softly, slowly, like they had all the time in the world.

And although he had wanted to wait until he was married, he decided that maybe it was null and void if you were being sent off to war, and so, under the light of the half-moon streaming in through Janet's window, they made their last night their first.

FORTY-TWO

The Pegasus II

San Francisco
   1966

Hog was sitting on a turned over milk crate in the back alley behind the Pegasus. He was smoking a cigarette, deep in thought.

Janet took a seat on the stoop and dropped a beaten-up copy of *The Great Gatsby* down next to her.

"What's up, kiddo?" Hog asked. Even though he was only a few years older than her, he always managed to sound fatherly.

Janet gave a shrug.

"Most of the boys come back, not always in one piece, but still." He took a drag. "It's the psychological shit that gets them the most." He pointed to his head with his thumb, nearly catching his hair on the cigarette.

"Everyone leaves," she said.

"Not everyone."

"Everyone I've ever loved has left."

Hog put his cigarette out on the ground and reached for the crumpled box in the back pocket of his jeans. He held out the box to her, but she shook her head. He lit a cigarette and handed it to her anyway. "Do me a favor and just hold it," he said, lighting another one for himself. "It's pathetic smoking alone. Not as bad as drinking alone, but still."

Janet held it, watching the tip burn, and then, without really thinking, she lifted it to her lips and inhaled. And then she started coughing up a lung.

Hog laughed. "You'll get used to it. Just go slow. Take a smaller inhale."

She took a small puff. It was horrible, but not so horrible.

"Lena and Alex haven't left," Hog said.

"Not yet, but they will. They're both going back to school in a few weeks."

"It's not like they're leaving *you*."

"They're going back to Santolsa."

Hog frowned and took another drag. "I'm from Santolsa."

Janet tried to look surprised.

"I tried to block it out. I have bad memories of that place."

"Me too," she said, taking another small puff of the cigarette in her hand.

"But it's not so bad really. Maybe you could go back with them."

Janet shook her head. "I want to be here when Dale comes back."

Hog gave her a look. "What else are you going to do?"

"Work here," she shrugged.

"You can keep working here on one condition."

"Yeah, what's that?"

"That you only work here part-time, and you go back to school, get your high school diploma and then you go to college."

Janet let out a laugh. "I can't afford to go to college."

"Sure you can. You're smart. Mayumi can tutor you. You'll get a scholarship or something, or you'll go to one of those colleges for dropouts that don't cost much."

"A college for dropouts?"

He nodded. "I know some guys who did that, it wasn't so bad. You could get a teaching certificate at least."

"Teaching?" she laughed.

"You'd be a great teacher. You're always reading books, teachers are always doing that. And you're nice and kids need nice teachers. All my teachers were assholes. I might have turned out totally different if I'd had a teacher like you."

Janet felt her heart leap.

"All those teen boys would like you too," he winked.

She rolled her eyes at him. "Shut up."

"You're a beautiful woman, Janet." And it didn't even sound creepy, it just sounded honest.

She felt her heart swell and looked down at the cigarette burning in her fingers. She tapped it and the ash fell. "Lena said we'd see each other again, me and Dale. You know she has that weird psychic thing she does."

Hog nodded. "There are more things in heaven and Earth, Horatio."

"You know Shakespeare?"

He gave her that winning smile. "In another life I might have gone to college too."

"Why not this one?" Her heart skipped a beat as she thought that this could be the moment things could change. Maybe this was one of those timeline shifts Lena had talked about. Maybe Hog would do something with his life, take a different path. Maybe this was where it changed. This conversation, here and now. Smoking a cigarette with her dad, changing the whole universe.

"You know what I want to do with this one?" he ran his free hand over his messy curls. "I want to travel, see the world. Meet people, have experiences. That's why I like working here, I get to meet people, be a part of everyone's story. That's what I really want. To be a part of a story, you know?"

"You're part of my story," she said.

They both inhaled together, and it was beautiful. Being here with her dad, talking like this. It was everything she had never realized she wanted from her dad.

"College could be an experience," she added.

He shook his head. "It's not my thing. Too many rules, and I heard you have to show up on time. Here I can do what I want, and that suits me. When Mayumi finishes school we're going to go on a big trip. All around the states, then Mexico, Peru…"

"But what if," Janet started. "What if you went traveling and something happened to you?"

"Like what?"

"I don't know, like you got lost or hurt or kidnapped or… you got in some kind of trouble?"

"Those things can happen anywhere, even at college."

Janet sighed. So maybe this wasn't it. This wasn't when he changed his mind. But Mayumi had two more years of school, so she still had plenty of time to try to change their futures. Janet wasn't going to stop trying. No matter how many cigarettes she had to have with her dad, she would help him change his path.

"So, Lena had a vision or something? About Dale coming back? Tell me about it."

Janet nodded. "That's the only thing keeping me going right now…"

And it continued to be the only thing that kept her going, long after Dale's letters stopped. Long after the war ended. Through every other relationship Janet tried and failed at over the years.

And Janet eventually lost count of how many times she wished Lena had never said it, because while she still believed there was a chance he would come back to her, nothing and no one else could ever fill the hole in her heart that his leaving had left.

FORTY-THREE

The End of Summer

San Francisco
   1966

Alex and Lena stood in the hallway, a pile of bags sitting between them.

Janet was standing with her arms folded against Dale's army sweater that she had hardly taken off for weeks.

"So," Alex began. "I guess this is goodbye."

Janet shrugged. "I guess so."

"It's been fun." Alex shook her head. "It's been more than fun. It's been a total trip."

Janet laughed. "It really has, hasn't it?"

"So, what's next?" Alex asked her, moving a strand of Janet's hair into place.

"Well, Diamond Jones is moving in this weekend and I'm pretty sure she's going to be tidier than both of you."

Alex gave her a playful nudge. "After that?"

Janet took a deep breath. "I guess I'm going to just try to keep busy while I wait for Dale. I'm going to try to get my high school diploma, and then maybe community college. Hog put this weird idea into my head about teaching."

Lena gave her a smile. "You'd make an excellent teacher, Janet."

"You really think so?"

Lena nodded. "I *know* so."

Alex rolled her eyes.

"And then," Janet carried on. "I don't know, keep protesting the war until it ends, burn my bra, go to Woodstock, watch the moon landing?"

Alex pouted. "I'm so jealous!"

"Come back and visit anytime."

Alex looked at Lena. "Could we?"

Lena frowned. "I'm not some time machine you can just use to go to rock concerts."

"Woodstock is not just a rock concert! It's one of the greatest historical events of all time!"

Lena just sighed.

"You should get going if you're going to make the midnight bus back to Santolsa," Janet said. They still had plenty of time, but this goodbye was hurting her heart and her head, and she wanted to rip it off like a Band-Aid, not just pull one hair out at a time.

Alex threw her arms around Janet, squeezing her tight. "Good luck with everything," she said, muffled into her neck. "Thank you for the best summer of my life. I will never forget this."

"You too." Janet forced the tears back.

"You'll see us again," Lena said giving her a warm smile.

Alex gave Lena a playful shove. "Stop *doing* that."

"I know it." Lena moved in and gave Janet a hug so warm and fuzzy that it made another tear fall, and then

Lena whispered into her ear, oh so quietly so Alex couldn't hear. "The Eights have failed, we must protect the portal ourselves."

Janet wanted to ask her what the hell she meant, but the words wouldn't come. She was choking up.

And then Lena and Alex picked up their bags and left.

And Janet sat in her bedroom and finally let all her tears fall.

Later that night, when she was all alone and found herself thinking about Dale and David and Gran and her mom and her dad she felt as if she was going to break into a thousand tiny pieces. Alex and Lena had helped her keep it together over the summer, but now she felt herself slipping.

Janet remembered that night at dinner when she'd had those two glasses of wine and how it had really taken the edge off. She'd felt *good*. Life had felt just a little bit easier when she'd been tipsy and that was was how she wanted to feel right now. How she *needed* to feel. Like things were just a little bit easier.

And so she walked downstairs and into Mario's back room and took a bottle of wine.

Interlude VII

Middle of nowhere
    1966

Alex had been in that half-awake half-asleep state of nothingness for hours. Lena had fallen asleep straight away, the bus bumping over the road seemed to lull her to sleep, while it had the opposite effect for Alex.

She would never forget the summer of 1966, but Alex missed home. She missed her parents, she even missed her brother, Nick. She missed the Internet and streaming TV and music. Being in 1966 was like living in slow motion, it had been great for a while, but now she just wanted to go fast again.

Her heart ached as she thought about what Lena wanted. For Lena, even 1966 had been too fast.

Alex really loved Lena, but she wondered, not for the first time, as she breathed in the powdery scent of her golden hair, if love was going to be enough for them. They were from two different worlds, and they were both going in totally different directions.

Lena stirred and Alex reached out to run a hand down her hair.

"Where are we?" Lena asked groggily.

"In the middle of nowhere," said Alex. "Somewhere between where we were and where we're going?"

"Where are we going?" Lena asked, sitting up and looking at Alex with bleary eyes. Her hair was sticking up on one side and it made Alex's heart ache. She really was so beautiful.

"I don't know."

"Well, I hope we're going together." Lena reached out and took Alex's hand in hers.

"Lena?" Alex began.

"Mmmm?"

"What you said to Janet, about her and Dale, was it true?"

Lena sighed. "Sometimes it's better to give people hope than to tell them what is true."

PART THREE

FORTY-FOUR

The Escort

Santolsa
    1983

Janet parked her car in her usual space in the staff parking lot of St. Christopher's High School. It was another beautiful sunny day in Santolsa, but inside she felt a storm brewing.

It had been two weeks since her birthday. It had never really felt right to celebrate, since her birthday was also the anniversary of her mom's death. Gran had always understood and never made a fuss. Instead of doing anything on her actual birthday Gran would buy a cake on a random day the month of her birthday and say it was because it had been discounted at the store. They both knew it was a birthday cake, but they never called it that. They would slice it up and eat it in front of the TV and Janet would get to choose what show to watch.

But this year wasn't just any other birthday, it was her *actual* day of birth. Her driver's license said she'd just turned 33, but her real birth certificate said she was just two weeks old.

She reached into her purse and pulled out the bronze chip they had given her at her last AA meeting. She'd stopped going after that meeting. It had been ten years since her last drink, and she was good. She was done. She hadn't even felt like a drink in at least three years.

But today she needed something to hold onto.

After that summer in San Francisco everything changed. Everyone started leaving. First Dale, then Alex and Lena. A year later Mayumi, her mother, had decided to do her final year of college in Paris. Of course Hog, her father, had gone with her. When her parents returned to San Francisco, they got an apartment nearby, but they only stayed a few months before they were off again. They both had the travel bug and after Paris they never stayed in one place long enough for Janet to even know where they were. She tried to follow them once and ended up spending a year teaching at a school in Mexico, but before she knew it, they were off again, and she had signed a contract that kept her where she was until the end of the academic year.

The only person Janet had stayed in touch with all those years was Diamond Jones. In fact, it was Diamond who took Janet to her first AA meeting. After that first meeting, she bought Janet a second-hand sewing machine. Janet had found sewing to be so therapeutic. When she was making a dress, she was completely consumed by the fabric, the color, the shape. It became her therapy. Diamond had eventually moved to New York City to take a job as a human rights lawyer and although they still wrote and called, it was never the same.

Hog had sent Janet a postcard from Nebraska about nine months ago. He said they'd gotten married, and that Mayumi was pregnant, but there was no return address.

Janet had taken off from work and spent a month in Nebraska trying to find them, but they could have been anywhere by then.

And so, another birthday had come and gone. Just like every birthday had. No gifts, no cards, just sadness and sitting alone in a motel room in Broken Bow, Nebraska wondering what went wrong and feeling more alone than ever.

This time her mom really was gone.

Janet had spent years trying to chase her parents, trying to change things, trying to do something, *anything*, to save her mom, and to help her dad change his path. She'd always remembered what Lena had said about changing timelines if you wanted it enough. Surely Janet wanting her mom to live was big enough to change a timeline.

But perhaps some things were set in stone after all.

Or maybe she missed her chance, messed it up and could have kept her alive if she'd tried harder, done more, done something different.

It felt like she was losing her mom all over again and she really didn't think that she was strong enough to lose one more person after all she'd lost so far.

Janet didn't know when Hog was going to bring the baby, *her* as a baby, to Gran. She'd seen Gran around town, and they'd exchanged pleasantries a few times. Janet had wondered if she should try to befriend Gran, try to be there when Hog brought the baby. But what would she say? What would she do? Whatever was going on with Hog was happening *now*. He was only going to leave her there once it was too late to change things anyway.

Maybe things just needed to play themselves out.

Janet was tired.

She was tired of trying to change everyone else's destiny.

She slipped the chip in the pocket of her pleather skirt and flipped open the glove box, grabbing a bottle of pain killers. She took two dry and threw the bottle in her purse. She was going to need them today.

Resting her head on the headrest she closed her eyes and said a prayer to a God she still didn't even know if she believed in. She didn't even know what she was even praying for, she just didn't want to feel so sad anymore. She didn't want to feel so alone. She didn't want to be caught in an endless loop of everyone she loved leaving.

She put her hands on the steering wheel and took a deep breath.

Here and now.

Apple and peach.

Apple and peace.

A small smile spread over her lips as she took herself back to that night in the 24-hour diner and on the midnight bus from Santolsa to San Francisco.

And in that moment of remembering she knew, even if that was all she got, she would be grateful for it. It was too precious. All her happy memories were too precious to let the unhappy ones drown them out.

So she took another deep breath, and held Dale in her heart, as she always did. His memory would get her through this, it always did.

And then she went in to face the day.

Vietnam

1970

The first explosion hit, and Dale flew backwards. It wasn't the first time he'd come this close to losing a limb, or worse.

The war had been nothing at all like he'd expected. He'd thought he was going to do his duty, to serve his country and do *something*, be a part of something bigger than himself.

He wasn't prepared for just how much it would change him.

That boy who had been wrapped up and tangled in Janet's arms that last night in San Francisco was just a ghost to him now.

Two years ago, after he'd been burned in the explosion and spent six months in the infirmary, he'd been given his papers. He'd been allowed to go home. But how could he go home after seeing what he had seen? How could he go home after doing what he had done? How could he ever face Janet again, looking how he did now? When he looked in the mirror, he still didn't recognize the person who looked back at him. His scars had never healed, and they never would.

How could he go back to Janet's apartment now, like nothing had happened, like no time had passed? How could he go and pick up where he left off?

How could he ever face her with *this* face?

So, he'd chosen to stay. He was a soldier now. War had aged him, hardened him, and changed him. His scars didn't affect his ability to see or run or fight, and he was grateful for that, because that was all he was good for now.

So here he was, in the middle of the jungle, knowing a second strike was about to hit, and trying to guess which direction it would come from.

He stilled, waiting for it to come, and for a moment he thought about just letting it take him. Letting it finish him. He could end this pain right now.

And then there was a sudden calm that washed over him. Almost like he knew this was it. This was how he would die. With honor, with courage, doing something important. And he was at peace with it.

So, he just stood there and closed his eyes, and in that moment, knowing he was about to die, he saw Janet.

They were in the 24-hour diner, sharing apple and peach pies. Then they were back on the midnight bus, and he was watching her fall asleep, the headlights from the trucks gently passing across her perfect face. And then they were in her apartment, that last night. His lips were on hers and she was pulling him towards her...

And in that moment, he was just grateful. It wasn't much time they'd had together, but it was beautiful, and he was so thankful for every moment they had shared. And whatever happened next would be alright, because he had known what it was to be in love. He had felt a love so pure and true and nothing could take that from him, not even death.

The second explosion should have taken him. He had been standing right where it hit, but now he was on the ground a few feet away and someone was dragging him behind a tree.

"You're heavy!" a girl's voice said.

He startled. There, right in front of him was Lena. He rubbed his eyes, but when he opened them again, she was still there. Why was it Lena he was seeing now? Why was Lena the last thing he would think of as he lay dying?

"You're not dying," she said, leaning over and gently putting a hand on his arm. "I just saved your life."

"But… why?"

She shrugged. "I owed someone a favor."

And then she just disappeared like she had never been there at all.

FORTY-FIVE

Margaret

———————

Santolsa
    1983

Janet was teaching third period English when there was a knock on the door and a girl with chestnut brown hair poked her head into the classroom. She looked absolutely terrified.

"Can I help you?" Janet asked.

The girl stared out at the class with her eyes wide. "I'm just in the wrong room," she squeaked.

"What class are you looking for?"

"Uh," the girl began, stumbling around for her words. "English. Mrs. Willis."

Janet's heart nearly lurched out of her chest. For a moment she had thought the girl said Mrs. *Williams*. Dale's name. She thought of that night when he asked her to marry him… if he came back…

"This is English, but there is no Mrs. Willis on the faculty," Janet said, pushing the memory away, like she had become so good at doing over the years. Push it away, put it in a box, close the lid.

"Huh? Yes there is, is this some kind of joke?" The girl was clearly embarrassed at being so lost and was getting defensive.

But Janet had sworn that when she became a teacher, she would always treat her students with respect. She wouldn't be like all the teachers who had made her high school life a living hell. "I wasn't expecting a new student today, but come on in," she said, welcoming the girl and trying to make her feel at ease. She could sort this all out at the office later. "I'm Miss Bates.

"Miss… Bates?" the girl whispered.

And before Janet had a chance to say *yes*, the girl had fainted and fallen on the floor.

"She's dead!" screamed Leigh, a girl who had so much potential but was more interested in maintaining her social standing than doing any homework.

"She's not dead," said Rochelle, a girl who really didn't have any academic talent, but was excellent at manipulation, a skill that would probably take her far. "Take a chill pill, Leigh, she's just fainted."

"Someone help her!" Lacey, a girl who had a heart of gold but put up a good front, called out frantically.

"Horace!" Janet shouted over the noise. "Go get the nurse." Horace was fast. Horace was reliable. A good choice for this. Horace pushed up his thick aviator glasses, jumped over the girl on the floor and was gone in a flash.

Janet pushed through the crowd, pushing Leigh and Rochelle back and kneeled on the floor. "Can you hear me?" There was no response. "You're OK, we're getting help. What's your name?"

Nothing.

"Can you tell me your name?"

The girl opened her eyes and began laughing. "Look at you all!" she giggled.

Janet frowned. This girl was clearly having some problems in life. "What's your name?" she asked again calmly.

"Look at you Mrs. Willis!" she pointed a finger in Janet's face and smiled. There was something about the gesture that unnerved Janet. It was like this girl *knew* her. She had the name wrong, but there was a recognition in her eyes, like this was not the first time they had met.

Lacey started blabbering on about concussions and something she had seen on *Dallas* last week. Janet asked if anyone saw the girl hit her head. A concussion could explain that weird look on her face, couldn't it?

The girl on the floor was still giggling at everyone and pointing at June-Belle's eyeshadow and then she locked eyes with one of Janet's favorite students. He was known as being a bit of a bad-boy, but he was smart. One of the smartest in the class. Janet was hoping he would go far, if he just got the encouragement he needed.

"Sammy Ruthven," the girl said, before her eyes closed again.

Janet had never seen this girl before. The girl didn't know where she was, or who Janet was, she'd made up the name of a teacher on the faculty, but she somehow knew Sammy Ruthven?

Janet didn't know what in the hell was happening, but she thought she should probably try to find out.

And so she took the girl to the nurse.

FORTY-SIX

The Box of Memories

Santolsa
1984

Janet reached into the drawer of her nightstand and pulled out the small wooden box. It had been a long time since she'd spoken about Dale with anyone, even though he had never been far from her thoughts. If she was honest with herself, it had been the main reason things had never worked out with anyone she'd tried to date since. She knew no one could ever make her feel like she did when she was sixteen and in the throes of young love. Maybe it was time to accept that relationships just weren't like that when you got older. They weren't full of magic, they were just... practical. She decided to call Ray later and see what he was doing. Maybe she could still make it work with him. Maybe it was time to settle down, maybe it was time to *settle*, period.

She took the box downstairs to where Peggy was sitting on the couch and looking up at her curiously. Janet opened the box, and there he was. Dale Williams, dressed in his U.S. Army uniform, looking as handsome as ever, frozen in time as an eighteen-year-old with a bright smile and a bright future ahead of him. Janet took the photo in her hands, knowing in that moment, that no matter what, she would never love anyone like she had loved Dale, and maybe that was just how it was going to be.

She passed the photo over to Peggy and looked at the other photo in the box – the one of her parents. The one *she* had taken that day at the protest. She didn't know why she kept it hidden away like this and made a promise to herself to find a frame for it and put it somewhere she would see it often.

Janet didn't have anything to remember David by. No photos, no ticket stubs or other scraps of memories. But he still lived in her heart. It had been different with David, but the truth was, she had loved him too.

Peggy took a moment to look at the picture of Dale. "He's a real hottie, Janet," she said, before handing the photo back.

Janet smiled as she took the picture back. "He certainly was. We couldn't keep our hands off each other. And at that time, it still turned a lot of heads to see a white girl and a black boy together. Even here in 1984 there are people who have a problem with it."

"Even in my time," said Peggy, shaking her head.

Janet put the picture back in the box and placed it down beside her before returning to her dinner.

"You still think about him," Peggy said.

Janet nodded. "Every day. And I dream about him all the time."

"How did he…?" Peggy asked.

Janet shrugged. The truth was, she didn't know. She still didn't know how he had died. She had certainly explored all the worst-case scenarios at one time or another. "I think that's the worst part. I don't even know what happened to him. He was missing in action."

"I'm so sorry, Janet." Peggy reached out for Janet's hand.

Janet put her hand on top of Peggy's and nodded. It had been so long since she'd talked to anyone about this, and as much as she had made peace with her past, the heartache sometimes felt brand new, like her heart was ripping into pieces all over again.

But having Peggy here helped. In fact, Peggy had helped her more than she would probably ever know.

"Thank you, Peggy, now let's watch the movie." And she got up and pressed play on the VCR.

FORTY-SEVEN

The Dam

Santolsa
1985

Janet sat on the couch with her legs curled up and he passed her the Bryan Adams mug full of hot cocoa.

It had been sixteen years since she'd seen him, and it was bringing up so many feelings she had managed to keep buried for so long. It was like a dam threatening to burst open in her heart. She had so many questions. She wanted to know where he had been all this time, why he had never tried to find her before, how he had found her now. She wanted to know if he was married, if he had kids, she wanted to know *everything*.

He sat across from her, a cup of cocoa in his own hands. He looked older, tired, worn out. He had wrinkles and streaks of gray in his hair, but at the same time, he somehow looked exactly the same. It was like so much time had passed, but also, none at all.

"Why are you here?" she finally asked. "After all this time?"

"I found him, Jan," he said, running his hand through his shoulder length not so dark anymore hair, an old habit she was so familiar with.

Janet shook her head. "David," she started, shaking her head, "What are you talking about? You found who?"

"I found Dale."

And the dam burst.

FORTY-EIGHT

The Gardener

1985

Salt Valley

The Salt Valley council office wasn't much to look at – just an old brick building with a sign out front, it was even uglier inside. Janet didn't know how anyone could work in these tiny cubicles in these soulless offices. Teaching wasn't always easy, but at least she could get up and walk around during her classes.

"Can I help?" asked a woman wearing thick round glasses, her gray hair in a low bun who was sitting behind what appeared to be the reception desk.

"I'm looking for someone, I believe he works for you in the parks department."

"We can't give that information out." The woman pursed her lips.

"It's… he's someone I knew… before Vietnam. He was…"

The woman's expression softened slightly.

"I didn't know he was still alive." Janet was usually so good at keeping her emotions in check, but she felt her lip waver.

The woman tutted. "Name?" she asked.

"Dale, Dale Williams."

The woman flicked through some files on her desk. "He's out in the square."

"In the square?"

"Yes. Right out there." She pointed back through the door that Janet had walked in.

"I'm sorry, what do you mean he's right out there?"

"The man you are looking for, this..." She looked down at the files again, "...Dale Williams. He's working in the square today."

Janet shook her head. She couldn't compute. "Are you sure you have the right person?" she asked.

"Are you?" asked the woman.

"I... I honestly don't know," Janet said.

"Well, there's only one way to find out." The woman closed the files and picked up the ringing phone, signaling that their exchange was over.

Janet walked back the way she came in a daze, back through the front door of the council office, past her car in the lot and across the road to the square. It was really nothing more than a quadrangle with a few benches, some old, cracked paths, a bit of grass and a few trees and bushes, but in that moment she could have been anywhere. Her heart was thumping so hard she thought she might explode.

It had to be a mistake. David didn't know what he'd seen. It had been a long time. The woman at the desk was confused. There must have been a different Dale Williams working for them.

And then she saw him.

And then he saw her.

He dropped the shovel he was holding, and it clattered to the ground.

Tears burst from Janet's eyes, the dam breaking, opening up as sixteen years, no, thirty-three years' worth of everything finally exploded in her heart and she ran to him.

Everything in him told him to run, to turn away, to push her back, to say no to this. He didn't want her to see him like this, he didn't want her to see who he had become. *What* he had become.

But his feet began to run towards her, not away, and he felt his arms opening, and his heart opening and suddenly it was 1966 all over again and she was in his arms once more.

FORTY-NINE

Starting Over

____

1985

Santolsa

"What happened to you?" she whispered, finally letting go and taking a step back to look at him. One side of his face was covered in burn scars, and his body was different, harder, scarred and tough all over.

He turned his head to the side, so she couldn't see his scars, a habit he had obviously developed since his injury.

She reached out to touch the side of his face.

He flinched and pushed her hand away. "I'm not the person that I was," he said.

"Neither am I." She reached out towards him, and he grabbed her by the wrist stopping her. It wasn't the gentle touch she once knew, it was something different. But she knew he was still inside. The Dale she knew and loved, still loved, always would love, was still in there.

She held his gaze until a single tear fell down over the scars, and his hand was finding its way into hers.

"I didn't ever want you to see me like this," he said.

"You think I care about *this*? It was never about how you looked. That was just a bonus."

"Vietnam changed me, Janet."

Hearing him say her name was like hearing angels sing.

"The things I saw. The things I did," he added in a whisper.

"I've done things too, remember?"

"I'm not right. I have nightmares. Visions. It never ends."

Janet took his other hand in hers too, noticing the skin on his hand was also scarred and wondering if the scars covered his whole body. She didn't care if they did. "Let me help you."

He let out a laugh. "I don't want your pity," he spat.

"It's not pity, Dale. I love you, I always have, and I always will."

He shook his head. "You don't even know me anymore. How could you love *this*?"

"So, let's get to know each other all over again."

He just stared at her for a moment. "You know why I came here? To Salt Valley?"

She shook her head.

"Because you said you would never come back to Santolsa. Because you said it was the worst place in the world and you would never be caught dead here. I figured it was the one place you wouldn't find me."

"Santolsa does something to people, it always calls them back. I think you knew that. I think you knew I would end up back here. I think that's why you came back to Salt Valley. You *wanted* me to find you."

He dropped her hands and took a step back.

"Remember what Lena said?" she asked, letting him take the space he needed.

He blinked at her. "*Lena?*"

"She said we'd see each other again."

He shook his head. "This is going to sound crazy, but I think Lena saved my life."

"It doesn't sound crazy at all. Lena has… powers."

"Powers?"

"What time do you finish work? I'll tell you everything."

"I'm just finishing up now."

"Let's go somewhere and talk."

He gave her a look. "I don't think it's a good idea."

"Why not?"

"Because I don't want you to have to deal with all this." He gestured to his face and down his body.

Janet stepped towards him again and put her hands on his shoulders. "I told you I'd wait for you, and I did. I'm not about to let you go now."

It was the first time in a long time that anyone had looked at him without just seeing his scars. Someone who knew him from before. Someone who knew who he used to be. He had spent all this time thinking she would be disgusted by him, but she was looking at him the same way she always had. Her green eyes lighting up like he was the most amazing thing she had ever seen.

"Is there someone else?" she asked, dropping her hands.

He laughed. "No, there's no one else. Do you have someone else?"

She shook her head.

"You *should* find someone else, someone who's not deformed, someone who can look after you."

She threw her hands in the air. "So it was all bullshit?"

"What?"

"All that stuff about being mine forever?"

"I meant it at the time."

"Oh, but not anymore?"

"Of course I'm yours forever," he sighed. "That doesn't mean you have to be mine."

"I *am* yours forever," she said, stamping her foot on the pruned leaves.

And he knew that she meant it.

And something in his heart felt like it clicked back into place, like it had been dislocated for so long and now it had been shoved back in. It was painful as hell, but it felt right.

And so they went for pie at his favorite diner in Salt Valley and they ordered apple and peach pies and she looked at him the same way she always had. And then he invited her back to his small ground floor apartment and they made love like it was 1966 again.

FIFTY

The Wedding

Santolsa
1986

Janet was dressed in a fluffy white robe, sitting on a bed in the Santolsa Motel on the edge of town, her bridesmaids fussing over her, fluffing up her hair and trying to get her veil to sit right.

"It needs to go a little higher," Peggy said. "Otherwise, you can't see it behind her hair." Peggy was dressed in a strapless taffeta peach gown with a billowing skirt that stopped at her knees. Her hair was big and curled, a crown of plastic flowers in peach and white sitting over her forehead.

"If it goes too high it will flatten her hair," said Diamond Jones. Her dress was made of the same peach taffeta, but in halter-neck style that fell to the ground. Her hair was dotted with plastic flowers in the same peach color.

They both looked beautiful.

But the day was bittersweet. Here she was with two of the most important people in her life, but there were so many people missing. Her mom, her dad, Gran, Alex and Lena…

"Janet?" Diamond was giving her that look. "You still want to do this?"

"Of course! I've waited my whole life for this day," she said.

"Then why do you look so sad?" asked Peggy, sitting down next to her on the bed.

"I guess I'm just thinking about everyone who couldn't be here."

Diamond nodded. "Mayumi wouldn't have missed this for the world. She'll be here in spirit, you know that."

Janet nodded, fighting away a tear.

"And if we knew where Hog was, and we got an invite to him you know he would've been here with bells on." Diamond said.

Diamond Jones didn't know Janet was a time traveler. It was nice really, to have some people in her life that didn't know. It meant she could pretend to be normal. But it often felt like no one knew all her secrets. Diamond Jones had been there to help pick up the pieces when Janet's drinking had gotten out of control. Something she still hadn't told Peggy about. And Peggy knew that Janet was a time traveler from the year 1999 but she didn't know all of Janet's secrets. And neither one of them knew about the night of the job for the Eights. Only David and Dale knew about that now.

She'd told Dale about most of it of course, Dale had blamed himself for her drinking at first, but he was glad that Janet had Diamond and had found the help she needed. She'd tried to tell him about time traveling a few times, but the words hadn't come. It was OK, she would tell him in time. Or she wouldn't.

Where you were from didn't matter. It was where you were going that was the important thing. And Janet's future was with Dale.

Peggy twisted the small diamond engagement ring on her own hand. "I keep thinking about the people who won't be able to come to my wedding too. My own parents won't get to see me get married. It's funny you know, when I was living with them, they never had time for me, they never even really knew me. But now that they are… well, I miss them."

Janet reached out to Peggy and pulled her in close. "We might not have our families here, but we have each other, right?"

Diamond sat down and put her arm around Janet. "We are your family, Janet."

"You're my aunt Janet, you *are* my family," said Peggy.

Janet let out something that was part laugh part cry. "You're right, you two are my family, and I'm so grateful for you both, more than you will ever know. You've both saved me."

"Don't cry, your mascara isn't waterproof," Peggy reminded her, giving her a squeeze.

Janet patted underneath her eyes. "Still OK?"

Peggy nodded.

"It's time to get dressed," Diamond announced.

Janet put on her wedding dress – a long flowing sixties style dress in white chiffon with floaty cap sleeves and a high collar. She looked at herself in the mirror and almost didn't recognize herself. For most of her adult life she never thought she'd get married. She never thought she'd find anyone after Dale. But she'd found him again, and he still loved her, and she still loved him. And now they were going to be bound together in holy matrimony in the one place neither of them ever thought they would ever end up in.

"You look so beautiful, Janet," Diamond said.

Peggy looked like she was about to cry.

"Don't you start," Janet warned. "Your mascara isn't waterproof either."

Janet and Dale exchanged vows underneath a Joshua tree at the back of the Santolsa Motel in front of a few of their close family and friends.

And it was the happiest day of both of their lives.

FIFTY-ONE

The Party

———————————

Santolsa
1986

"Mrs. Willis!" Peggy called out over the music. "I can finally call you that!"

The wedding reception was nothing fancy - a buffet of frozen pizza, garlic bread and spring rolls served in the ballroom of the Santolsa Motel, which was really just the bar with the tables moved to the sides, but it was perfect. They'd hired a local band to play covers of all their favorite songs and everyone was having a good time.

Janet grinned. "I guess you were right after all."

"It's so… modern, taking just half his name."

"I am from the nineties, remember?"

"Oh, yeah, I keep forgetting!" Peggy shook her head.

"And you know I spent a good chunk of time in the sixties and seventies fighting for women's rights."

"I'd love to hear more about that. Maybe you should write a book."

Janet raised an eyebrow. "Maybe one day I will."

"I wish I could do something that cool, like all the stuff you did back then."

"You have your own path to walk," Janet reminded her.

Peggy's face twisted. "There's something I need to tell you, about the future."

Janet shook her head. "I don't want to know."

"I think you should know this."

"Why?"

"It's about how long you and Dale have together."

Janet's eyebrows drew together. "How will it help me to know?"

"Maybe you can do something, maybe you can change it."

"I'm tired of trying to change everything."

"But if it could save someone you love?"

Janet shook her head. "I've spent most of my life trying to save people I love. In the end, everyone has their own journey, their own story, their own timeline."

"But…" Peggy continued.

Janet cut her off. "Look," she said, picking up a champagne flute of Mello Yello from a table. "One way or another, everything ends. Either he'll leave me, or I'll leave him, or I'll die, or he will. It doesn't matter. What matters is what we do today. So many people waste their whole lives worrying about the future. I don't want to be one of them."

Peggy looked thoughtfully into her own glass of Mellow Yellow.

"Life is short, Peg, no matter how much time you have. So, look after the time you have. We are all guardians of time, really."

Peggy gave a slow nod.

"May I cut in?" Sammy Ruthven slipped an arm around Peggy's waist, and she beamed at him. He was dressed in a light blue suit, his hair was slicked to the side and one piece kept falling into his eyes. Peggy reached out and pushed it back.

"Of course," Janet said, smiling at the young couple in love.

"Congratulations." Sammy let go of Peggy just long enough to give Janet a quick hug. "I wish you both so much happiness together."

"And you," Janet replied, sending them off onto the dance floor with a wave of her hand.

"Miss Bates!" Lacey threw her arms around Janet's neck. "I'm so happy for you!" she grinned.

"Oh, thank you Lacey. I hope you are enjoying yourself."

Jack appeared behind her with a big smile on his face. "Best, wedding, ever."

And he pulled Lacey back onto the dance floor.

Janet couldn't help but smile as she watched them move around the floor - Peggy and Sammy, Lacey and Jack. Everyone was right where they needed to be.

"Could I have this dance?"

Janet turned around to face a ghost from her past.

David.

It may have been a strange choice to invite him to her wedding, but he was such an important part of her story that it didn't feel right not to have him here.

She gave a nod and he led her to the dance floor, resting his hands on her gently, leaving plenty of space between them. They began to sway to the music of the Kinks singing about a girl called Lola.

"Thank you, David," she started, "for helping me find my way back to Dale."

"Thank you for helping me find *my* way," he replied. "If it hadn't been for you, I wouldn't be here. I wouldn't have gotten out of the Eights. I would never have met Georgia or had my three beautiful children."

"I never asked you, whatever happened to Abigail?"

David rolled his eyes. "She was a piece of work."

"*You* were also a piece of work back then too."

"I'm sorry, you know, about what I did in the bar that night."

She shook her head. "Water under the bridge."

"One minute Abigail was everything to me, the next, she was just gone. After I joined up with the Eights in San Francisco we got a place together and things were great for a while. She was learning English and I was learning patience. Then one night she took that dictionary and my car and just left. I heard from a friend in the Eights a few years later that someone saw her in Wisconsin, but I don't know."

"Do you think she ever made it back to her time?"

He shook his head. "I doubt it. I don't think she really understood how she got here in the first place."

"I hope she's OK, wherever she is."

"Me too. I feel like such a jerk for the way I treated her."

"We were young, we were all just working it out."

"I hope you're happy too, Janet."

"I am," she smiled.

"Georgia!" David stepped out of Janet's arms and embraced his heavily pregnant wife. Georgia was nothing like Abigail or Janet, but the way David looked at her was like she had stopped time.

Georgia gave Janet a hug and wished her well, before the two of them took their places on the dance floor.

The band began to play their song. They didn't really sound like Sonny and Cher, but it was close enough.

"May I have this dance?"

And there he was, her *husband*. The man that she had waited sixteen years for. The man she had waited *thirty-six* years for. And every second had been worth it, to be here now, to have his hand reach for hers and to look down and see the gold band across his finger, matching hers. Proof that this was real.

"You may have all the dances until the music stops," she said.

"Well, here's hoping it lasts forever, then."

She put her glass of Mellow Yellow down on a table nearby and Dale took her in his arms, and they danced like it would be 1966 forever.

FIFTY-TWO

The Hospital II

Santolsa
2004

The Salt Valley Hospital had become Janet's second home this last year. The appointments, the short stays that turned into longer stays that turned into one long stay that never ended.

Janet had thought many times over these years about what Peggy said she knew about the future. About how much time she had with Dale. Janet had obsessed about it, released it and let it go, then obsessed about it again. If she'd known, maybe there *was* something she could have done. Maybe they could have caught it earlier or found some other treatment.

But they'd had nineteen beautiful years together, and after losing him once, every day she woke up in his arms had been a blessing for them both.

Dale should have died in Vietnam. It was Lena who had saved him and given them this gift of time together.

One night while they were lying in bed late at night on their honeymoon in Red Rock Janet had finally told Dale that she was a time traveler. She thought he was asleep and so she simply whispered it up into the roof of their cabin. "I'm a time traveler," she said. "I'm from the future."

"I know," he had mumbled into his pillow.

And that was the only time they ever talked about it, and she was thankful for it. It gave her peace. It gave her a here and now.

"I'm ready to go," he whispered to her now. "We got more time than we were meant to."

"It's not enough," she said, gripping his hand, mascara staining her cheek as a tear fell.

"It would never be enough," he said.

She reached out and brushed a tear from his own cheek.

"I want you to be happy," he began. "I don't want you to wait for me this time."

She shook her head. "This time, you wait for me to come join you wherever you're going, OK?"

He nodded his head slowly. "I'll always wait for you."

She pressed her lips to his forehead.

"Tell me a story," he said.

"A story?"

He nodded.

"I don't know any."

"Yes, you do. Your life is full of stories."

"OK, I'll tell you the best one I know. It's about a girl who met a boy on a midnight bus to San Francisco."

"I like that story," he said.

And so, she began the story, and she told it to him until he fell asleep.

FIFTY-THREE

The Recruit

____

Santolsa
2016

It a was late afternoon just before summer break and Janet
was sitting at her desk in her English classroom grading
papers. She didn't want to miss the sunset, so she bundled
up the last of the papers and shoved them into her bag.
She'd do the rest at home, or maybe she'd just sit on the
back porch and reminisce. She'd quit smoking many years
ago now, but once in a while Janet had the urge to light
one as she sat and thought about the past. She'd only ever
taken it up because it reminded her of her dad. Whenever
she had a cigarette in her hand, she felt like he was with
her. But Peggy's nagging had eventually won out, Janet had
put her own health first and quit.

That's what old people did though, they reminisced.
They had more time behind them than ahead, so instead
of making plans and worrying about the future, they

thought about the good old days and relived them on their back porch, watching the first stars appear.

It was just like time traveling, really. You could be anywhere you wanted if you just took yourself back there in your mind.

Janet had many places she liked to re-visit. The midnight bus, the Pancake Palace, that whole summer of 1966. The day she saw Dale again in the square, her wedding day… There were so many good memories to choose from that there was always something wonderful to think about in the evenings.

And yes, there was a lot of sadness too, but that was life. No one gets through life without it.

"Janet?" a soft voice asked from the open door of the classroom.

She looked up from the pile of papers, and there stood Lena. She hadn't aged at all, she was still sixteen, so young and pretty.

Janet gasped. "*Lena?*"

Lena nodded and rushed at her, giving her a warm hug and squeezing her tight.

Janet mumbled into her hair, "how are you here?"

"I'm a time traveling witch, Janet," she laughed.

Janet's head was reeling. "Of course, but…"

"I'm here to recruit you."

"Recruit me for what?"

"You remember how I left the coven? Well, we need a replacement."

"But that was decades ago."

"For you it was. For me, well, I just got back from San Francisco with Alex. I just said goodbye to you yesterday. I had a vision on the bus that I was to see you here and recruit you, so here I am."

"I don't understand," Janet said, rubbing her forehead.

"You are my replacement, Janet," Lena said. "You are to go at once to the year 1888 and help Sister Maria and Sister Catherine to start the school. You are to be one of the founders of St. Christopher's High School. We've been watching you and you've been deemed worthy."

Janet laughed.

Lena frowned.

"You're serious."

Lena nodded.

"I'm not a witch, Lena," Janet scoffed. "What can I possibly bring to the coven?"

"Magic comes easy to those who have a pure heart, to those who have looked after others, and to those who have proven themselves to be honorable keepers of time. Sister Maria and Sister Catherine will teach you the rest."

"Sister *Catherine*? From when I was at school?"

"Yes, I believe you already know her," Lena gave a smug smile. "It will be a great adventure with many perks. You can work with time magic to slow down the aging process, even reverse it slightly."

Well, that sounded good.

"And you can time travel, sometimes. As long as you don't influence anything too much."

"Oh, like you did? I know what you did for Dale. I know you saved him."

"I did it for you. To thank you, for your service."

Janet laughed again. "This is too much."

"Aren't you used to that by now?" Lena said, folding her arms across her chest.

"I don't think I'll ever get used to it."

"You have some time to get your affairs in order. I'll come back for you on the last day of classes, just before the summer break."

Janet thought about it. There was really nothing left for

her here. Dale was gone, Young Peggy was back in 1983, Old Peggy had her own life now with Sammy and her work at a school for the deaf in Elko and Jack and Lacey had made a wonderful life for themselves in L.A.

"Will you come?" Lena asked.

Janet sighed. "I think you already know I will. But who will take my place to protect the portal in this time?"

"Peggy will be your replacement here, and one day she will join the Nuns of Santolsa too. Sister Maria and Sister Catherine will finally die of old age, and then I will return. And then you, me and Peggy will be the new Nuns of Santolsa… and we will do things differently," she grinned.

And Janet laughed so hard she thought she was going to burst.

Interlude IX

Santolsa
  1888

It was a balmy Saturday evening in 1888 and Sister Janet was about to sit down at the desk in her room of the abbey which looked out over the Nevada desert. The stars were shining so bright, much brighter than they had shone in her time. Although she had traveled back to help Sister Maria and Sister Catherine open the school and keep the time portal safe, she refused to wear a habit in the abbey. When they went out into the world it made sense, and Janet was surprised just how differently she was treated dressed as a nun, even by non-believers. There wasn't a lot to choose from clothes-wise in this time, but Janet had thankfully found an old (well, new in this time) sewing machine. It was clunky and difficult to use but Janet had been able to make herself some loose-fitting dresses, and now she was dressed in a pair of long bloomers which were actually very comfortable and an oversized nineties style tee she'd made out of calico.

It wasn't so bad being back in the nineteenth century, not really. Janet missed some of her creature comforts like frozen pizza, her record player and hot showers. But she remembered her favorite songs by singing them loudly and off key in the garden and Sister Catherine had been working on developing a type of pizza that was nothing like the ones Gran used to make, it would be a while before she'd get her hands on a pineapple, but they were made with love.

Sister Catherine and Janet had become good friends, and even Sister Maria was softening a little. She often remembered Lena's words – that one day Peggy would join the nuns of Santolsa and Lena would return.

But when she found herself fixated on it, she took a deep breath and tried to bring herself back to the here and now.

Sister Catherine had assured her that Peggy and Sammy would have a long, full life together before Peggy was recruited and that brought Janet some comfort. She had also told Janet about Alex and Lena. They had had one of those on again off again love affairs for decades, meeting up in various times and places over the years. Sister Catherine had said that the way Lena moved through time it was hard to follow her timeline, but she didn't think their story was done yet.

Janet was actually enjoying the slow pace of life here. Her days felt longer, and the evenings spent sitting outside watching the sunset felt as if they would last forever.

There was no point in hurrying time. Whatever her destiny was, it would find her. For now, she would just enjoy the long evenings, her favorite time to think about Dale, to hold him in her heart and keep him alive in her own way.

And each night, when the sun had gone down, Janet

wrote. She wrote about all the people she'd ever loved. She wrote about her mom and dad, about Dale and David, about Peggy and Sammy and Jack and Lacey.

She had finally found the words.

But she still had one more story to write.

Janet picked up a pen and a piece of paper and began.

The Nuns of Santolsa, she wrote.

FIFTY-FOUR

The Beginning

Santolsa
  2016

Janet sat at her kitchen table, butterflies in her stomach as she stared into the bottom of her old Bryan Adams mug, meditating on the coffee that had gone cold. She'd lost a lot of things over the years – things that had cracked or broken or disappeared, but this mug was one of her constants.

She took the last sip, not for the taste, for the caffeine.

It was days like today she almost felt tempted to light a cigarette, take a long inhale and invoke some of her father's guidance.

She wondered what he would say about all this. He'd probably just laugh and say life was a trip.

And he would be right.

Because today was the day.

Today was the day that she would give Peggy... no, *Magz* the key.

It seemed like just yesterday that Peggy had time traveled back to 1983, stuck her head into the classroom, freaked out and fainted on the floor. But it was thirty-three years ago. Almost to the day.

But today wasn't the day Peggy would go back, or arrive, or however it happened. She wouldn't go back until later this week, but today she would see Sammy Ruthven's face in the yearbook for the first time. She would hold the key in her hand, and all the pieces of the puzzle would fall into place.

Today the wheels would be put in motion.

Janet didn't know exactly how this day would play out. She didn't know if it would all go to plan. She was really just going off what had happened all those years ago, and what Peggy had told her had happened. That was her script, that was how she knew what to do and what to say.

She toyed with the idea of not doing it. She wondered what would happen if she didn't give Peggy the key, if she made a different choice, or what if this Peggy, this *Magz*, made a different choice?

Janet had learned some things over the years. One was that no matter how set in stone things appeared to be, they could sometimes still be changed. The other was that some things, no matter how desperately you wanted them to be changed, just couldn't be.

There was no rhyme or reason to it, and Janet had given up trying to understand in the end. She'd chosen to look at life as a great adventure rather than a series of good or bad things that happened. Adventures always contain both.

But there were so many good things that had happened.

And grief was just love turned upside down and inside out.

Loss only hurts because you had loved so much.

And Janet had loved with all her heart. She had lost Dale twice, but she had also found him twice, and in the end, they'd had so much more time than she ever thought they would. She was grateful for it all.

She was grateful for Peggy, who had become a daughter to her, and for Jack and Lacey and their daughter Alex, who had been one of Janet's best friends that summer they had all lived together in San Francisco.

She was grateful for Diamond Jones who had helped her to deal with one of the hardest times in her life.

She was even grateful for David, for Jonas, for the Eights. Without them she would never have found her way back here.

And she was even grateful for Santolsa. A town she once couldn't wait to put in her rear-view mirror. No matter how much she tried to run from it, it had always called her back. She'd found her peace with it. She'd found her peace here.

She'd found contentment.

Janet stacked the yearbooks on her desk, heart racing. She pulled out the 1983 yearbook and double checked that the key on the old yellow ribbon was still in place.

She'd worn the key on that ribbon that whole summer. At the time she didn't really know why. It wasn't like she needed to use it. But in a way, it had been her connection to the past. Apart from her military boots, everything else she'd ever owned, and everyone else she'd ever loved back in her time was gone. But by wearing the key, it was like she could stay connected to them, to who she had once been. She felt like if she had that key, she could use it anytime and go back.

But after Dale had gone to Vietnam, she knew no matter what, she could never go back to her time. She knew she'd stay in the sixties until they turned into the seventies and even the eighties to wait for him. So, one day she took the key off and put it in an old book that Lena had left behind. And there it had stayed until this morning.

Students began to file into the classroom, scraping back chairs and talking loudly.

Janet pretended to be busy with some papers, but all she was thinking about was Peggy.

It had been so hard to be her teacher these last few years and never be able to tell her the truth. Magz, as she was called then, had struggled so much. She'd been bullied and she was lonely, and Janet had wanted so many times to throw her arms around her, tell her that she already knew her, that they were friends, that they were *family*.

Most of all she just wanted to be able to tell her that everything was going to be OK. That she would travel back in time and fall in love, that she would make so many wonderful friends, that she would marry the love of her life, have a long and full life with him and that she would finally be *happy*.

The bell went for first period and Janet gave a start.

"Good morning class," she began, her voice wavering ever so slightly. "I have a new assignment for you, it's going to be lots of fun, I promise."

"Fun?" scoffed Jim.

Janet ignored him. Jim was not worth her time or her energy.

"Each of you will be given a St. Christopher's yearbook from a different year. Your assignment will be to compare the high school experience from then with now." Janet grabbed the stack of books and began passing them around the classroom. "I want you to get creative, think of this as historical fiction, write me a story."

Janet threw the 1983 yearbook on Magz's desk.

Magz sneezed.

"Magz!" Janet reprimanded. She was about to hand Magz her destiny, and she wasn't even paying attention!

Magz looked up sheepishly.

"Have you even heard a word I've said this morning?" Janet asked.

Magz looked around the room nervously before mumbling an apology.

Janet looked at Jack. Oh, *Jack*. She wished she could tell him everything too. She wished she could tell him that he would find love too, that he'd be rich and happy and successful, and all would be well in his life. She wasn't sure he could handle knowing he'd have a daughter who would time travel back to 1966 with her witch-nun girlfriend and spend a summer with Janet listening to records, serving pizza and protesting.

So instead of telling him all that, she just said – "Jack, can you fill Magz in on anything she may have missed so far this lesson?" before throwing the 1984 yearbook onto his own desk.

Janet sat back down at her desk, pretending to grade papers, but she was watching them both out of the corner of her eye. Magz and Jack.

Peggy and Jack.

She watched as Magz opened the book, her eyes lighting up, almost as if she knew. As if she knew that this was something special. That *this* was the magic she had been waiting for.

She watched as Magz looked through the pages of Sammy Ruthven's yearbook, the man who would one day become her husband. If only she knew!

"Is this you Mrs. Willis?" Anastasia called out, bringing Janet back to the present moment.

"Let me see." Janet stood up and walked over to Anastasia's desk. She put her black rimmed reading glasses that dangled from the gold chain around her neck onto her nose. She took the book and saw her younger self smiling up at her.

"Why would you work in this dump for that long?" Mindy mumbled. Janet just ignored her, like she did with all her most annoying students. Life was too short to bother with them when there were people like Peggy and Jack who needed her.

Janet grinned down at herself. "Why, yes, that is me!" She held up the book, smiling as she pointed to the picture. "Gosh, that was some time ago. 1980. I was Miss Bates then."

She wished that she'd known how pretty she was when she was younger. She'd always thought that she had been very plain, nothing special, but too late she saw the truth. She really had been beautiful. Janet leaned back on her desk, flipping through the pages.

"There's a lot of nuns in here," Jack said.

"Yes, the nuns!" said Janet. "There were quite a few nuns around in the seventies but by the early eighties we only had a couple left. They've all gone now, and you'd hardly even know we were Catholic these days. Even daily prayers seem to have gone out of the homeroom windows." She shrugged. "It's a different time."

Anastasia's hand shot up again, but she didn't wait before she spoke. "Have you always worked here Mrs. Willis?"

Janet's face twitched. "I've worked here most of my adult life. I had quite a few years off during the nineties." Janet and Dale had gone back to San Francisco to relive their youth during those years. She didn't want to run into her younger self in Santolsa, so they disappeared for a while. Dale had worked for the parks department and spent his days keeping Golden Gate Park looking beautiful. Janet had worked part time as a tutor and tried her hand at writing novels, but she could never quite find the right words to tell her story.

"Why would you come back to this hell hole?" scoffed Jim.

Janet looked at him with daggers in her eyes. She wanted to teach Jim a lesson, so she told the truth. "My husband became terminally ill, and we wanted to be around friends and family before he went, and when he did go, I just stayed." She took a breath and steadied herself. Of course, she stayed. Where else would she go? San Francisco had been theirs together. She'd been alone in Santolsa long enough to know she could be alone here again.

The class fell silent.

"Sorry for your loss Mrs. Willis," said Anastasia politely.

Someone dropped a pencil.

"It was a long time ago." Janet slowly lowered her glasses. "I had so much happiness and joy with my husband that to be sad about his passing would be a dishonor to him and the beautiful, if short, life we had together."

She would always be sad that she had lost the love of her life, but to be here now, knowing that she would be a part of helping Peggy and Jack and Sammy and Lacey find love, that was something wonderful. Even all the students who had walked through her classroom door had felt like her children in one way or another.

Even Jim. She hoped in some way she had made his

life better and sown some seeds to help him become a better man.

Janet looked over at Magz. "We had more years together than many couples in love are given." And it was true. She had gotten her second chance with Dale. They had been given more time than she ever thought they would have. It was a blessing so many people didn't get. She knew she was lucky to have known that kind of love, even if it hadn't lasted forever.

But it would last forever in her heart.

"But you," Janet called out to the class, waving the book around. "You have your whole lives ahead of you, so much happiness and tragedy still to come!" She slammed the book closed and threw it back to Anastasia who let out a yelp.

Janet grabbed the 1978 yearbook off Jim's desk and waved it above her head, the sleeves of her black silk blouse billowing out. "These books are a testament to the lives of the people in them, so please don't think of this as just an assignment. These people lived, some of them died. I don't want a report on the facts. I know the facts, I was there." She threw the book back down onto Jim's desk. "Choose someone in your yearbook you can identify with, or someone you find really interesting for no apparent reason. Who do you think you would be friends with? Who would you avoid? What events grab you? I want to know about a night out with your new friends in the sixties, where did you go? What music did you listen to? What did you eat at Dee's Diner?"

"Dee's diner was around in the sixties?" Jack laughed.

"Yes Jack, Dee's has been on that same corner of town since the fifties. If those walls could talk, my gosh, they would have some stories to tell. I was a regular there myself in the old days." She smiled, thinking of all the coffee and conversations she'd shared with friends there over the years. She thought of her first day in 1966 with Annabelle the Avon Lady and of Jack's future in the past, flipping burgers which would lead him to opening his own diners and becoming the Plant Based King of California. She smiled.

"Did you grow up here?" asked Anastasia.

"Well, yes I suppose I did," Janet said. "Let me tell you something." She began walking through the desks. "Teenagers in the past did all the things you do now, they got into all the same trouble you get into now, they just had to plan their misadventures face to face or call each other on landlines."

"What's a landline?" asked Mindy.

Janet raised an eyebrow and continued. "I want to know about the auditions for the school production of Romeo and Juliet in 1975. That was quite a show, the girl who played Juliet went on to become quite famous, and I can't wait to hear all about the greatest night in history. It was 1982 and the year the St. Christopher's Chariots last won a basketball game!" The class laughed.

"Tell me," she continued, waving an arm towards Magz and Jack, "about the high school prom of 1983."

Janet didn't know why she'd said that. The *prom*. Suddenly she was back there, trying to save Sammy. The radio reporting the news incorrectly. *Nick*. One of her favorite students, such a good kid with a bright future ahead of him, gone too soon. Her legs felt weak, as if the entire past was finally catching up with her.

"What happened at the high school prom of 1983?" asked Anastasia.

Janet shook her head. "Nothing."

After a short moment, Janet composed herself. "I urge you though, please do not Google anyone. And definitely do not contact any of these people through email or otherwise. As far as you are concerned these people are still in the past. Contacting them is completely unnecessary and I'm sure they'd all be very annoyed to know that their personal information is being used for a historical fiction class assignment and I don't want to have to explain that to anyone."

"Can we like, Google the time and the place and stuff?" asked Tom, one of the quiet achievers of the class.

"Yes, of course! Do your research on the time period, that's part of the task. Just spare me the phone calls from the kids I taught in the past. I really don't want to speak to them."

Janet couldn't help herself, she had to ask Magz what she was thinking.

"Did you find anyone to write about, Magz?" she asked.

"Maybe this guy." Magz tapped his picture with her pink pen. "Sammy Ruthven."

Janet's head began to spin and then it felt like it was splitting in two. It had been a long time since she'd felt this kind of headache.

"Uh, is something wrong Mrs. Willis?" Magz asked.

"Magz." Janet grabbed her shoulder. Maybe there was still time, maybe she could still fix everything. Maybe Nick didn't have to die. She couldn't save her mom or her dad, she couldn't save Dale, but maybe she could still save Nick. "You are, Sammy Ruthven is…" She put a hand to her mouth, what was she doing? She couldn't tell Magz anything. For all she knew, telling her now would change everything, it might stop the bad, but what if it stopped all the good too? What if in saving Nick, Sammy died in his place?

She had to let it go.

"Sammy Ruthven is what Mrs. Willis?" Magz looked up her with a concerned look and put her hand on top of Janet's.

Janet looked down at their hands, one on top of the other. Her hand so much older than it had been when she had first met Peggy all those years ago, but still, it was all so familiar. Janet glanced over at Jack.

"Uh, I'm still deciding," he said. Janet nodded, turned, and walked back to her desk. She sat down and just stared out the window. It was all too much. She needed a moment. She needed some pain killers, she needed a cigarette.

Finally, she looked back over towards Magz.

And she realized, this was it.

This was the moment.

Magz was frowning as she searched the pages of the book.

The bell signaled the end of the lesson, and while the rest of the class hurriedly closed their books and scraped back chairs, Magz was still busy flipping through the pages.

Janet's heart raced at the thought of her finding the key, the key to her future, the key to Janet's past.

Magz stopped and pulled out the key, strung on the old yellow ribbon. She stared at it blankly, reached out and rubbed it between her fingers, and then Janet watched as she grabbed it and put it in her pocket.

The End

Or is it just the beginning?

<h1 style="text-align:center">Author's Note</h1>

———————————

I first started writing *Class of 1983* when I was a student teacher at a high school in Sydney, Australia in 2008. I was teaching English and Drama and often found myself in the book room picking up class sets of books and plays for my classes. I would always take my time, shutting myself away in the small room that smelled like old books and felt like a little quiet haven away from my students and the other teachers. It was a public school and a little rough around the edges (like so many of the schools I taught in), and most of the books looked like they had been there since *I* was at school. I found myself feeling like this book room was out of time, that it could take me back to my own teen years in the nineties or anywhere else I wanted to go.

Of course, I always came out back in the present, but it was fun to think about. And the more I thought about it, the more it turned into an obsession, an idea for a cool story, an actual novel, and then a three book series!

Sharing the *Santolsa Saga* with you has been a dream come true. I am in so much awe and gratitude that people have actually read these books and enjoyed them. I really hope you enjoyed this last one and I hope you liked the ending, or the not-ending, because this series doesn't really end, it just starts all over again.

These books have many "themes" but one of the things I really loved exploring in the *Santolsa Saga* was the concept of eternity. This story doesn't end, you could start right at the beginning again, and continue the cycle. And our stories don't end either. We can time travel anytime we like. All we have to do is stop and remember the past, the good times, the people we've loved and lost and they are right here with us again. And to visit the future all you have to do is think about what you want your future to be and then do everything in your power to make it happen.

I made the *Santolsa Saga* happen, and you can make your dreams happen too!

When I first started pitching *Class of 1983* to agents and publishers, I got a total of 100 rejections. I won't pretend that wasn't crushing to the ego, but I knew there was someone out there who would "get" this story, so I said screw it and self-published.

The success of these books is all down to you the readers, and I can't thank you enough for picking these books up and giving them, and me a chance.

If you enjoyed this final installment and the other books in the series, it would mean the world to me if you would consider posting a review on Amazon and/or Goodreads. It only takes a few minutes, but reviews are like solid gold to us indie authors!

If you would like to receive updates about what I'm writing next (there is a standalone YA romance in the works and another series percolating in my brain!) head over to www.victoriamaxwellauthor.com to sign up for the newsletter or find me on Instagram —

www.instagram.com/victoriamaxwellauthor or Facebook –
www.facebook.com/victoriamaxwellauthor

And if you have any questions or just want to say hey,
I'd love to hear from you! You can reach me at
hi@victoriamaxwellauthor.com

Acknowledgments

Thank *you* for reading these books, for your emails and DMs, for telling your friends, for sharing on social media, for your reviews. You have no idea how many of my days you have made and how much gratitude I have for you. Thank you for coming on this strange and beautiful journey with me! My gratitude is never ending and I'm sending you so much love and wishing you nothing but the best for your life.

To my amazing beta readers who asked hard questions, pointed out problems, got super into continuity and 1960s history with me and helped me shape this book into something wonderful. Thank you Gaby, Aisling, Dagmar, Maria Saraphina, Eliza and Cheryl for all your feedback and support!

To the New Age Hipster community - thank you for supporting me with my woo woo work so I could make time for my magical fiction too!

To my fake friend Hannah, who isn't fake at all and is actually one of the realest people I know – thank you for your constant support and love and for Fake Shit Movie

Club and all the bad movies we've watched that made me realize maybe my stories aren't so bad after all. To Nicole – thank you for your support, words of encouragement, lunches you didn't let me pay for, vegan cake and impromptu spiritual healing sessions in coffee shops. To Hope who was there at the start – your support has always been incredible, and I feel so honored to have you in my life. I'm always time traveling back in time to Marly Bar in my mind and dancing with you to bad early 2000s pop music. To all my other friends and mentors who inspire me constantly – Lauren, Giselle, Vanessa, Dot, Elle, Emma and everyone who has had my back. Please know I've always got yours too!

To mum – thank you for inspiring me to write and for leading the way. To dad – I travel through time every day to revisit the precious times we had together. And to Ian – the love of my life. I am so grateful I met you on that grey London day that was the start of our story. May our story never end.

xx

About the Author

Victoria Maxwell is the best-selling young adult fiction author of the *Santolsa Saga* series, author of *Witch, Please: Empowerment and Enlightenment for the Modern Mystic* published by HarperCollins and the *Angels Among Us Oracle* published by Rockpool Publishing.

As well as being a YA author, Victoria is the creator of New Age Hipster, a spiritual home for good witches, light-workers, starseeds and spiritual seekers.

An ex-high school English, Drama and Autism Specialist teacher, Victoria is a lifelong lover of magic and stories. Her interests include road trips, stone circles, book shops, thrift shops, vegan pizza, sweet potato fries, rainy days and 80s movies.

Connect here : hi@victoriamaxwellauthor.com

www.ingramcontent.com/pod-product-compliance
Lightning Source LLC
Chambersburg PA
CBHW030800200726
48285CB00013B/320